FRIENDS ALONG THE WAY

BY JULIA MARKUS

Uncle
American Rose
Friends Along the Way

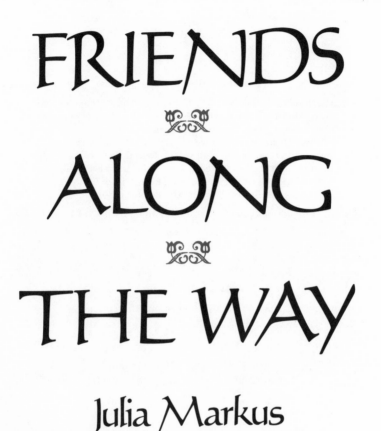

FRIENDS

ALONG

THE WAY

Julia Markus

HOUGHTON MIFFLIN COMPANY

BOSTON   1985

Library of Congress Cataloging in Publication Data

Markus, Julia, date
Friends along the way.

I. Title.
PS3563.A672F7   1985   813'.54   84-25263
ISBN 0-395-35357-2

Printed in the United States of America

V 10 9 8 7 6 5 4 3 2 1

The author is grateful to Mary Delaplain for
permission to quote from "Maybe She Go."

For Patrick, with love

PART I

GARIBALDI'S WALL

I

I first saw Alice Blanders Russo at the American Center in Rome. She was sitting in the back gardens under the shade of a tree. Sunlight dappled her lap. She wore a scoop-neck blouse and a black skirt wide enough to suggest that she was collecting sunlight as she sat. I've known her now for many years. Winter, summer, spring, full-cut skirts and low-cut tops. In the late sixties she still had nylons with seams running down the back. All clothes return to fashion. Yet Alice never looked in or out of fashion. Her taste stressed durability, but I think she knew, cat-center, the effect was timelessness.

Sitting under the tree, she was doing something uncharacteristic. She stared. Since it was the first time I saw her, the image stayed with me. She did it once more, recently. It completed a circle. And started this story.

She stared straight ahead, past the Center's rustic cottages, past the extensive back gardens. The Center is a large villa enclosed on its north side by the city wall. This is the wall Garibaldi stormed, leading his One Thousand into Rome, leading

Italy into nationhood. She stared at the bricks embedded in the wall, but the look in her eyes had none of the nostalgia of historical research. She was asking the wall a question, and when she didn't get an answer, she seemed put out. She sighed. Then she saw me.

"Why, hello," she said kindly. "Come, sit down."

"I don't want to disturb you."

"There's room for two."

I sat down and introduced myself. "I'm Betsy Lewis." We began to talk.

All my conversations with Alice blend; it is as if through the years she has been telling me one story. I hear her voice now, slow, modulated; I hear her opinions, fair and informed; and underneath the pleasant blur, I hear that story. I know we talked about politics that day. And somehow as she talked, softly, steadily, husbands dropped out. I swear I counted three. Nick Russo was on her mind. Her last husband. He had been a fellow at the American Center in the early fifties, when it reopened after the Second World War. That's when she lived at the Center. Leo. Leo kept intertwining. Leo wasn't a husband. Can I remember the first time she mentioned him? "*Tosca* will be playing next summer," she said. "Leo can get you tickets."

Leo can get you tickets. It was nice of her. Offering friendship, offering freebies. I remember how I pictured Leo before I met him. A short man, fifty, fifty-five. Blue suit and tie. Sensitive, intellectual, a bureaucrat working for national TV. Glasses. A stable man. Someone you'd settle down with after three husbands. Ha!

Five foot two, eyes of blue ... Men must have found Alice beautiful in her day. Her long irregular nose wouldn't have ruined the impression, nor the rather wide hips under her wide skirt. Even that afternoon at the Center, the hatch marks beneath her eyes and the little lines at the sides of them seemed acts more of concern than of time. The crevice formed by her breasts touching was mysterious, as if she had something secret tucked between them, farther down.

But she wasn't really beautiful. The more I think of it, I realize it was her very lack of classical beauty that abetted her. You can grow more and more attractive; character piles up with years. A cache. But true beauty has a breaking point. It stretches as tight as it can, then it snaps. It must have been that way for Maple Blanders — Alice's mother. Alice hadn't a picture of her, but I found her in two histories of the stage. Now there was a beauty. Millions of mirrors never prepared her for the mirror she would one day have to face. I doubt Alice powdered her nose without seeing, in the compact's small glass, the absence of her mother's megalomaniacal fate.

We got on to America. This was 1968, the autumn after Martin Luther King, Jr.'s assassination. We had both been in Rome at the time. April, Martin Luther King. June, Robert Kennedy. Violence, riots in the streets. I told Alice how much Dr. King's assassination had affected me. It brought up all my memories of my old friend Salmanda and what had happened to her because she was black. It made me feel so helpless. We talked about civil rights in the back gardens, and Alice's eyes lit up. At the heart of history Alice always defended the underdog against her mother. I talked about suppression and linked it to the Italian Risorgimento, and I talked about my research on Anita Garibaldi, too. That's what I was doing at the Center that day, using the library. Alice read me as greedily as she would a newspaper. She's interested in everything, I thought. She asked me, "Why don't you come to dinner?"

"Everything happens to me!" I told my husband when I got home. I had an uncanny knack of meeting special people. Much more than Doug had, though God knows he was in the right business. He never did see people the way I did. He didn't see anything exciting at the heart of things. I respected him for that. But for me, entering Alice's apartment was entering a new world.

The apartment was not exceptional — the first unexceptional apartment I'd been to in Rome. Usually you climb up four, five, six flights of stone stairs, examine the construction, and make stabs at the century. Finally you enter a labyrinth of good taste. Then out again to the terrace and The View. You freeze in the winter, and the landlord thinks Americans are crazy to prefer an "attico" — their attic is our penthouse — but you're paying for the picturesque, the characteristic, the individual. You're paying for being in Rome, goddamn it; you want to stand high above the old city and name domes.

Alice didn't have a terrace, though she'd lived with Leo since the late fifties, when terraced apartments were dirt cheap. "We hadn't one lira extra to spend on frills," she'd say. It was a policy statement.

Her apartment had four small rooms, but she was a genius at working with next to nothing. Everything was bright and clean and cleared out. Each chair was made to sit on, and the round dining room table surrounded by pictures on the wall was so inviting it could have had conversations with itself.

"Oh, it's lovely here," I said. "It's special." Doug gave me a look. He was thirty then, tall, slim, with light brown hair and eyes. His look was bitchy.

But the fact is, the extraordinary women of the world do not wear signs. Why the honey of life should stick to Alice's lips and the disappointments and failures be brushed off like pollen from her blouse was not at first clear. I remember the night when we all began to worry whether the fish we ate might be as polluted as the Mediterranean. She said she planned to eat as much fish as she could ingest before she died.

She was a slow eater. She brought to her table everyone who came to Rome with an idea. She herself never imposed an idea on anyone, and in a group she was often very quiet. It was as if she supplied the pasta and chicken dish, fruit in season and local wine, and we supplied the impressions of what we were doing and seeing and where we thought we were.

Alice knew where she was. She read the Italian paper that Leo brought her early each morning and got to the American Center often enough to catch up with news from the States. She was self-educated (married for the first time before she had a chance to think). Everything in print would always be something new to learn. She had the avariciousness of the self-educated.

I didn't. I picked my sources. I was twenty-six when I came to Rome, fresh from my master's degree. For me, college had been the road past the confusions of youth, the way out of my home town. I was in Keats's town now, repeating his words. Beauty is truth, truth beauty. I didn't realize how green he was when he wrote them; he was younger than I when he died. Rome was truth and beauty to me. Newspapers were a means for perfecting my Italian. I got my facts from esoteric sources: archives people had overlooked and nifty reading rooms. All ordinary events interested me as long as they were a hundred years old. But the people, the extraordinary people I met — people were like books of life to me. Their surroundings mirrored their souls, their words were unforgettable dialogue, and their lives were worked out along a pattern I can only describe as destiny.

The man I thought at first glance that night might be Leo turned out to be Bev Brewster, a Southerner once he spoke, though he had lived in Rome forever. He was portly, which hid a lot of raw physical strength, and he had wiry, pure white hair. "Of course I'm in demand, my dear Betsy," he said after I expressed astonishment at all the Italian films Alice announced he had been in. "I fall. A self-respecting Italian wouldn't be caught dead falling." With that, he clutched his hand to his throat and staggered. He managed to drop dead on Alice's floor without knocking against any of us.

"Really, Bev," Alice said.

"Now I recognize you!" I said. Bev smiled up at me. Then he rose from the dead to tell me I was Pisces — wrong. To tell me I was Italian American —

"How'd you know that?"

"The same way he didn't know your sign," Doug said.

"Doubting Douglas, doubting Douglas all the way," Bev replied.

No Leo that night. He worked late. It was a few months — around Christmastime — before I met Leo. And what a meeting!

Better than one of Bev's movies where he's a mother superior or a dumb American tourist gorging himself before he flops.

I invited Alice and Leo to dinner on a Friday when Leo would definitely be free. "Nothing fancy," I said, as if Alice valued fancy things. "Nothing fancy," I repeated to Doug, who was a very good cook and arranged food on a tray like a still life even before nouvelle cuisine. He shrugged. "It's up to you."

Then I worried. Should I invite other people? Who should I invite? Bev was so lively, but he was on location. Alice had hinted that Leo's English wasn't too good. Which of our group of American acquaintances spoke good Italian? Who did we know? Who were we? We weren't exciting; that I knew. It's a tribute to Alice's long reach on people, names, and places, a tribute to her harsh mother, her early wealth, being a Blanders and leaving all that, that though now she lived in Rome on the little she had, with a companion for her quiet years, I thought one should be exceptional oneself to know her.

I knew how I looked from the outside. The young wife of a busy man, dabbling in the culture of Italy by researching an earlier foreigner there, Anita Garibaldi.

How did Doug look from the outside? Douglas Shaw. The connoisseur with the right credentials and a justly reputed eye. I was still admiring the reasons I had married him: his integrity and his eye. I was still interested when he traced the provenance of a drawing. I was still fascinated by the skill with which he bought and sold. I couldn't do it. I never saw Doug try to buy at the lowest possible price or hold out for top dollar. When I complimented him on his business acumen, I got a warm response, sure, but I also got a dry eye. What the hell was going to bind the four of us together except clam sauce?

But the Friday I made my clam sauce (Mamma's recipe), Leo would be able to point his finger to the front page of every newspaper in Rome and say, "I'm having dinner right here." (The picture of our door full of holes.) "With these people." (The picture of me with my hands in front of my face and Doug following.) His cohorts would believe him. What did Nano, the librarian of the American Center, once say to me, and not nicely: "Ah, so you know Leo Conti. He's a phenomenon, that man. A phenomenon." No, no one who knew him would doubt that Alice was introducing Leo to the couple who hit the front page of every daily in Rome. Alice's magic and Leo's magic conspired to a world of pictured people.

To set the stage for my being the darling of the paparazzi by the Friday I met Leo, let me describe our apartment. I picked it out. I didn't want a prince's salon decked out with Old World trappings on loan from Doug's auction house, as fitting as it would be for an associate of Ward and Humphries. I was very suspicious of Italy at first. I knew it from family stories. My grandfather left Italy to get away from old things, and I wasn't going to rush back, the first Lewis with a college education, to set myself up in some leaky and drafty pleasure dome. I like straight lines. I liked the modern apartments that sprang up in Rome in the sixties, when the crane stood out against the sky like a cross. I persevered. We ended up in a regular neighborhood on the Vatican side. Via della Buona Fortuna was a tortuous street wandering down a hill. On the top was the Swedish convent of the Sisters of Good Fortune, as well as the older apartment houses where many of the tenants were poor and had lived for generations. In the curve halfway down the hill, progress began in the form of newer pastel-colored apartment buildings. Ours was one of the first of those to be built. We had the top floor in the apartment house on that curve. From our terrace we saw one dome — St. Peter's — enough.

Every time the three Sordi kids kicked against our shared wall, Doug would give me a look. Meeting Mr. Sordi on the elevator late at night stirred up the contention. Mr. Sordi was in his mid-thirties — thirty-seven, I'd find out. He owned the jewelry store in the neighborhood. What a night owl! Didn't his wife mind? When we got home the same time as he, he'd never say hello. The three of us would play elevator in the elevator, pretending our uninhabited bodies were being shipped upstairs.

When I'd pass by his store, Sordi would often be standing in the doorway with his arms folded across his chest, like a businessman. He'd stare right through me. He was the living reminder to both Doug and me that Via della Buona Fortuna was not Doug's idea.

"What the hell is that?" Doug said. It was Thursday night and we were getting ready to go out to eat gnocchi. They make those light little potato balls every Thursday in Rome. Usually they're eaten up at the midday meal, but our local trattoria saved some for us. Every week. We were regulars.

I stopped combing my hair and listened to the noise from behind those modern walls. "Well . . . if we were in America, I'd swear they were shots."

"Goddamn."

"Come off it, Doug. So the kids have firecrackers. It's almost New Year's. They're kids. We're going out. It's not so bad." In this apartment I'd become the defender of noise. There's plenty of time for quiet after we're dead, I'd say. (I believe it.)

The intercom rang. "Now what?"

"I'll go see."

It was the portiera on the intercom. She couldn't reach the Sordis. Would I go over and tell Mrs. Sordi to call down? There was something about understanding a foreign language that inclined me to do what I was asked as a proof that I understood.

I went out to the small hall we shared with the Sordis and rang their bell. The loud popping noise stopped, but no one answered. I rang again. Pop! Pop! Pop! The door was shaking. I stood there and watched it. The moment before death must be as long as it's reputed to be. The door was moving toward me before I realized I was being shot at.

I ran like hell back into my apartment and slammed the door.

"Doug! Shots! Shots!"

"Shots?"

"The children. Oh, my God, the children!"

"Firecrackers, firecrackers, Betsy," he said calmly. He didn't believe me. We both saw our marriage as a way of keeping my imagination from running wild.

There was a blast at our door. The maniac had come out in

the hall in pursuit of me. One blast, two, three. Then he slammed back next door. "Shots," I said.

We moved into the study, away from the connecting wall, and stared at each other. Our life together was full of small things going wrong. I could blame myself for popping sounds and try to compensate for having gotten my way. But shots?

Our phone was ringing ceaselessly and it was drawing the madman's attention. He was responding to it with volleys. I crawled back into the living room, reached up, and brought the phone down to where I lay, protected by the couch.

"Buona sera! *Paese Sera!*" The voice greeted me cheerfully. It was the evening communist paper — sort of a Red *Daily News.* "Signora, for courtesy, what's going on?"

"What's going on? You're asking me? Get the police here! There's a maniac loose. There are women and children inside that apartment. Get the police here before it's too late!"

It will take time, the reporter explained to me. It seemed that the maniac was also firing down the hill from the back window. The block was cordoned off. We had to wait. In the meantime, could I answer a few questions? And again, he persuaded me because we were speaking in Italian. Crouched on the floor, I told him everything, from the firecrackers to being shot at through the door.

"Street of Good Fortune," I said to Doug after I crawled back into the study. "When will I ever learn?"

Doug had a lot of curiosity. He went out onto our terrace from the study and circled over to our back window, where he could see shots flicker down the hill. It was dangerous. But I don't think he thought in those days that fate could get sloppy with him.

When he returned, he said he'd seen cops moving up the hill. A while later we heard a cop at the Sordis' door. "Sandro. Put down that gun. Come talk with me, Sandro."

There was a long pause, like a child catching his breath after a tantrum. Then another volley of shots.

"Sandro. Sandro." A second cop's voice.

"Sandro?" I whispered to Doug. "Alessandro? Doug, it's Sordi himself! Sordi? Oh, my God, he's done his whole family in!"

Sordi sobbed pathetically, as if in agreement.

"It's okay, Sandro. It's okay. Put down your gun. Let's talk."

Sordi spoke through his sobs. Thick, indistinguishable words.

"I understand, Sandro. Okay. Okay. Put the gun down and let me in."

The silence increased. Sordi had been the one member of the household you'd never hear. Then he opened the door.

The cops led Sordi away. They already knew what it took me time to realize: he had been holed up there — thank God — alone.

The apartment was a battlefield. Though we knew we shouldn't be there before the cops, we entered with the portiera. She was a stocky country woman with a bland moon face. Her eyes had opened wide with caution the moment she got off the bus in Rome. They stuck. No amount of blinking could wipe away what she saw. The administrator of the building arrived a few seconds later. He was a balding middle-aged man who carried himself self-importantly, like a frog. The four of us tiptoed through the apartment together.

Sordi had shot at everything that made a sound. The intercom was knocked off the wall in the hall. The living room walls were full of holes and crumbling plaster. On the little round table by the couch there was an empty bottle of Sambuca, the sides of which were crystallizing with the drops of the liqueur that had missed his mouth. On the couch was the newspaper. It was as if Sordi had sat down with a drink and the news, and then decided on a shoot out. The portiera made simpering noises; the administrator shook his head.

Sordi had done everything to the master bedroom that he hadn't done to his wife. There was a big oil of the Madonna (worthless, Doug opined) over the matrimonial bed. Sordi had shot it and the surrounding plaster, though the Virgin still hung on at a cockeyed angle. Her picture appeared in the papers, along with us and the door.

"I don't understand it," said the administrator, returning to the living room with us. "I just repainted for them."

"Looks as if you'll be plastering this time," Doug said.

The man looked around with incredulity. I have always believed that landlords and their representatives exist on an entirely different level of reality from their tenants. "I don't understand," he repeated.

By now the reporters appeared, together with the police. I explained my part in the proceedings and had a look at my bullet-drenched door with them. Then Doug and I went out for gnocchi. We came back about one in the morning — too early for Sordi, usually. When we walked off the elevator at our floor, the paparazzi stood up from the railing and we were greeted by a barrage of flashing lights. I put my hands to my face. That's what Leo saw on all the front pages Friday morning, me hiding something and Doug behind me looking strained.

The four of us stood in front of the door. Leo examined the holes in it; Alice stood next to him. Leo was much younger than I had expected. Perhaps he was in his late thirties or early forties. His face was alive with curiosity, and he was enormously handsome. Man-handsome. He had a wide face with well-defined cheekbones and thick salt-and-pepper hair. He was tall for an Italian, as tall as Doug, but he looked bigger, more muscular, broader. He wore his suit without losing contact with what was under it. When he looked up from the door, his beautiful gray eyes seemed momentarily remote. "A poor shot, Sordi," Leo said, and then he smiled. His teeth were European, irregular. I wished I were his tongue.

He was so different from what I imagined a woman wanted or got for her quiet years, that Alice not only grew younger as I looked at her, but became more mysterious. I realized I had pigeonholed Alice with my admiration, put her into a reality I understood. It was a home-grown reality, one I had tried to share some years back with my old friend Salmanda. Life once more turned out to have a lot of edges. Looking at Doug — tall, slim, contained — I wondered. Had *I* gotten what I imagined a woman wanted for her quiet years? Looking at Leo, my heart lit up.

We had plenty to talk about at dinner. "You see," I said, "Sordi's jewelry store is next to a pocketbook store. I never thought a thing of it. Sordi standing outside his store, the pocketbook lady outside hers, their arms crossed over their stomachs. She" — I almost said she was older than he — "wore rouge and had a pinched face. Mrs. Sordi's a beauty, even though she sings off-key through our walls. The pocketbook lady's not a sympathetic person. But neither is Sordi. I knew he came home late with liquor on his breath, but I figured he played cards with the boys. Actually, he was having an affair with the pocketbook lady. It's always the quiet ones, right? The pocketbook lady's husband found out about the affair, and Wednesday night he beat Sordi up.

"I hear Mrs. Sordi never questioned Sordi's arriving home so late. It seems he's a problem drinker. She knew he was out playing cards and drinking. There was nothing she could do. But when he came home with his face knocked in and his clothes full of blood, she asked him where he'd been. She didn't buy his answer. I don't know if he threatened her or if she put two and two together, but the next day she left, the maid left, the three kids left. That's what the reporters were doing here last night. Waiting for her. For some reason they thought she'd be back.

"And what happens? I get home from dinner. I'm surrounded by reporters. Lights start flashing. Suddenly I'm in *La Dolce Vita*. Paparazzi, paparazzi everywhere. This isn't happening. This is Fellini's Rome. I'm in a film. Well, I'm not one of those children faking a vision. Remember them running back and forth pointing to the invisible Madonna while the TV lights keep exploding in the rain? Great scene. And I'm not Anita Ekberg making love to the photographers with her eyes as she mouths a pizza. I'm closer to Mrs. Steiner. I don't know yet that the kiddies and hubby are dead. I'm getting off the bus and the reporters are swarming around me. Why me? I'm stunned.

"So what do I do? I protect myself from the glare of the lights and the paparazzi. I put my hands over my face.

"What a mistake! I'm in Italy. I'm on the front page. I'm the other woman!"

"I don't know why you hid your face," Doug said.

"I just told you," I said in English to make sure.

"In a very exaggerated version."

"Dear Betsy," Alice said, "you had a night for yourself."

"And I had a day," Doug said. "Sordi's father was here with his lawyer. I said we didn't want a cent. All we want is our door fixed on the double. He came back with two lawyers. I don't know if it's my Italian, but they thought I was holding out for more! They got up to a half a milione before they said take it or leave it."

"Why, that's eight hundred dollars," Alice said. "What did you do?"

"I took it."

"Do you know what the police told me?" I continued quickly. I hadn't wanted Doug to take the money. "A man's home is his castle. Sordi could have shot his rifles off till kingdom come. Two rifles in a house full of kids and a storehouse of ammo. He could have shot all the Madonnas off all his walls."

"Don't exaggerate, Betsy!"

"What do you mean? He's only liable for shooting out the window and shooting at me. Not for what he did inside his apartment. His apartment is his castle. But he came out of his castle to finish off our door. The papers quoted me wrong. Old Papa Sordi thought his son was gunning for me. So I think Doug was right. If he didn't accept some money, the whole family wouldn't sleep, thinking we'd prosecute. Papa Sordi had to pay us off and the two boys on the street who got skin wounds. He had to fix the apartment and our door. But I imagine with all that done, Sordi will still be in jail for a long time. I won't have to worry about him shooting through the wall."

Leo smiled. He sucked a clam from its shell and then wrapped a final fistful of spaghetti around his fork. "Had he killed anyone, he'd be out in three months."

"Three months!"

"Certainly," Leo said. "That would be a crime of passion. He would have gotten three months for killing you."

"Well, what's he going to get for what he did do?"

"Three days."

"Three days?"

"Time enough to sober him up." Leo's smile broadened. It said, Betsy, I know this city. Its ironies are second nature to me. I'm Roman. No absurdity surprises me. I'll surprise you.

"Leo," I said, "our block was cordoned off; the tenants in our building were terrorized. He blew holes in things. He disturbed the peace. He'll be in for more than three days. God, he's not coming back here!"

Leo got up from the table. "What a sauce!" he said. "What a cook! I'm stuffed." He looked at me, his eyes full of fun. "Three days. Every man does something like this once in his life. Three days."

Every man. That's exactly what the woman at the milk store said the next day, and my favorite waiter from our gnocchi place, and the administrator himself. A man's a man. It happens.

"You mean he's going to come back, that madman, and live a wall away from me?" I asked the administrator. "Everyone knows now that he's a drinker and he's very dangerous when he's drunk. What about your paint job? What about your plaster?"

"Signora, these things happen in a man's life. A man's a man."

THE FAULT IS MINE. Mrs. Sordi confessed in the headlines of all the Saturday papers. That's what the paparazzi had been waiting for on our landing! A woman shouldn't walk out on her husband because she hears some trivial gossip. It was Mrs. Sordi's fault that she was jealous. Her jealousy caused Sandro to drink a bottle of Sambuca and try to shoot the Madonna off the wall. She broke down while she gave her confession, fully realizing what she had caused dear Sandro to do. Because of Leo's explanation, I realized that Mrs. Sordi's confession was a legal ploy. His lawyers were setting the stage for a crime of passion. She and they needn't have bothered. Sordi was released the next day.

Money, putty, plaster, paint. Things smoothed over. Once Sordi's face was healed, all traces of his mistress's husband's fist removed, he rang my bell. He stood in the doorway in his suit, white shirt, tie. His balding pate gleamed clean.

"I'm sorry, Signora," he said.

"Non fa niente," I answered in my automatic Italian. It's nothing. I was suddenly sorry that he had to stand there because he had a rich papa and a shamed wife and because of them he had to look into my eyes. Maybe he believed what he read in the papers, that he tried to kill me, that he opened the door and pointed his rifle directly at me, that I ran and he shot the door. Misquote and picture.

Would I have said "non fa niente" nine years ago, when Salmanda was in trouble? But that was in America. What was Rome if not the monument to reason? (Remember Dante's Virgil? I did.) The grand churches, the rooftops, the ruins, the fountains, the squares. The music of the intellect rang so clear that the dissonance of absurdity set up strong flashes of color. *La Dolce Vita* again. Steiner's suicide aside, and his wife's getting off the bus, Rome was Fellini's Ekberg, big tits bobbing, wading through a baroque fountain while the sweet civilizing clarity of Nino Rota's music toned things down.

I never saw Mrs. Sordi in the hall again, nor did I hear her sing. I'd walk by Sordi's store and see him standing outside his door and the pocketbook lady standing outside hers, both staring straight ahead, arms crossed, defying the neighborhood with tarnished imitations of their former bella figura.

One day in late spring the Sordis moved out. The portiera said they moved in with his papa. That summer his store closed, though his name was not immediately taken off the sign. I heard he went to work for his father. No more shoot-outs. From now on Sordi's sad story would be contained within four walls, hushed in the bosom of a family. A man's home is his castle. He'd had his once.

"Enough of Signor Sordi," Doug had said finally on the night of the clam sauce. He turned to Leo. "What do you do for national TV?"

Leo put down his cognac. He held out the palms of his hands. "I work."

℀ 2 ℀

Leo had been a worker at the American Center in the early fifties, and it was there that he and Alice met. She had come to Rome to be with her husband, who was on a grant. And her husband, Nick Russo, didn't like Leo at all. He thought she was too friendly toward him. Alice knew all the workers by name. For her, food was served by people, dishes were washed by people, lawns and hedges were clipped by people. When she saw a person, she'd speak. It was not only a way of practicing her Italian.

It bothered Nick. I can understand. I mean, in my home too, Italian Italians were not to be trusted. After all, if they were upright, honest, and hardworking, why were they still in Italy? Nick had a very pronounced Italian American's suspicion of Italians. Once in Rome, he began to think that maybe the Second World War itself had been a ruse for Italy's seeking American aid. Perhaps he thought this because the war was still so evident. The people were poor and took what they could get. He'd have been one of them if his parents hadn't come to America.

But he wasn't one of them. He spoke what he thought was Italian. It was an adulterated dialect, a sort of peppered English that wouldn't travel farther than his parents' table and his old neighborhood. He was constantly annoyed when the workers pretended not to, or didn't, understand him, and waited for the signora, Alice, to repeat. Leo did this a lot, to rub it in. Nick had married an older woman. It must have annoyed him to see Alice admired by an even younger man.

Nick was a slim, lithe guy from Baltimore, with a punch-in-the-nose face. Full of energy. He couldn't sit still. And when he talked he gestured, and when he thought he moved. The wrong body type for an intellectual. One night in New York his girl-friend had taken him to a party Alice was giving. He picked Alice off her feet and kissed her hard. Nick got what he wanted. Directly. Always. His big bad moods came when he doubted he'd get what he wanted directly, always. According to Alice, Nick was one of those men to whom you just couldn't say no.

At least she couldn't. His big brain and his restless, active body hit her directly. There was nothing in the way he spoke English or in his manners that set the stage for his accomplishments. He was not a Blanders, cushioned by wealth and beauty in the early days and alcoholism and narcissistic delusions later on.

These true-grit, no-nonsense guys can be pricks. When Nick won the Center's fellowship in jurisprudence, he told Alice he was going to Rome. "What about me?" she asked. He told her that if she could raise the money, she could come too.

"Oh, Betsy, you should have seen Naples after the war. The ship docked, and Tullio, the Center's chauffeur, was there waiting for me. I half-expected Nick would have come along to meet me. It was a dreary twilight. I sat in the back seat of the limousine. I felt so useless. I watched desolation fall like night. You'd think the war had ended yesterday, not more than seven years ago, or that it was still going on and we were following the troops into Rome. Bombed-out buildings, rubble everywhere. Poor Naples! Children, so many children, with so little

to eat. Then at night, along the road, prostitutes by their bon-
fires, the shadows of the flames on them like devils licking.
Everything so ghostlike and eerie. Nothing as I expected. I was
being driven through the shattered outsides of things. I cried for
Naples, for Italy. I cried all the way to Rome. Then we were at
the American Center. Nick was waiting for me in the guard-
house. When he saw me he said, 'Who died?'"

Afterward Nick regretted not having gone to Naples to greet
her. He regretted having said, Who died? Alice was no stranger
to his vacillations. They had a fiery reconciliation. And according to Alice, they had a great time at the Center, for a while.

The Center's a funny place. It's all those classical scholars
and legal scholars and artists and architects and town planners
and archeologists living together in their own private America.
The Greco-Roman-Christian tradition, the best that has been
thought and said, drives them dizzy after a while on top of their
hill. Of course, Alice explored Rome and made friends and per-
fected her Italian, and Nick went away on a lot of research trips,
using the Center simply as a base. Their personal problems
didn't spill over till the end.

Intrigues developed at the Center. They still do. I've seen the
complaint book in the office. It sits under the fellows' mailboxes,
open, with a pencil tied to its spine. TOO MUCH OIL IN THE SAUCE.
Bored wives sleep around, everyone drinks, an acidy wine, probably from someone's uncle's vineyard, was served gratis at
lunch. By the late sixties, when I knew it, errant classical scholars not only occasionally threw up in the fountain in the inner
court — PUKE IS NO GOOD FOR THE GOLDFISH — but at least one
artist's wife OD'd. That was a first. By the last time I was there
a few fellows looked as if their unnaturally wide eyes were *not*
staring unblinkingly into the future. I'd go crazy if I had gotten
a grant and had to live there, I used to reason beyond the pang
of envy and annoyance of having applied and lost. Why is it easy
to believe winners don't deserve to win, that they are lucky, shallow, and have prominent relatives? And why is it such a shock,
after you've won a prize or two yourself, to see that people think

you are lucky, shallow, and have prominent relatives?

Grantless, I used the Center's library often. Luckily I had almost all my index cards filled by the autumn I met Alice. For afterward, every time I went to the Center I was distracted. I couldn't help imagining how it had been in the early fifties, when Alice met Leo there. I'd take more breaks than usual, sitting in the courtyard on one of the benches dedicated to Americans who lost their lives during the First World War. My eyes would go over the ancient fragments neatly placed into the peach stucco of the opposite wall and I'd think of Alice's story. I'd think of Nick's jealousy of Leo as I walked over to the fountain and watched the goldfish gulp. Or when I'd look up over the loggia to see if I could catch any of the grantees walking around their rooms in their underwear. If I wanted more sun, I'd take a break in the extensive back gardens, where I had first met Alice. The Center was built in the early twentieth century by an American millionaire. If not authentically Old World, the extensive villa is a terrific compilation of the type of imagination that once led to it. It is a very contemplative place if your nerves hold up. WHEN IS THE PLUMBER COMING TO ROOM 416? EMERGENCY!!!!! I had plenty of time to reconstruct what happened that day in the fifties when, as Alice put it, Nick lost his fountain pen.

"Where is it?" Nick asked.

He and Alice were in their room. They had an outside view; from their window they could see down to Rome. Alice had placed his desk by that window. She walked over to it and carefully went through the drawers.

"I don't see it," she said. "Can you remember the last time you used it?"

"It was here! It was right here!"

She kept quiet.

"You don't give a damn, do you? You'd be happy if I didn't send this!" He held in his hand the letter she had typed for him and left on his desk for signing.

"Nick, it's your decision."

"Really? So you think I should leave the firm? You like the letter?"

"I think Burt Adams had his hopes pinned on you. He gave you time off to accept this grant. Of course he doesn't have to offer you the salary you can get in Ohio with Keeger's firm. But Ohio isn't New York, Nick."

"Really? You mean Ohio isn't New York? All this time I thought Ohio was New York, and now you tell me it isn't. Cleveland. At least Cleveland. Come on, Cleveland's New York, isn't it, Alice. Isn't it?"

"Oh, Nick."

"Don't 'oh Nick' me."

"Why are you doing this? You're good at what you do, Nick. You'll be good anywhere. I'll go with you anywhere."

"That's just it. There's New York and there's Anywhere. You're such a snob, Alice. You think New York is the only place in the world. Well, I don't."

Well, of course he did. According to Alice, that is. In New York he had been Burton Adams' fair-haired boy. And Burton Adams was a scholar of international law. He could get you a grant. And Wienlohf. Wienlohf could get the clients. Adams and Wienlohf. It was like Harvard and E. F. Hutton. You couldn't beat it. It was the big league. Until Nick left for Rome, he had been willing to climb that staircase to paradise as slow as the rules. Nicholas Russo. He saw his constellation laid out against the heavens on a clear night.

Nothing changed, except that he had his thirtieth birthday while at the American Center. At the same time he received an offer from Keeger Associates in Cleveland that more than doubled the salary he would go back to at Adams and Wienlohf, and it foretold a partnership.

So he looked at Alice, his eyes burning with contempt. "Here, here!" he screamed and he crumpled his letter of acceptance to Keeger. It wrinkled up sounding like one of the tin cans she used to crush during the war. "Now are you happy, you bitch?"

"Nick! *I'm* going to have to retype that!"

"Don't you think I know what's going on between you and the kitchen help? You know where it is! Don't you think I know who stole my fountain pen?"

FOUNTAIN PEN MISSING!

"I hear Nick lost his fountain pen." Yanoff came over to her in the salone during tea that afternoon. The salone of the Center is a huge room with large-scale history paintings by Anonimo and Circo Di. The original owner of the villa was no Berenson. There's a grand piano, a pool table (he played pool), Persian carpets, and plush sofas. Yanoff was in his thirties then. I was to meet him years later, in the seventies, when he was quite well known and living in New York. I asked him then if he remembered Alice Blanders Russo. It took him a moment. "The blonde," he said. He was as offhanded as Alice, who has always called his work "melted nudes." She name-drops "Clyde Yanoff" as if his fame were an indictment against modern art. She's not too hot on modern art anyway. She sees nothing pretty in the dearrangement of the human form.

The Center is the type of place where you can say "I hear Nick lost his fountain pen" with all sorts of nuances. Especially in the grand salone. It gave Alice the willies when Yanoff said that. She said she didn't know why. I think she knew why.

It had to do with Leo. He modeled naked for Yanoff in his off hours. Here are two of Leo's favorite stories. He probably told them to Yanoff.

The first one's a story Leo tells on Alice. It occurred in Trastevere during the Feast of Noi Antri, late August, Alice's first summer in Rome. Nick was away on an organized trip to some hill towns. Alice was alone. Who's left in Rome in August? She walked down to the festa from the Center. She took that wonderful route past the sheets of water cascading from the Acqua Paula to the Spanish church with Bramante's little temple (the Renaissance in a nutshell) in its courtyard. Then she descended the stairs that led along the wall of the Arcadian Academy. The Arcadians were eighteenth-century Romans of good family and artistic inclinations who sat in their club's green garden, writing verse about and dressing up like sweet-smelling shepherds of an age gone by. You have to be made of gold to mourn the Golden Age.

I think of those dazzling Romans, glinting, so near the side streets of Trastevere. On those streets the wrinkled black-clad women still sit outside their tottering medieval ruins. They still cook outdoors on little charcoal braziers, red ripe tomatoes, alive with the smell of earth, by their side. Wives nurse. Children stir up the noise of the street. If the eighteenth-century Arcadian gentlemen had peeked over their walls, they would have encountered the Golden Age. The experience would have done a hell of a lot for their poetry.

Down walks Alice to the native quarter of Rome. Here live people who were Roman in the days of Rome. Their festival is in August, when those who live on the right side of the Tiber are at the beach, in the mountains, out to lunch. Noi Altri. We others. The old, old feast of people who have always had their Roman origins and their poverty to celebrate.

Alice walks down the jagged scar of a side street to the wide, flat, modern thoroughfare, Viale Trastevere. The street looks like Anytackytown, USA, at Christmastime. Colored lights are strung up. Under them the avenue is lined with game stands, food stands, buy-some-things stands. In the fifties you could buy wooden things. Now you can buy plastic things. The food stands haven't changed. The most popular are still those where the huge, long roasted pigs stuffed with herbs, the famous porchetta di Ariccia, are sold. Alice was standing in a crowd, looking at the pig from a distance. Its face was tanned and crisp. Its body had been cut open, cleaned, and reconstituted so that the layer of gleaming white fat surrounded a mound of green herbs pressing flesh.

Suddenly there were two hands in front of her. In one hand there was half a loaf of coarse-grained country bread, in the other a tan package, at least three ettos of the pork.

"Are you hungry?"

"Leo! Why, I'm starved. But —"

"But." He gave her the bread so that he could take her arm and lead her down the street to where the wooden tables were set out in front of the wine shops. The tables were very crowded, people everywhere. He spoke to a group quicker than she could understand, and two places opened up for them. He seated her there with the food and went into the store, returning with a liter of white wine and two glasses.

"Here," he said. "You have to learn to push or else you will die of hunger in Rome, Signora Alice. Especially in August, when the Center's kitchen is closed. What are you doing in Rome, anyway?"

"Where would I be?"

"Where is Signor Nick?" He said "Signor Nick" as if it were a joke.

"My husband's on a trip. Right now he's probably at Gubbio."

Leo poured wine for them. Took out his pocketknife and cut the bread.

"What a feast!" she said.

"What a man, that husband of yours, leaving you in Rome to starve."

"Oh, I'm old enough to take care of myself, Leo. I wanted to stay in Rome. I needed time alone to catch up with many things. And I wanted to see the feast."

Leo smiled as she talked, as if he didn't believe her. Or maybe it was she who didn't quite believe she wanted to be alone. She spoke in a slow but accurate Italian. Still, he might not have understood every word. It hardly mattered. The people. The wooden tables. The porchetta sandwiches. The wine. Here she was in the middle of the festival. She felt part of it suddenly. "I'm so glad to be here. You must let me pay my share, Leo."

He ignored her comment.

"You have enough mouths to feed," she continued. He had told her about his life. Of the wife he had had to marry. Of her desertion. Of how she left their son with him.

He shrugged. "Forget Naples." She had told him of her trip from Naples to Rome after she had disembarked. Of the desolation of the war still all around her. "The war's over. Let's enjoy ourselves."

"I am enjoying myself. But how can we forget the war?" She looked at his open shirt, contemplated his naked neck. "Did you have to sell your medals during the war?"

It was a tipsy question. She'd admit that whenever Leo told the story. Sometimes she just comes out with things.

The night in Trastevere he looked at her attentively, trying to see what she'd just said. She wasn't like the other women he had known. She always said more than he expected. But this time? He pointed to his neck to make sure. "You mean?"

"Yes. Did you have to sell your saint's medal?"

He burst out laughing. Alice looked around to see if anyone was there to notice.

He hunched over the table toward her. Pushed away the scraps of food and the paper. Poured more wine. Then he told his story. "I don't need a medal around my neck," he said, as if it was a secret. "I have my honor."

"Your honor?"

"Yes. The priest came to me. I remember the night. A night like this, Signora Alice. Hot and beautiful, only without you, without porchetta, without wine. It was during the last days before occupation. I was fifteen, the right age. Perfect." He raised his thumb and forefinger to form an O. "The priest took me into the sacristy. It was quiet. We were alone. We could hear my stomach growl. He lit a holy candle and held it up so I could see what he had in his hand. Like this!" Leo raised one hand above his head and then looked to what was dangling from the other. "Saint Christopher carrying the world on his shoulders on a nice chain — all gold. Gold. I can see it now. But what the priest wanted for his gift I could not give. I preferred to go hungry. He kept the medal and chain. I kept my honor."

Alice's eyes widened. "You mean . . . ?"

"Look all around you! Look at them. Do you see one man without a chain and a medal?"

"You mean to tell me . . . ?"

"Every single one of them, Signora Alice. There's not a real man left in Rome since the war. The priests have made every one of them bend over. I tell you their secret to warn you. There's not one left who's not a fag. So stay away from them all!"

The second one's a joke: the American and the prostitute.

The American meets the prostitute outside of Castel San Angelo and they bicker about the price. When the price is settled they go to a room. Only then does the prostitute tell the American she has the curse. No matter. He's willing to do it from the rear. After they've had sex, the American complains about how bad things are in his country, how high taxes are. "You think you have it bad," the prostitute says. Here Leo dropped his falsetto and said in a deep voice, "What about us in Italy? Do you know how hard we have to work for a piece of bread? By day, I'm a construction worker."

Alice laughed when Leo told this. "Imagine, Betsy. 'By day, I'm a construction worker.' Poor Italy."

No wonder Alice warned him to be careful of how he joked in front of Yanoff, that day in the fifties after Yanoff approached her about Nick's fountain pen.

"I'd be careful of Yanoff, Leo."

"I know how to handle him," Leo answered.

"I don't trust him."

"Neither do I."

They were far out in the back gardens, near the old caretaker's shack that was now a studio, Yanoff's studio that year.

Leo said, "I hear Signor Nick lost his fountain pen yesterday."

"How did you hear that? Do you see what I mean about Yanoff? He told you."

"Today Signor Nick was not at lunch. We had to send the poor man a tray."

"*Nick*, Leo. *Nick*. Why must you always irritate him? Signor Nick. The way you say it! Why must you be so rude to him? Don't you think he notices? He has so much on his mind."

"He has a big head. He can carry what is on his mind."

"He has a big brain, Leo. He's a very talented man. He has

ideas about people and society. He can be rude, too, I know. He doesn't realize how uncaring he sometimes seems. But we can't be everything to everyone in this world, Leo."

"You don't have to defend him to me. I wash dishes. I pose for a few lire. I have nothing on my mind. He'd be angry at you for defending me. I'm not one of his people. I'm not in his society."

"I'm defending him to me, can't you see?"

"Don't cry. Did he hit you? If he hit you —"

"No, he didn't hit me. It's self-flagellation. He's hitting himself. He's up in our room, insisting on retyping a letter. He's getting himself wound up on erasures. He'll have a floor full of discarded copies before he'll call on me. He'll blame it all on me. I can retype the letter. But I can't tell him what he wants to hear."

"What's that?"

"He wants to hear that I think he's doing the better thing by leaving New York, by accepting an offer in Cleveland. And he may be. Who am I to say?"

"You don't think so?"

"I know they want him in Cleveland. I know how attractive a firm can make an offer sound. When a firm in America is wooing you, it's just like a courtship."

"Then there's the marriage. What happens after Signor Nick is deflowered?"

"Really, Leo."

"Well, I made you smile."

She stretched, reached up, and touched a leaf. "I don't know how it will be after the honeymoon."

"You should know."

"That's what he thinks too. He knows how rocky things can get for him."

"Excuse me. After the honeymoon, does the firm take away money, position, a free hand?"

"I doubt that — as far as money and position go. But I'm not so sure about a free hand. Nick will be meeting some very conservative clients. He may not, in the long run, if he wants money and position, have such a free hand."

"Poor man. He'll have money, a good position; he'll have you.

Hello, Lawyer Russo, people will say as he walks down the street. But they won't know how he suffers. They won't know he can't do everything he wants. Such a shame. Too bad his parents didn't stay in Italy. Not only would he have learned Italian properly, but he could have done errands for the GIs when he was a kid. He could have put toilet paper, sugar, beans, under his overcoat and run them home to his mother. Then when the Center reopened, because he was so industrious and never got caught, he could be recommended for a job in the kitchen. No money, no position. Never mind. In the kitchen of the Center you are allowed not only one, but it is demanded that you have two free hands."

She looked at him steadily. "The more people have, the more they want."

"I want you," he said. "If I had you, I'd be happy forever."

A week later, Nick lost a navy blue sweater. He slapped Alice hard across the face. "Get it back, you bitch."

"He hit you," Leo said. They were in the loggia. There were people around.

"No."

"What's wrong, then? Was he offered more money? Are they going to make him President of the United States? What new tragedy has hit that big brain you say he has in his big head?"

"He lost his blue sweater."

THINGS ARE DISAPPEARING. LOCK YOUR DOORS.

"I hear Nick lost a sweater," Yanoff said to her the next day. Yanoff was thin, medium height; he had burning black eyes. He was a dry man, his humor a matchtip scratching against flint.

"How did you hear?"

"Your husband told me, my dear. I commiserated with him. After all, we have something in common. He has things taken from his room. I have things taken from my room. I lose things too."

She knew what Yanoff was getting at. So did I when she told me this story. Alice never had to spell it out for me. None of us spelled things out in Rome. We relied on the sophistication of the city and our own sensibilities to clothe our vagrant imaginations in tact.

"You're interested in human nature," Alice would say to me when she realized she was talking on and on about Leo and the old days at the Center, or when she realized she was telling me something very private about Leo and Nick and her. By saying it, she immediately and momentarily turned her experience into something objective. We were on a field trip together. She couldn't talk too much for me. I used to be such a good listener, back in Rome, when we were the best of friends. Alice's words were as clear as water and I held a cup to them. I could imagine what went around the Center while Yanoff and Nick Russo were losing things. SEX SUSPECTED! The blue plate special. SEX GOING ON! SPRING SEX SCANDAL!

It is May. Nick has accepted the Cleveland offer. The terms are set. May, June. At the end of July, Alice will be gone from Rome. She looks concerned, tense. She won't cry uncle. All she has to say is Cleveland is New York, that the Big Apple will regret its snobby pay scale, that Nick Russo has made the best of all possible decisions in the best of all possible worlds. Whenever Nick looks at her now he sees his shadow. This wonder boy from Baltimore came from nowhere and studied with the best. He almost set the firm of Adams and Wienlohf on its head. He didn't marry a virgin in the Church. Now he's beginning to want for himself what his mother, who speaks broken English, has wanted for him all along.

What's wrong with that?

Alice kept quiet. Personally, I don't see anything wrong with it myself. Alice always put it that Nick couldn't live with himself because he thought he had sold out. In one way or another he had to obliterate the New York years in order to find peace. At the time, I accepted Alice's diagnosis: "It's a terrible thing, Betsy, when a man blinds himself to everything except measuring success by money." What I didn't understand then is why, loving him so much, she didn't yes him. Maybe Cleveland *was*

New York. After all, my marriage wasn't based on great passion; still, I knew when it was essential in our relationship for me to yes a man. Not Alice. After Nick accepted the offer, he always saw the unexpressed no in her eyes.

But when Leo looked into her eyes, he looked into a mirror. She was as reassuring as his face, and almost as familiar. She'd come to him, a late war reparations gift, from across the seas.

Leo's early days weren't so different from those of the rock stars later on. With the rockers of the sixties it was a flood of girls. They were everywhere, those girls. After concerts there was a stampede. Unlisted phones, unlisted addresses. Open your door, chain still on, girls slid in. There were the mornings after — strange girls in strange motel rooms, strange girls in your bed. Walk down a country road and open your mailbox. Strange girl. If there was a DDT or TAT or Roach Motel for strange girls, they'd come crawling out of the sinks, from under the floorboards. You'd find them writhing on tile bathroom floors, sliding out from under radiators. You couldn't shave without looking past your lather in the mirror to the heaps of miniskirted, long-haired, smooth-legged, small-assed strange girls from the night before.

It's got to be hell after a while, all these strange girls looking for something, crazy for somebody, all obsessions pinned on you. So you'd OD or find another way to die or go into therapy or go to India or find a girlfriend or marry the goddess and call her mother or get smart in business and rich as Croesus and send your logos to the moon. It's got to leave a bitter taste — everyone, including yourself, fucking your mind. It's your talent, it's your God-given, devil-powered talent, that sets the electricity snapping through the electronics of the room.

With Leo, the consequences were different. He wasn't talented or cerebral or eccentric. He was very sexy and he was very nice. His equipment included an empty stomach; he was thankful when he got enough to eat. He knew when an Italian fucked him over. Like the girl he had to marry. The strange girls in Rome all had papas and the Church. He stayed away from his neighborhood after it was too late. He didn't go to the baptism of his son.

He hung around the Americans. He was damn lucky he was sympathetic. Even when his English made no sense, he did. I think for many Americans, he *was* Rome. He realized this quickly, and for him it was a benediction. After the war, by the fifties, he had already gone through rock star confusion. He had learned to know when he had had enough. I'm not saying he made any sweeping renunciations. Through his life, whether or not he played it well, women would always be his trump card. What I am saying is, as young as he was when he met Alice, he'd been through a lot. He loved her.

Alice's talent for romance must have come from her mother. She grew up in a household where romance happened. Men arrived with flowers, poems, baubles. Boring men, probably bringing offerings to the outsides of things. Nothing was too small or too big for Maple's *whoop!* of acceptance. When it came to taking, Maple Blanders was as democratic as all get-out. She saved wrappings and ribbons, got them neatly tucked out of harm's way, just in case she had to draw blood. By the time Alice was born, Maple's acting career was over. Alice said that after years of marriage she assumed a new role, the virtuous wife and mother. Richard Blanders was a big man in New York politics. He had handcrafted her career. Who knows how many of Maple's suitors were after him? He died unexpectedly.

"Daddy's ill," Maple told Alice. "I'm going to take care of him." Dramatically underplaying her words, she then walked into her bedroom, stretching an arm out behind her to close the door. A day and a half later the police broke down that door. Maple was in bed with the corpse. Richard Blanders, whose stink had alerted the household, was stiff. It took more than an hour to maneuver him down the winding wooden staircase. Alice watched the inhuman descent of her father while Maple wailed her goodbyes.

That summer Alice was eleven, and Maple had a new way to keep a suitor at arm's length. When necessary, the widow, resplendent in flowing black, would have Alice walk with her and the gentleman in her gardens that overlooked the Hudson. On command from her mother, the little girl would uncoil the rope attached to the old elm and lower Daddy's ashes from the branches. Alice eloped at fourteen.

She had found romance. She was quite infatuated with her first husband, twice her age, dashing, handsome, rich. "He's a wastrel," Maple warned her. Save your wrappings, honey; Mommy's telling you true. Alice had a son by him so young that Brad Jr.'s age never seemed to date her. But Brad Sr. was definitely a child of the twenties. He seemed to go out with them — *crash*. I see him in a tux and a top hat. I see him with Alice and Brad Jr. in the little basement apartment that appalled his parents and that Alice insisted on after all his squanderings. Living in a tenement they could afford was perhaps Alice's first taste of independence. Here the no-frill policy began to emerge. People could actually live without admirers, servants, champagne, and Daddy's urn swinging from a hundred-year-old elm. I see him after his parents lost everything, losing himself. Now he is a blur, sitting in his room in the sanitarium. He fades away. I am left to think he died a drunk, somewhere, I don't know where, out of reach. The tux tattered, the top hat flattened. He's as unreal as the crazy things we do in youth, against experience and someone else's better judgment.

She doesn't talk about Number Two too much. I think he kept her. I think she did him for Brad Jr.'s college education. Married him reluctantly. When she saw Brad Jr. knocked to the floor, and Number Two in a drunken rage looming over him, she got hit right between the eyes with what she thought she had done for someone else's welfare.

One and Two were husbands. Lovers I don't count. They peek through in some of her stories, especially after she started to go to business. She just had a nice way of having lovers without letting them obtrude.

Then there was Nick.

She had tried to dissuade Nick from marrying her. She hadn't considered it wise. She told him the age difference wasn't propitious, that he was just starting out. She knew his Italian mamma didn't like the idea. She was in awe of his strong, down-to-earth mother, who worked her life away to educate her son. She was everything Maple hadn't been. Alice respected her, just as she would look up to Leo's mother. Maple was dead by the time of Nick. She had spent her last years trying to get the New York papers to run an exposé of Alice, who allowed Maple Blanders to walk around Manhattan. One month the *Times*, one month the *Telegram*. She'd go from daily to daily, toting what she salvaged on the way. Alice never could get her committed. She inherited her mother's brownstone by default.

Nick's glamorous older woman came with a brownstone and a past. He loved it all. She tried to be fair about it. She told him he could share it all, but best not to marry. Nick was the sworn enemy of a no. Maybe she knew it. He was the love of her life. How fair could she be? He wants what he wants when he wants it. And I was weak, she'd often say. I gave it to him. And that was no good for him either. He needed a more demanding woman. Someone more like his mother, who'd say, Nick, you do this and you do that. Someone who'd keep him in line. Alice would say, "You do this and you do that," imitating an Italian accent. I loved the way she said that; it was tough and warm and without malice. Yes, she'd repeat, someone more like his mother or his second wife.

Well, whatever Leo and Alice were or were not doing, Nick was sure they were making a fool of him. It was one thing to leave Alice in New York to raise her own fare, beg her in passionate letters to come to Rome, not meet her in Naples, then in a blaze of self-recrimination and doubt set a fire between them again. After all, Nick was a young man just starting out, a brilliant man susceptible to the torments of talent. Alice was older, tested. She was not the most up-to-date minute hand you could buy, racing round the hour. The world as well as Mamma Russo must see he could have done much better. For her, who owed him, *him*, to take up with Leo Conti. He'd kill that bastard, he'd kill them both.

And what did Leo's looks and youth mean anyway? Everyone

in the Center knew about him and Yanoff. "Sheer nastiness," Alice said. Poor Leo. Life was tough. By day he was a construction worker. Let him who has an empty stomach cast the first stone. That's the way Alice saw it, I'm sure, though this was a subject she alluded to rarely in our conversations. It was a significant entry only under the category World War II, brought out just in the direst emergency to illustrate the lunacy of nations.

The way Leo said "Clyde Yanoff" made me think of the relationship differently. Alice would bristle when he said what a good painter Yanoff was. But Leo loved to recount to us that, on his first visit to the States with Alice, he went to see himself in a museum. All the bitterness about what happened at the Center had faded.

I can understand that. Yanoff was probably the most intelligent and sensitive person Leo had met up to the time he met Alice. And he spoke a fine Italian. He was someone Leo could talk to, someone who could show him more. Sometimes I think Leo's acute grasp of the ironies of life owes a lot to what he learned from Yanoff. What could a woman give him? These strange girls were bred in individual bodies, but they shared a mind-set. They could tease him, make him hard, go hysterical, give him guilt, give him a son. Girls are dumb. Alice was a first. She brought something to him. She made him hard, she made him think. Any time he saw her at the Center, he had an overwhelming desire to touch her, hold her, love her, talk. I think she was the first woman, perhaps the only woman, he ever really loved. I also think he was already riding high, posing for Yanoff's melted nudes, when he met her.

And when Leo rode high, he was reckless. Boy, I've seen that myself. He taunted Yanoff by taking what he wanted from his room. Why not? I don't mean to make Yanoff and Leo out as a marriage of true minds. The bottom line is they were a colonial situation.

So when Yanoff heard Nick Russo was losing things, he retaliated. He told Nick, emphatically, that he, Yanoff, was losing things too. The implication was deadly. Leo Conti was servicing one sophisticated fag and one lonely older woman. As a statement, that sure is ugly. But in a place like the Center, statements are evaded, implications draw attention the way eggs served outdoors on a hot summer day draw bees. BUZZ, BUZZ, BUZZ, went the Center, relishing, embroidering. And since the villa was a closed circuit, pitched on top of a city none of the grantees called home, the gossip became part of the local language, became a custom overnight. (Hey, I can't find my toothbrush. Who's been fucking Leo Conti around here?)

Leo and Alice are in the back gardens. She's warning him about Yanoff. The clear blue sky itself seems the source of an even flow of light, but the sun takes careful aim. It glints the head off the marble colossus of Jesus Christ that looks down on them from the neighboring convent's roof. There's the smell of moist earth, new grass, and small spring flowers. Lunch is over and the kitchen cleaned. Everyone is asleep now or resting. When Leo lifts his arm to take a drag of his cigarette, Alice can smell his sweat.

"Don't worry about Yanoff. He needs me. Let's go in the studio. I'll show you what he's making of me right now."

"I'm sure the door's locked."

"I can get in."

"Yanoff would be furious if you broke in. That's exactly what I'm talking about, Leo."

"He won't know. Leave it to me. Come on, Alice."

"No, Leo. It wouldn't be wise."

"I can't talk with you like this. I want to be with you. Soon you're going to leave."

"I wish I were gone already. The sooner we all go home, the better for you."

"The better for me?"

"Yes. I'm afraid we are going to cause you trouble."

"Trouble? Please, Alice, come inside with me."

"No."

"Then where? When? Are we never to see each other? Here, take this."

"What's this?"

"It's my address, if you're so afraid of trouble. Flora, my sister, she'll always know where to reach me if I'm not home. Come see me."

"What purpose would it serve, Leo?"

"We'll take a walk. Like we did last summer. A walk. One more walk. Is that too much to ask? I love you, Alice. I'll always love you. When you leave, my life will walk away."

"Leo —"

"Just one walk. Is that too much to ask?"

"Leo —" What Alice saw was a blur approaching them. It was Nick, running, crouched, cut in half by a Rumpelstiltskin rage. Leo, disappear! That's what she was trying to say. Don't let this happen. Here comes trouble!

Nick came between them and grabbed Alice by the shoulders.

Leo restrained him from behind. Nick twisted free and faced Leo. "Keep your hands off me, you bastard!" Nick yelled.

"Leo!" Alice demanded. And then she called him "caro." She called him "dear" so that the intimate "tu" of her address would in no way sound as if she were commanding a child, a servant, or a dog. "Leo, dear, please go. This is between Nick and me. I'll be okay."

"Caro!" Nick screamed.

"Bravo, Signor Nick. You pronounce that well."

The two men were about to square off. Alice wedged between them and held on to her husband. Alice is unusually strong. "I won't have this. Do you want to wake everyone? Do you want everybody to see? Are you so bent on making a fool out of me, Nick?"

"I want my fountain pen back, Conti. Do you understand? I want my sweater. I want —"

"It's dirty, Nick. Plain dirty. You're in control. One punch at you and Leo loses his job. I won't have it. Do you understand? I won't have this boy on my conscience. You just be careful, Nick, before you go too far!"

She bossed him and he stopped. (You do this, Nick, you do

that.) "Get out of here, Conti," he said instead. "Get out of here before I kill you."

"Listen to him, Leo dear. Please! For me."

"Va bene, Signor Nick. For her, I'll get out of here before you kill me," he said, mocking Nick's awful Italian. Then attempting English, he said, "But you touch her, you make her hurt, I kill you. Capisce? I kill you. English is semplice, Mr. Nick. I kill you." Then he turned and walked away.

"Thief!" Nick called after him. "Ladro!"

Turning to her, sweating with rage, Nick said, "*Dear* Leo, huh? The briefcase, the one that was too expensive for you to like —"

"I said it was lovely, Nick."

"Well, it's gone. The pen. The sweater. The briefcase. Three strikes. That bastard's out."

"Nick, what are you saying? Who are you accusing? What proof do you have? It's all malicious rumors. Sheer nonsense."

"Look at you! Defending that trash. You don't give a shit about my briefcase. You don't give a shit about me. You let him in our room. For all I know he's in my bed while I'm out! What do you care about what I've lost? It's all the same to you. Where's that love, all that love for me? Where have you been while I've had all of these problems, all of these decisions to make? What do you care? You don't give a damn for me. Aren't I young enough for you, Alice? Don't you get enough of what you like for free? I'm sick of paying the bills, hear me? I don't care who hears, who knows, who thinks what. I'm not about to pay for your lover. Stay here. Starve with him. I wish you *would* get off my back. But him — if he knows what's good for him, he'd better give me back every single thing!"

A few days later Leo did not show up at work. He had heard the rumor that he had been denounced. Denounced to the police. It was a stupid, evil rumor. He ran scared.

Leo's sister answered the door. Flora was tall and big-boned with a lot of dark matted hair. Maybe it was being stuck with

Leo's looks that soured her. Anyway, she had none of his grace.

"What do you want?" she asked Alice.

"I'd like to see Leo."

"He's not here."

"He said you'd know where he is."

"Who are you?"

"I'm Alice Russo."

"I don't know where he is."

"Well, may I leave a message?"

"Make it quick, okay? I'm alone with the kid. My mother's out. God knows where my brother is."

"Alice!"

"Stay away from the door!" Flora yelled at her brother. Then she turned back to Alice. "He makes fools of all women, Signora. Why shouldn't he make a fool of me? Come in."

"Come in, Alice. Come in," Leo repeated. "Flora, do something with Cosimo. Disappear, okay?"

Disappear? She and his three-year-old son? She shrugged.

He took Alice's hand. "Come with me."

Alice sat in the kitchen. It was a big room, the living room as well, and judging from the cot, someone slept there too.

"Here," Leo said, "Flora made coffee. Just like teatime at the Center. May I serve you, Signora?"

He sat across from her and poured the coffee. "You're an angel to come here."

"Yanoff told me he saw you yesterday morning."

"Did he?" Leo rubbed a hand over his face.

"You should have stayed at the Center and gone to work."

"And been arrested?"

"That's nonsense, Leo. Yanoff told me he was kidding you. No one's denounced you. It's a rumor. A nasty, ugly rumor."

"How do you know?"

"I know."

"Your husband thinks I'm taking something from him. I wish I were. Don't you think his Italian is good enough to go to police headquarters and report me?"

"Is that what Yanoff told you? It's not true."

"How do you know?"

"Nick swore to me he'd done no such thing."

"You believe him?"

"Absolutely. He's very sorry for losing his temper."

"He's wooing you."

"Perhaps, but he's also very sorry for losing his temper," she repeated. "We had a long talk."

Nick had asked her forgiveness. It was late last night. He'd come back to the room. "It's this." He had handed her a letter. She sat up in bed. Turned the lamp on. A letter from Burt Adams: "We'll feel your loss at Adams and Wienlohf. Certainly, however, you owe it to yourself to accept what you consider to be the more beneficial offer. I can only wish you the best of luck in your career."

"What about it, Nick?"

"I don't know." Tears rolled down his face. "Alice, do you think I've done the best thing?" He sobbed.

"Oh, Nick."

"Forgive me, Alice."

She did . . .

"Leo, I don't deny that he is missing things," Alice continued. "But now he admits he doesn't know who's taken them. It's not just he and Yanoff who are missing things from their rooms. Yanoff made up that little fantasy. It suits him. There's thievery at the Center, that's certain. I assume it's one of the grantees who's never needed a cent."

"I take what I want from Yanoff."

"You do?"

"He wouldn't denounce me. You say your husband didn't?"

"I know he didn't. He might have liked to hurt you, but he didn't. No one's denounced you. So please come back to work."

"Do you think with all the men out of work in Rome, they'll keep someone who has been called a thief, someone who was rumored denounced?"

"Of course they'll keep you."

He smiled. "Until August, when the Center's kitchen closes. Until August is better than nothing. Who told you I should come back?"

"No one."

"Ah, you see!"

"I see you're an innocent man. Don't let the world make you out a guilty one. You say they'll fire you in August. If you're so sure of it, of course they will. But if you insist on your rights, you'll keep your job. You can't hide. You must not run away. You must be there. You must let everyone see you. You must insist on your rights. You're innocent!"

She was making her point by clapping her open hand on the table. He took her hand in his and kissed it. "You're an angel to have come here."

When he had heard the doorbell, he was sure it was the police. His stomach had leaped into his mouth. Then he saw Alice, as determined and as beautiful as a celestial avenger, in the hallway with Flora. He was startled at first. She had come for their walk. Yet panic was not conducive to desire. What if he couldn't give her pleasure that day? But fears of that had receded as they drank their coffee and as they talked. No denunciation. No police. Alice right here, alone in the kitchen with him. He went over to her, knelt down, and buried his face in her lap. She comforted him. She kept telling him things would be all right. Then he surprised her. He took her by the waist, and when he stood up, she was being carried over his shoulder like a child or a sack of flour. He took her to another room.

The blinds were closed in Roman fashion to keep out heat and dust. The room was dark and cool as night. He deposited her on the bed. She could feel the embroidery on the bedspread. He was holding her, telling her he loved her, building up to the passion he had promised her, the one walk they could take. He had his hands under her blouse when he felt her body go against him. She put her hands over his, stopped him, and sat up. "Nick is expecting me," she said. "He knows I am here."

"What?"

He sat up too. "You told him you were coming here? Why did you do that?"

She didn't answer. She got off the bed and straightened her clothes. Leo was furious. She felt misunderstood.

"Come back to work," she said.

He got off the bed. "Okay." That's all he said.

At the door she said, "I'll see you at the Center tomorrow."

Leo returned to work the next day. He was arrested mid-morning.

"How well I understand," Alice said to me. I was telling her about the trouble my old friend Salmanda had had with the law. "Being black or being as poor as Leo was."

"Did Leo have trouble like that?"

"Well, yes . . . at the Center. He was arrested there."

"Arrested?"

"Nano never told you?" Nano, the librarian at the Center, was so homely that he often spoke into a world of spite.

"No, he never said a word."

"I thought he might have."

"Listen, Alice, don't talk about it if you don't want to."

"I don't mind telling you, Betsy. It says so much about human nature. Here was Leo who had nothing, yet someone obviously thought he had much too much. All that kleptomania at the Center that year. Nick losing his fountain pen, Clyde Yanoff losing one small thing after another. Someone blamed Leo. Someone denounced him to the police."

"Who?"

"I don't know for sure, though I think it was one of Clyde Yanoff's cruel jokes. I'll never forget Carl Forester's face. Imagine, the police coming right into the president's office. The Italian police at the American Center. You know, he came from quite a family, Carl. A Chicago family. He was so well mannered. Manners and pots of money. He had beautiful silk suits made for him in Rome. He called Nick and me in. He was livid with rage. 'Russo,' he said. *Russo*, can you imagine? 'Russo, did you file that denunciation? Do you have anything to do with this?' Nick was furious too. The way Carl said his last name, as if there were something wrong with an Italian last name, as if Nick couldn't be trusted.

"'I have nothing to do with this, *Forester*. You can take the whole place and shove it, as far as I'm concerned.'

"'That's your idea of loyalty, is it?'

"Well, Nick didn't even know what he meant. After all, why shouldn't the Center give him a grant, pay his passage both ways, feed him meals? He hadn't denounced Leo. No one denounced Leo. It was like trying to find a fascist after the war.

"It was a terrible prank, you see. The denunciation was signed Signor Inu Endo. Do you know that joke? What does the Italian call the homosexual? Something like that. It was going round the Center at the time.

"'Carl,' I said when things calmed down and the two of them were trying to sort through all the rumors. Carl was scared stiff that this affair would hit the papers. 'What about Leo Conti?' I asked. 'He's a poor man. His being denounced is a prank. Is the Center going to put up his bail?'

"'Bail, Alice?' Nick looked at me as if I'd grown dimwitted. 'There is no bail in Italy.'

"No bail. Can you imagine, Betsy? Why, if it weren't for Nano's conniving . . .'"

Nano came from the same neighborhood as Leo, worked for the GIs and then for the Center, like Leo. He's still there. His office is in the basement of the library, where flat slices of light cut through the gloom way above his head. Nature visited Nano when he was in his mother's womb, toyed with the idea of deforming him, and then decided against it, but barely. Left him with a massive head on a short body. The heavy head is always pulled down, hunching his back after it toward the work on his desk. Every bill of lading at the Center goes through him. He smiles only when he catches an error. Americans often assume Nano is a nickname for Antonio. But an Italian nickname is as direct as an Italian stare. Nano means dwarf. Signor Nano, we called him respectfully. Mr. Dwarf.

He probably smiled when Alice walked down into his office

that day. He had a soft spot for her. "How's Signora Alice?" he'd always ask me. "When is she coming to tea?" He must have smiled at Alice; there were plenty of errors then, and I think he quietly adored blond hair. Also, Alice used to speak to him softly, with a tinge of regret. And that day, years ago, he could help her.

He rose. "Sit down, Signora Alice," he said.

"You called for me, Signor Nano?"

"That scoundrel Conti has caused me a month's work in less than a week."

"It's hard on you."

"Yes, indeed. Yet there is no reason it should be hard on you."

"An innocent man is in jail."

"Conti? Don't you worry about him, Signora. He's a phenomenon, that man."

"Is he?"

"He was born lucky. I've known him ever since we were boys together. He's immune to the confusion he causes all around him."

"Right now he's in jail."

"Pity the other inmates. Pity the warden. Pity yourself. Pity your dear husband. Pity me."

"He has caused you much work, dear Signor Dwarf. *That* I can see."

"Yes, he has. That's why I say, Don't you worry. I see you at meals with those heavy eyes. I see you, forgive me, angry with your husband. Part of my reward in this matter would be to save you trouble, Signora Alice. If I see you so sad, I lose, how do you say, part of my incentive. Do you understand?"

"I'm not so sure. Are you saying there is something I can do?"

"Yes. You can let me handle this. Do not worry. Go on about your life. Let me tell you directly, between us. Your husband did not denounce Conti."

"I know he didn't. But do you know who did?"

Nano put his hand up. "The denunciation has been revoked."

"Revoked?"

"It is a comedy of errors. The search to identify Signor Endo.

The police are embarrassed. It is mortifying all around."

"Oh, Signor Nano, you've cleared it all up?"

"I did not call you in to congratulate myself."

"But it's marvelous! You deserve congratulations. You deserve a reward."

"My reward is to see you smile."

"Well, I am smiling! And Leo . . . he'll want to reward you, I'm sure."

"Conti? By the time he's released, he'll have forgotten he was in jail."

"I don't understand."

"I do. I know him well."

"What do you mean, by the time he's released?"

"This is Italy, Signora Alice. Not New Jersey. These things take time."

"Time?"

"Formalities. There are ten hands for each piece of paper. It won't do any harm for Conti to wait."

"Wait? How long?"

"Now you are unhappy again. Believe me, Signora, it will not do that scoundrel harm to wait. A man thinks in jail. Look at Hitler. It will give Conti time to exercise another part of his body, forgive me. Maybe he'll come out with a plan."

"Leo Conti is a poor man. You know he has a son to feed."

"He should have thought of that. He should think, I am a poor man, before he creates a son to feed."

"That is none of our business."

"Excuse me. If I could do something to make you happy, I would. Forget Conti; for you I'd do it. But it comes back to the fact that he's a poor man. Justice is justice, that is certain. For a rich man, however, justice is swift. For example, how could I say to my cousin, There's a small man, a man like us, in your precinct. Make the paperwork fly for him. What is his, how do you say, incentive? Do you understand?"

"Without incentive, how long will the paperwork take? How many days?"

"Days? Weeks, months, Signora. I cannot predict. Time. It

takes time. And if there should be an error, a small mistake . . . Well, Conti will have time to try to think."

"If he were a rich man, how long would it take?"

"That too depends. He must have the right connections. My relative, for example, is a dependable man. If the rich man knew my relative, my relative would direct him through the right channels. My relative would make sure the ten hands complete the paperwork, that nothing is lost. He'd be out in a few days."

"I understand."

"Believe me, Signora, if it were up to me, I'd have my relative do it, just so you would smile. And my relative would do it as a favor for me. But the ten hands, Signora."

"How much would it cost?"

"Forty-five thousand lire."

"Forty-five thousand lire? Why, that's more than Leo makes a month, I'm sure."

He shrugged. "In dollars it's nothing. Not even a hundred. But forty thousand. I can try to get it done for forty."

She didn't answer.

"The scoundrel's not worth it, I know. Trust me. Let me see what I can do. I'll start at thirty-five."

Alice opened her pocketbook. She searched for her wallet, found it, unfolded it slowly. It was difficult for her to bring out the money. She was carrying more than usual, for no one was leaving money in the rooms. Once the lire were on the desk, however, she felt a flood of relief. The higher she counted, the more she wanted Nano to take it. Twenty-five thousand. She took out her change purse, fumbled, unlatched it, then poured the change out on his desk.

"There, you have it! Every last lira I have."

Twenty-six thousand, six hundred, and ninety-five.

"He's not worth even this, Signora. But for you, for you, I'll see what I can do."

Why wasn't she happy after that? Conti was out of jail. All's well that ends well. That was Nick's point. Leo had been fired. That was her point.

"How the hell could they let him come back?"

"It's not fair, Nick."

"What's not fair? He's free, isn't he? When in Rome, don't forget. That's how they do things here."

They were in their room; the sun was pouring through it. Nick was putting things in his briefcase. No one had stolen it. He hadn't looked hard enough, that's all. He had apologized to Alice for his earlier suspicions. He made light of his jealousy. Leo Conti was annihilated by his absence. The better man had won.

"Alice, are you sure you don't want to come?" Friends.

It was his last trip before they left. No, she had told him a few days ago. She'd stay in town, sort out books and papers, systematize the packing. Yes, that makes a lot of sense. It made Nick nervous to be stuck in the middle of preparations. You're gonna love it there, he had said the other day, including her. Soon he'd be back in the real world.

"Cheer up, will you! Come with me if you want to."

"No, Nick, I'll stay here," she told him again.

He grabbed his suitcase. He kissed her. A prelude to his running off to his office. "Goodbye, dear," she said automatically. "Have a good time."

He left her there in the sunny room. She looked out the window. She'd go down to Rome. A walk would do her good. It would loosen the cold stone at the bottom of her heart. She missed Leo. His absence told her something sad about the future.

She went to Campo dei Fiori. The square is a vegetable market in the morning. In late June cherries and asparagus make their appearance, and the tomato stands expand into varieties. Poor Bruno was burned at the stake in this square, for thinking, and his dark green statue, with its hooded, shadowed face, fights a losing battle to remind shoppers that something unjust happened here. Alice looked up at him; he stared down. What happened to him wasn't fair. Life. He got a statue out of it. She knew lots of people who got statues out of life. That's what Yanoff strove for. What does it mean to them, she wondered. What did the stage mean to her mother? What did those horrid canvases mean to Yanoff? He protected them childishly, drove Nano crazy the past month with picky arrangements to ship them out. He was on a boat now, along with his suite of gigantic melted Leos, satisfied. He didn't give a thought for the real Leo any more than her mother ever gave a thought for the real Alice under the flouncy baby doll dress. The Bruno made her angry. She found herself walking toward the periphery of Rome.

Leo opened the door. It was siesta time, but he was awake. He looked at her as if he were staring past bars.

"Did you tell your husband you were coming here?"

"My husband's on a trip," she said. "Right now he's probably being received by the mayor of Gubbio."

Gubbio, that's where Nick had been that August night when Alice had walked down from the Center to the Feast of Noi Antri and was surprised by Leo's outstretched hands.

"Ah! Dear, characteristic Gubbio. What I owe to that town! Come in, Alice, come in."

They sat in the kitchen. He made her take off her stockings. He prepared a bowl of warm water. He washed her feet. She watched him. He was very serious. With one big hand he held her foot, with the other he washed. When he was finished he dried each foot and massaged it. "Does that feel good?" he asked her.

"That feels very good," she said.

"You were right the last time you were here. This is better."

She did not go into what she had been wrong about the last time she was there — he *had* been denounced; he *did* go to jail. He was kissing her feet, her ankles. He was reaching up her legs for her.

There were other people in the house. She was musty after the long, hot walk. These things went through her head, then left her. He got up from where he had been crouched and locked the door behind them, closed the blinds. "This is my bed," he whispered. He took his mattress from the cot and laid it on the floor.

For the next two weeks they lived in a state of sheer recklessness. During the days she'd come to him. And at night he was insane enough to come to her. The first time was the first night. At two in the morning there was a hand on her face. "Leo!" "I'll be quiet, I promise." He undressed. He slipped into her bed. "This is madness," she told him as he put his arms around her. He agreed. She grew sore from love and was herself in a state of frenzy. Then it had to end as abruptly as it began and he was beside himself.

"I want you to stay with me!" he demanded.

"Leo, I can't."

"But you don't love him."

"Leo, I never said that."

"Then who am I to you?"

"Why, you're Leo. My dear, dear Leo."

"I love you."

"I love you."

"Then stay with me."

Of course it was impossible. Logistically, where? Economically, which one of them had a penny? Emotionally, she was Nick's wife.

Leo swore he'd never speak to her again. She was a betrayer. She was the only thing in the world that kept him alive. He would die. I'm dying right now, he said.

She insisted that he was not dying. He insisted there was nothing left to live for.

"Your son," she replied. "Your little son."

He was brutal. He bruised her the last time they were together. But Nick didn't notice a thing.

She stacked books, packaged them, signed declarations, and sorted. She was numb at the core. Nick had the right attitude now. He was up, up. He didn't notice a thing. Or, to be more accurate, he was where he would always be. In his own world. He had made peace with himself. He was happy enough with what stretched in front of him to be magnanimous to Alice. He was okay now. Conti was out of sight. Yanoff had gone home; he wasn't there to give him the needle. The firm had found them a place. Keeger himself had sent a glowing letter. Nick didn't notice a thing.

And she slowly became more hopeful as it came time to leave Rome, to be driven back to Naples. Nick's good mood was infectious. She tried not to feel so left out. What could there be for her and Leo? What they had already had in those two weeks. When you came right down to it, she might be leaving to go to an entirely new city, but that was where she belonged. She was going home.

The last night at the Center, she woke up at about the time that Leo used to appear, and once up, she just couldn't get back to sleep. She knew he was near. It takes a piece out of your common sense when you feel so close to a stranger. She resisted. But he would not recede. Two-thirty. Three. It would be dawn soon. Was he really there? Was it a dare? There was only one way to clear her head. She slipped a robe over her nightgown and crept out of the room and down the stairs.

A year and a half of my life, she thought as she walked through the courtyard and out into the back gardens. As she walked through the grass she convinced herself that she had been imagining it; Leo couldn't really be there. This was simply her way of saying goodbye.

"Alice!"

"Ssshh!"

She put her hands to his lips. "You're crazy, absolutely crazy. What am I going to do about you?"

They made love standing. Her legs were around his waist and her head was thrown back, her hair catching against the wall. He was filling her up with pleasure. She could feel him from her cunt up through the throbbing on the left side of her neck. She was having wave after wave of orgasm. He was not giving up. "You're going to drive me crazy too," she said. "No, no," he said. "I'm going to bring you back."

They must have looked wild and beautiful, touching that force. He with the body of an undernourished athlete; she, soft and abundant, woman through and through. When I met them years later, I could feel electricity running through the air.

He came finally, the way a man comes when he's doing more than coming, when he's having orgasm too.

"I don't know if I'll have the strength to make it to the boat," she whispered.

"Good," he said, contentedly. They were lying on the ground, on their damp and dewy clothes.

Goodbye, they said to each other finally.

"Alice, I love you. I'll always love you."

Her last words were "I'll write."

3

She wrote.

She kept Leo informed, sharing with him her days and her new friends, not to mention her new job in Keeger's office, the people who came to dinner, the films she saw. Writing in Italian, she must have conveyed the habits of the Americans in a very droll way, which would have suited Leo's sense of the absurd and sense of humor. These accounts were her staples, like the jars of anchovies in oil and pickled artichokes that she would later keep on the ledge over her kitchen table for him. They were similar to the newspaper clippings from the Italian papers that she would later put in folders marked *Italian Politics, The Mezzogiorno, Trattorias Outside Rome, Walking Tours* . . . She was Maple's daughter, but the scraps she saved were days. She hoarded them to share.

I imagine that she wrote stoutly about Nick's success in Keeger's firm, and his acclimation to Ohio. In the very bluntness of these reports, Leo would be able to hear her sigh. He would understand that Nick was mistreating her. He'd see through her

words as clearly as I would see her naked body through a nightgown — that summer in Italy when I was still putting her past
together in my mind. She was in the hallway. The sheer fabric
didn't hide a thing. Straightforward reports must have stirred
Leo's desire.

For three years Nick Russo wanted a divorce, and he didn't
want a divorce. He wanted her to leave, but he didn't want her
to leave. He wanted them to separate, but he wanted her to stay
in the same town. When he left her, she resigned from her sec-
retarial job at Keeger Associates and packed her bags. He
caught up with her in the train station. He begged her to
stay . . . in the same town, close to him; they'd still be friends.
When she refused, he boarded the train with her. The same Nick
who once swept her off her feet. He held her hand and cried all
the way to New York. Cried because he really was throwing her
away. He could count on Alice's love revolving around him. He
could count on her keeping a job, making a home, giving parties.
He was painfully nostalgic, now that he wanted other things. He
was young. He wanted children. Dynamic legal mind, soon to
be made partner in his firm, thirty-one, thirty-two, thirty-three,
sick of rentals, wants to build his dream home and fill it with
his own children. Please send picture. Please apply. Children?
Alice's child had children.

Back east, she moved into her son's house in Rutherford. Her
brownstone was rented out. After a while, she decided to put it
on the market. Brad and his wife had two small daughters. He
was a chemist and at the time worked in one of the industries
in the Jersey flatlands (now the Meadowlands), not far from
where I worked the summer after I started college with Salmanda.

Brad's his mother's son. Even now, when you're with him you
feel he understands expectations. He doesn't have them, though.
Maybe that's why he drinks. It's as if his early years with Alice
knocked something out of him — the spirit of adventure. I met
him only once, in Florida, last year. But that was my impression.

When his children were little, his wife wanted to go back to work. It was propitious, with Alice in their house in a daze. Leonore got a bookkeeping job in a bank and paid Alice to care for the children. Alice got room and board in Rutherford as well as two hundred dollars a month from Nick and the rent on the brownstone. Before Nick Russo could find a housewife of his own, Alice had become one for her son.

She cleaned the big house, she minded the children, she marketed. For one whole year she watched herself vacuum, plump up pillows, dust. She heard herself talking to children, reading them stories. She watched herself writing letters. Alice living like that? Imagine the state she was in.

Then Keeger came through. He was one of her many correspondents. He wrote that his two daughters and their two friends wanted to tour Italy that summer. Would she let him send her as well, as their cicerone and chaperone? Oh, yes, Leo wrote, come to Rome this summer, Alice. I am still waiting for you. She wrote back that she wasn't sure she could.

Alice has patience. She waits to see what happens before making demands. Time has often been her ally.

What was she waiting for? I'd ask myself, sitting in the Center's library. By then it was springtime in Rome and Alice was still telling me her story. How could she wait that long to come back to the heartstruck Leo? Now, if it had been me . . . Alice didn't realize the effect her life was having on me. She was telling me all that happened in order to remember Nick Russo. Nick Russo. I often wondered if I reminded Alice of him — right from the day she met me at the Center's back gardens. We were both Italian Americans, both from immigrant roots. I think he hurt her so much that she never talked him out. There were times I felt that for all her wisdom, for all the fullness of her life, when she spoke of Nick Russo she was still stunned. So she kept talking to me about her life with Nick, and I kept hearing Leo. I kept wondering, When will she leave Russo? When will she return to Leo's warm, strong arms?

In grade school, when the class read about Sir Lancelot, the teacher made us write whether we thought he and Guinevere should have run away together. We all thought it was a great idea. The teacher put a damper on our fun. She reminded us of King Arthur and of Guinevere's responsibility toward him. She taught us that it's not Christian to ride off into the sunset with another man. Had it been her husband Alice was waiting for? Often, I'd give up the library and take walks.

I'd take the walk down to Trastevere; I'd take the longer one across the river to Campo dei Fiori, trying to strike a balance between the riot of fruits, vegetables, and fish in the square and the statue of Bruno's shaded and downcast face. After all, how many women lived like Alice? Husband after husband, lovers too, sweeping her off her feet. Leo in the garden. Leo waiting for her to return. After all, wasn't she an exception. Didn't most women get married, settle down to responsibility, live without the heights of passion? After all, how long can passion last?

Alice's daughter-in-law hated the bank manager, who had no sense of appreciation. She quit. Two women in the same house all day? Alice would only be in the way.

Alice has a bunch of stories about college girls abroad. How often heads were washed and hair brushed, and gloves and gold and shoes and pocketbooks sought after. Not to mention all the clothes they brought. And all they didn't know. But four college girls were no match for Alice, even if she was just getting out of a debilitating depression. She's an indefatigable tourist. Keeger got his money's worth. The girls walked many miles to see much more than they wanted to, I'm sure. She gave them a break in Florence. Left them to shop the Ponte Vecchio themselves, while she preceded them to Rome.

Now, Alice is a good traveler, too good, if your idea of a vacation is to lie on a beach. She says it's because her skin can't take the sun, but I'm sure she thinks such loitering wasteful. Her frugality as well as her curiosity demands that she see everything. It's the secret of being a good tourist. Once you make the trip, some of the best things in life are free. It's all on the same ticket. Of course you *can* spend your time buying bargains and eating in overpriced touristy places and come home with a load of film to be processed. You pay your money, you take your choice. Alice goes overboard in her own way sometimes. She doesn't have the instinct for knowing when saving money is spendthrift. I think that's why her trip to Rome is a train story.

She doesn't remember how she got on the milk train to Rome, but I'll bet in some way she was saving very little money. She had wired Leo that she'd arrive "in the morning" and had named her hotel. But Leo couldn't wait. He rushed to the railroad station before dawn. His heart's blood was needed at the Stazione Termini to pump that train to Rome. I wonder if he'd ever met someone coming from somewhere else before.

Now he stands on the tracks at dawn, his early morning stomach stirring. He isn't going to eat or drink until he has Alice in his arms. Train after train arrives from the North without her. The day grows hot; the crowds press in. As each train depopulates, the terror grips him — maybe the cynic in his nature tells the whole truth. She's not coming. She's never coming. Still, he'll wait some more.

Meanwhile, Alice is on the milk train, swamped with the girls' suitcases. It is she who must cart half their possessions to Rome. The train has broken down three times during the night. She and the rest of the sleepy people in her compartment are told to disembark at a provincial train station. Off goes Alice, dragging her luggage. She stands on the platform. She's alone! Where's everybody? Still sleeping? Has she heard wrong? Suddenly, the train makes a jutting motion, as it has often during the night, each car thrown forward to a standstill. This time, however, the train puffs, starts up.

"Signora!" she hears from inside.

She gathers what she can amid the calls of warning and starts back. In a strenuous flurry of confusion, she gets everything into her compartment again. The men help her to redistribute all that luggage on the overhead racks.

"Signora, why did you get off?" she's asked when the train stops puffing and they are nowhere again.

"Weren't we told to?"

"Of course, Signora. But this is Italy."

Oh, Leo.

The American parachutist jumps out of the plane: For my God and my country.

The French parachutist is next; Leo salutes: Viva France.

The German next: For Duty.

The Italian. Leo shrugs: For the sign he reads near the exit. It is forbidden to jump.

At four-thirty that afternoon, the train arrives in Rome. There's a stampede for the door. She's the last one out. Suddenly she's in the air. She's in Leo's arms. In the midst of her disarray, they cling to each other. He is crying. She is crying. "You're here now," he says. "I'll never let you go."

She goes. The last night in Rome he was very upset. He tried to nail her with his passion. She said she'd be back. He didn't believe her. He should have. There was nothing left for her in America except to grow old. What was there left in Rome for Leo? No bail. No divorce. He was eternally wed to the strange girl. She had turned out stranger than he thought; ran away and left him with a son.

I wonder how it was from her point of view, when at sixteen or seventeen she had fallen in love with Leo. Had being young been like an opera for her? There she was in postwar Italy, torn with desire. Wild passion. I hear the sobs of remorse when her pregnancy turns him cold. Her screams when her father beats her. The hymn in her head when her father presents her to the Contis and Leo has to marry her. Love triumphs. An ecstatic shudder of submission. The curtain falls.

Life takes over. The household routine. The wild strange girl under the yoke of her mother-in-law and Flora while her husband is free on the streets. Enter a new man. A new escape. A new betrayal. And her little son, Cosimo, is left behind.

The Conti household. Mamma is the focal point. That fiery socialist who was pledged to the Resistance. Who somehow stirred her no-account husband to run messages during the war before he died. It was she who worked her hands dry on other people's floors. It was she who sustained her children. Here was Rome without Alice. Mamma out to work. Leo scraping by. Flora stuck at home, caring for her brother's son.

For Leo, Alice was like the dollar bills she enclosed in every letter from America, "for little Cosimo." She was hope kept alive. What was any other woman next to her? He slept around with the preoccupation of a man whose luck may change. Any day he might be up for something better.

So he was beside himself, full of passion and fury, that last night in Rome, when he once more had to let Alice go.

In America, Nick got wind of what had happened in Rome. The Keeger girls returned to Cleveland with tales of the adorable Leo. He wrote to Alice, back now in Rutherford, to tell her she was acting like a fool. He tried to void the two hundred a month he had agreed to when they first separated. She'd get alimony for having to live without him, not for corroborating his old fantasy about Leo. She'd get two hundred to live in a country where it was peanuts, not for Rome, where she could really live. I've always felt her longevity has served Russo right.

Nick was so riled up, he wanted to come to Rutherford to talk sense. He alternated between trying to show her something for her own good and wanting his money back. It was worse than the lost fountain pen and sweater, the idea that Alice might live in Rome. That's two hundred a month of his going to Leo Conti.

Far from him, Alice was able to write Nick, No, don't come. This letter made him wonder whether he and Alice had been hasty; whether he shouldn't come to talk about the two of them before the divorce was final. What did Alice think of that? The question occasioned more letters. It delayed Alice's departure, even though the brownstone was now sold. For a while it looked as though there was a possibility of reconciliation. Then Nick's girlfriend gave him an ultimatum: me or the trip to New Jersey. You do this, Nick, or you do that. Once Alice agreed to meet Nick, he never did show up.

Another year passed before Alice returned to Rome. She didn't take the direct route, either. Her sense of economy presented itself in the form of a freighter that made stops halfway round the world. "I had so much to bring with me, Betsy. Practical things. And I brought two of everything; toothbrushes, blankets, canteen cups. I know it sounds silly, but you name it, I brought two. I wasn't fool enough to imagine I knew what actually was awaiting me in Rome. All I knew was that I had enough to start a life there. But somehow I had this faith that I would share my life. Without even thinking about it, I brought enough for two. Why did I take the freighter? What was my hurry? With my limited means, when would I get another chance to see so much of the world?"

Don't hurry, my parents used to tell me; you have all the time in the world to grow up. That's how I felt by summertime in Rome, thinking of Alice crossing the seas, returning to the open arms of Leo. I was grown-up and left in a hot city with all the time in the world. A hot, sumptuous city. Fruit, vegetables, wine, cheese, pasta, bread made every day. Courtyards, fountains, domes, churches, squares. Rome was the living liberal arts. And I should be experiencing everything I had crammed for in college. But under the splash of that blue sky and burning sun, I'd walk aimlessly, daydream, sweat. On streetcars, thinking of Leo, I'd miss my stop. I'd give up, get off, and walk. And as I walked I'd see that every prince's palace had love scrawled on the walls, and in the street, car doors opened as I passed.

Many people say they can't work in Rome — or work up to capacity — because of the distractions. My distraction was Alice and her story of Leo, which she told me over lunch, over the phone, which she whispered to me as I sat next to her in Doug's car as the four of us toured Ariccia and Frascati in Sunday forays to the environs. I could feel her breath as intimately as I saw the broad back of Leo's neck. I couldn't get enough of it. Her stale, preprandial breath, the stubble that tracked its way up the sides of Leo's neck to his hair. You're interested in human nature, Betsy.

"Doesn't she ever shut up?" Doug asked me one day in Nemi.

We had walked a different way from them to the top of the hill from which you can look down to the lake called Diana's Mirror. The lake had been circled out of a crater some time during the Golden Age. Like everything I saw in Italy then, it had ripple after ripple of meaning, though the lake itself was as still as glass. I looked up at Doug's smoothly shaven face, saw the strain in his light brown eyes and the annoyance that tugged his lips toward his teeth.

"She has a lot to say."

He shrugged.

"And besides," I continued, "what else do you have to do on Sundays? Look where we are!"

"Frazer's lake," he said. He was referring to *The Golden Bough*.

"Yes. And here we are."

He put his arm around my shoulder. We had moments of harmony, Doug and I, maybe our best moments, high up somewhere, looking at a view.

It was at Bev Brewster's apartment that the subject of an extended summer trip with Alice and Leo came up, and it did so by sheer coincidence. We were eating out on Bev's magnificent terrace, in the middle of his blooming garden, right in the heart of Rome. The longer Bev stayed away from Georgia, the more pronounced his Southern accent and the more regional his cooking. I wouldn't have been surprised after a while to see Spanish moss dripping from his potted trees. Distance made a Confederate of him, just as versatility made a dilettante of him. He was a poet, a playwright, a puppeteer, and cartoonist, who made his living falling. He once cornered a pot of gold in the lyrics of a movie tune. He was an extraordinary conversationalist. Being so far from home, he seized the possibilities of our language. I believed him capable of finishing the novel he had long ago started. His curse was that there was nothing Bev Brewster couldn't do. This was the devil imp of his nature that didn't let the genius through.

"I won't go back to Gaeta," he said to me that day, after I brought the subject up. "I stop at Sperlonga."

I asked why. Gaeta was where my parents' people came from, and I was toying with the idea of going to visit.

"Why? My dear Betsy, I lost a perfectly adequate secretary there. She was a silly girl, I admit, but her parents thought Italy would be good for her. In more than one way, a tragic mistake."

"Tell Betsy what happened to her, Bev," Tony said in slow precise English. Tony was Bev's secretary that year, a blond boy from outside Aquila. He was short and lithe and hung on Bev's every word.

"She drowned," answered Rowena de Somebody (as I called her), who came from one of the oldest families in Rome, except that her mother was American. Rowena was extremely tall and thin, with an elegantly structured face and fine, long dark hair. She had all the grace one admires in high-fashion models, a charm that doesn't translate well to the day-to-day. Men abused her, which made her more vulnerable and more proud. It also made her contemptuous of women. The sun slanted across her face as she said that, and she smiled.

"Drowned?" I asked.

"Alas," said Bev. "And there I was in Gaeta, left with her journal, 'My Life in Italy.'" He paused. His thick white hair and his green eyes gleaming with fun gave him a Santa-like joviality, but he was a tougher nut. "She'd only been here six months, and I tell you! Well, I spared her parents *that*. I doubt posterity will miss 'My Life in Italy,' however much the NATO forces miss its authoress. I tell you she had an entire *fleet*. Christ stopped at Eboli and I stop at Sperlonga and that is that."

Bev took the big jug of wine in the shadow by his feet and motioned our glasses to him. No carafes at his table. Be it a fancy vintage someone brought or his carefully selected jug, "wine should be poured once," he'd say. Fine with me. The light white of the region made my insides as balmy as the day.

"How did she drown?" I wanted to know. "Is the water very rough there?"

"Smooth as silk," Bev said.

"Not that day, Bev," Alice interjected. They had known each

other for ages. Bev had once rented a floor in her old New York brownstone. That was when he had been included in a painting show at MOMA. There'd been a big party for it in the museum courtyard. Bev had arrived with his cohorts in an early version of glitter rock. "New York wasn't ready for me," Bev said. He left before it was. And he stayed away too long.

"It was not as smooth as silk, Betsy," Alice continued. "The poor girl got caught in one of those unexpected currents caused when sand parts, and she was carried away."

"That's horrible!"

No one seemed willing to share my reaction. They avoided death the way Bev stopped five miles short of Gaeta.

"It happens," Sid Lorraine said. He was a big wheel in textiles who always visited Bev when he passed through. "You live the life, Bev," he'd say. I think he lent Bev money.

"Gaeta's a bore," Rowena de Somebody said. "You should see Carrara, the mountains."

"I don't know if it would be a bore for me, Rowena. I feel I should look up my relatives."

"It's an experience you should have," Alice agreed.

"Why?" asked Bev, who told us when we asked that his parents were run over by a train in Atlanta as they tottered home after a ball.

"Bravo!" Leo interjected. "Why?" It was Alice who kept up with his family.

"Why?" Doug joined in. He never said much at these gatherings. I think he was bored. You don't have to come, I'd tell him. But he came. "Do you think they're going to be interested in Anita Garibaldi, Betsy?"

"That's not the point, is it? I could have been born there. Don't you think there might be something there for me?"

"No."

I knew what Doug meant. He meant *he* was interested in my work on Anita Garibaldi, and *he* wanted me to go to La Spezia on a business trip with him. But I thought it would be a good time to go to Gaeta, while he was away.

Why didn't I want him to visit those relatives with me? He would be bored. He wouldn't adapt to the local dialect. No. It had to do with why I kept my maiden name. I was very unsure of myself, moody. At times I got drunk and said the wrong things. I was often depressed, though I thought I had no right or reason. I hated domestic details and wanted to write. Doug encouraged my writing, supported my ambition, and sheltered me from myself. That's why I had gotten married, though I still wasn't sure I should have. I was sure of my name, Betsy Lewis, and the fact that my grandparents came from Gaeta. I think I became a historian on that basis.

I thought that the crack about my uneducated relatives' lack of interest in Anita Garibaldi made Doug sound shallow. So I covered. "Oh, you!" I answered. "I know what you mean. You're really saying you want me to go to La Spezia with you."

"Ah," Rowena said. "Then you could visit Carrara."

"And Pietrasanta," Alice said. "Betsy, it's lovely there. So many sculptors come to use the bronze foundry. My friend Tod Goldstein is there every summer. You'd love Tod and his wife, Betsy."

"Maybe she'll listen to you, Alice," Doug said. "Pietrasanta is exactly where I have to go."

"There too?"

"I told you, Betsy. I have to look over a whole suite of bronzes for Kaufmann."

"Samuel Kaufmann?" Bev asked. "Well, I'll be."

"I thought you were going to do that in La Spezia, Doug."

"I guess you didn't pay attention, for a change. I said we would stay at La Spezia at the beach. You're the one who loves the beach."

"La Spezia sounds so Shelley," Bev said. "But in season it is definitely postromantic. Hordes of heart-hunters. Such crowds."

"The beaches near Pietrasanta are never crowded," Alice put in. "It's so much more relaxed there. Tod always rents a cabina. It's lovely there, isn't it, Leo?"

Leo smiled at her. "Yes, it's lovely, anchovy." He pronounced

"Alice" in the Italian fashion — A-lee-chay. Pronounced that way, "Alice" means anchovy. It was his term of endearment.

They looked as if they were remembering something that made them very happy. I burst in, "Why don't we go to Pietrasanta together!"

Doug reminded me of my proposal late that afternoon. We woke from our siesta irritable from the heat after so much wine. He accused me of making plans without taking him into account. He was right. I had looked at Leo and Alice, and my fearsome enthusiasm had carried me away. Now I felt guilty.

"Don't you like Alice and Leo?"

"That's not the point. I wanted a few weeks of just the two of us."

"Traveling is always more fun with another couple."

"Well, Kaufmann and his wife will be there."

"Oh, those two are sure a lot of fun."

"What do you have against money, Betsy? It's Kaufmann and his kind who pay our rent. Everyone can't be a Southern fag or a maintenance man at a TV station. Everyone can't talk the ears off your head, like Alice with her 'Oh, Betsy dear.' What about me? Do you ever think about me? About the people I might like or want to see? You've just tied up the summer for both of us. The trip's on the firm. I thought we could stay at a nice place at La Spezia. Not worry about the cost. Now what have we gotten into? Sharing Tod Goldstein's beach umbrella? Why, he's an academic sculptor, for Christ's sake. We've only got a few years here, Betsy, and you're tying us up."

We compromised in the end. I said I wouldn't go to Gaeta that summer, and Doug said he'd go to La Spezia with the Kaufmanns by himself — it turned out that's where they liked to stay. Later, he'd meet me in Pietrasanta. For each other, we each gave up what we most wanted to do.

❧ 4 ❧

The week Doug spent at La Spezia, I spent in Rome. I felt that alone in our apartment, in the morning and in the long evening after the sun cooled off, I'd be able to consolidate my notes and work out the first draft of my study without distractions. This made a lot of sense. It glossed over the fact that I was wondering about my marriage, and for all I knew, Doug was wondering too. We didn't talk about it. He spent his days eyeing objects that increase in value, and I spent mine in the nineteenth century. We had an enormous investment in things that last.

So alone I limbered up in the early morning by looking back over the past year in Rome and writing down my impressions. At times I'd re-create my conversations with Alice word by word. That felt good. Then I'd get on with my historical writing. I'd break for lunch and a nap in the heat. Then I'd work into the night.

The day I had to leave the neighborhood and go to the center of Rome, I bumped into Leo. I didn't see him, but he rushed across the street to greet me. For some reason he thought I *had*

seen him. He joked that I'd ignored him because I was so popular. I had been walking along, pretending not to hear the re-
marks of the Latin lovers following me. Yet how could he think
I'd snub him? I said, "Until you called my name you were just
another Latin lover to me." He laughed.

We were at the Spanish Steps. When I looked up at him, I saw
the white steps, the flowers, the blur of hippie vendors, and, at
the top, the outline of the French church too. It was as if, with
his concern, with his smile, he were offering them to me. Man
of Rome, offering me his city.

I turned from him and pointed to the house that abutted the
Spanish Steps. "Keats died there," I said. He looked disconcerted; I swear he was about to condole with me when he
snapped to and said, "Of the heat?"

"Isn't it hot?" I answered.

How hot was it that summer?

He was sweating from rushing and I was flushed.

"Let's have a coffee; it's good for the heat," he said. I told him
my grandfather used to say the same thing. He looked newly
disconcerted.

He took me to the Caffè Greco. It's very expensive there. I
thought we'd stand at the bar. No, we'll sit, we'll sit, he insisted
politely, as if cost were the least consideration. It felt funny.
Wherever we went with Alice, we took our coffee at half-price at
the bar.

The Caffè Greco was the last place I'd have thought to enter
on a hot summer day. Its labyrinth of ornate rooms, the art on
the walls, the waiters in their tails, all the nineteenth-century
associations, seemed to me to blend with winter afternoons and
hot chocolate. In the summer one sat in the street under an umbrella. Once we left the bar area and began walking from room
to room, I realized what a tourist I still was. While I'd be outside
absorbing local color and sweating, half of Rome would be in
here, talking low and keeping cool. The Caffè Greco was air-
conditioned!

We gravitated to what I told Leo was my favorite room. The

old-fashioned oils, thick and lined, once the height of expatriate art in Rome, glimmered soberly from the walls. I looked for the oil of Garibaldi done by an Englishman. I could discern the muddy red of his shirt. Near it, there was a study of three naked women in a studio, turned academic by time. We sat at the corner table on the velvet couch. "Oh, how wonderful, Leo. It's absolutely freezing here!" He gave me his I-know-Rome look and seemed once again content and at the same time in control. I told him of my favorite grave, after Keats's, in the Protestant cemetery. The small tombstone has a drawing under glass of a young American, long-haired and bearded, a hippie from a hundred years ago. Under it one reads that the stone was erected "by subscription of the poet's friends at Caffè Greco." Here lay one whose name was really writ on water. Yet the dead boy's association with the caffè struck me forcefully. It brought the Caffè Greco up to date somehow. It was as if he had been buried in his T-shirt.

Leo got a kick out of my description, threw his head back, and laughed. When the waiter came, Leo surprised me again. Iced coffee was on the tip of my tongue. (To warm me up, I was about to quip.) Leo ordered whiskey and ice. What happened then was quite wonderful, I thought. We began to talk with each other so naturally that you'd think we'd always been the best of friends. Yet the conversation was somehow new. I began to realize that it was the Italian. Doug's Italian was decent; Alice's was completely grammatical, but its pace was much too slow. Alone with Leo, I heard my Italian take off. At least, I felt it did. Maybe it was the whiskey.

Leo did most of the talking. He talked of the war and after, of how thin and hungry he'd been, of the GIs giving him his first taste of whiskey. He compared the work on the wall with what Yanoff was attempting a century later. He talked about modern art as if he knew something. He showed off.

He had been living with a very intelligent woman for a number of years and he poached when she wasn't around. When he talked about politics or art, it was Alice he was speaking. Or

sharing. As he went on, I saw Alice patiently clipping out articles that were pertinent and adding them to her well-kept files.
I saw her simple kitchen and those anchovies in oil that she kept
for his bread. It was a well-nurtured relationship, theirs, kept
warm by a mother hen.

Alice had once told me that a worker at national TV made
scarcely the equivalent of two hundred dollars a month. It had
embarrassed Leo to have her talk about his earnings. "You're
wrong, anyway," he had snapped. On the second round of whiskey he told me that a worker at national TV made scarcely two
hundred a month. You'd never know it from the extravagant
way he ordered at the Caffè Greco — or maybe you would. Then
he began to talk about the union. I had never heard him so involved, though Alice had told me he was active. There are var-
ious unions in Italy, one for each political party, and there are
many parties. Leo was in the communist union, the strongest
one, the one most committed to the arts. Most of the big shots
Doug dealt with in the art world were quite fashionably com-
munisti.

I think Alice was uncomfortable about Leo's commitment to
Eurocommunism. Despite Berlinguer, she always saw the So-
viet Union at its back. Though she was for the workers, for the
underdog, her accurate grasp of grievance was counterbalanced
by a deep suspicion of any power claiming a method for elimi-
nating what was wrong. Her view of tyrants was impressively
one-sided. All people in power were candidates. They were selfish men of unrelenting will and monstrous ego. None of them
were beyond taking everything they could from you under some
fancy name and, when they were done with you, hanging your
ashes from a tree. You fought against them, although chances
were you'd lose.

Leo did not intend to lose. Nor was his animosity directed
against a particular person. No I've-come-for-the-rent-the-rent-
the-rent villain, à la Alice. He was alive with facts and figures.
Glowing with them. He was enraged by the meanness of the cap-
tains of industry. It was as if out there on the street he had just

become conscious of his own lot, and I was the first person he was telling. His intensity was surprising. I had felt a similar outrage when Salmanda got in trouble. Perhaps at that moment I understood him better than Alice did. And it was he who told me that day that he was running for the head of the union. Alice hadn't breathed a word. He broke up his discourse Leo-fashion, finally. He said that in the long run there should be no hostility between Russia and America, since, when the Russian delegates came to visit, they drank their vodka with Coca-Cola.

"I really shouldn't go away next week," he said, his new sense of responsibility turning him grave.

"We could change our plans," I said.

"You don't know Alice."

"What do you mean?"

"Alice wants to go."

"Don't tell me you're henpecked, Leo." I was teasing him. Alice had brought two of everything to Rome. She knew how to share.

It was as if he read my mind. He went back to his early days with Alice. He talked about how he had waited for her at the train station. He talked about her trip on the freighter, how seeing the world was more important than he was. How he had almost died, waiting for her. He became more and more outrageous. "Don't exaggerate," I said in English, imitating Doug's plea to me.

"I'm not exaggerating, Betsy. You don't know Alice. She's a very selfish woman."

"Alice selfish? Leo, really!"

He couldn't stop then. He continued on the theme, embellishing the absurdity, until I was laughing and he was one big smile. "Take today," he said. "It's my day off. She wanted me home, finishing the new bookcase. What did she care if I had a very important meeting?"

"If you have an important meeting, what are you doing here?"

"Some meeting," he said. "Bickering, bickering. We got nowhere."

"So Alice may have been right, after all. At least you could have gotten the bookcase done."

"No, no. She was wrong. In order to progress, we must be willing to dirty our feet in the shit of every day.

"Comrade!" he called. A startled waiter turned around. Comrade in a penguin suit. "Another round, comrade!" The two men smiled at each other. Leo's zest was infectious, even in that stiff place.

I was pretty high by the time we left. As we walked through the rooms of the Caffè Greco once more, Leo whispered conspiratorially, "She's going to take me out of Rome this summer because that's what she wants. Watch her more carefully, Betsy. I'm beginning to wonder how good a historian you are." With that, he opened the door for me. The heat hit me in the face. I reeled. Leo put his arm out to support me. "Watch her, but first of all, watch your step!" We went down the street arm in arm. "Alice is a very selfish woman," he said merrily. "You'll see. She does only what Alice wants to do."

Alice wanted to read her paper. I sat opposite her and Leo in our compartment in the train. We were in second class and I didn't have to worry about Doug being uncomfortable on the hard bench. Leo and I had window seats; Alice sat next to him. On her other side was a small man, a farmer whose bones surfaced as dry as the skin on his face. He wore a wide-brimmed hat and carried in his lap a package tied with rope. Next to me sat his wife? daughter? a plump country woman with a baby. They were sullen and left at the first stop. No one replaced them. A touristic triumph. With cheap tickets, we had just achieved luxury.

When they left, Alice began to read her paper out loud. Leo put his head back and closed his eyes as she read on in her exact Italian. "What do you think of that, Betsy, why . . ." And she began another. Leo told her to be quiet, he wanted to rest. For a while she was.

"Look at this," she said softly, and came to sit by me so that we could read a column together. Before long she was whispering it, word by word. I wasn't interested, but I didn't tell her. She sat hunched over her paper, her legs spread to hold it open on her lap. As she read I looked at Leo, his head thrown back and to the side, his eyes closed. I leaned my head back too and closed my eyes. Alice's whisper was persistent, as if she were after us. I opened my eyes. His eyes were open too. We looked at each other. I was going to say something to him. But I didn't. Alice read on.

Pietrasanta is a small Italian town that turns American in the summer. Sculptors come from all over to use the bronze foundry and the marble works. Or they used to. I think prices have gone up there a lot lately. Also, many sculptors are using foundries at home now, experimenting with new materials, new methods, new ways. Lipchitz cast there, and you'd see him, an ancient, tanned man with a white beard and a beret. Sometimes you just thought you saw him. The nature of his fame and the spirit of the place conspired, and there was more than one old man with beard and beret walking around the town square, attempting to make sculptures out of life.

Doug could spot a bronze cast in Pietrasanta anywhere in the world, the work is so fine. A modern work or a fifteenth-century work, he'd spot it. The town is close to the marble quarries of Carrara — the marble of Michelangelo. And that marble is transported to Pietrasanta. Though the church and the square are old, and the bronze workers and marble cutters come from generation after generation of bronze workers and marble cutters, in the summer the small Tuscan town is invaded by artists and resembles any other art colony, as it has for generation after generation.

What I liked about the town immediately was its simplicity. There was nothing particularly monumental about its oldness. Or anything more than bland about the new housing that was beginning to crop up outside the small historic center. Pietrasanta hadn't died of beauty; it manufactured it. The town was very much alive.

Doug had done a very nice thing. He had rented a cottage for the four of us, and since the Kaufmanns had spent an overnight there with him, he was charging it to the firm. It was a newly built cottage, with two bedrooms, bath, kitchen, sitting room, and a garden. This was his surprise. We wouldn't have to stay in the town's rudimentary hotel, and Alice and Leo wouldn't have to squeeze in with the Goldsteins. Kindnesses like this made my heart go out to him. Underneath, he was a wonderful man, Doug, and I knew that when we married.

That night the Goldsteins had dinner for us in the newish house they rented every summer. Tod is a lovable guy. Very generous and open. He's one of those introverts who are socially outgoing. He really likes people and wants to be liked. All the time you can figure out that his heart beats too fast, he's overprotective of his children, and in his fantasy life he's a hermit. Molly is very pretty and very timid. She and Tod met when they were teen-agers at Music and Art High School and were married before they realized they had absolutely nothing in common other than their rebellion against Tod's parents, who didn't want him to marry a Gentile. I think Molly would like to be left alone. Maybe her fantasy is that she could exist very nicely without the gregarious. The most enthusiastic I've seen her is greeting us. She rushed into Leo's arms and closed her eyes while they embraced. Wives Anonymous, I thought.

Tod was about five foot ten and bulky, with a long, fleshy face. His nervousness showed in the pockets under his eyes. "Alice," he said, as he embraced his friend, "be forewarned. I'm going to try to tempt you to stay with us."

Molly looked tired out from Tod's generosity. She was slim and blond and wore her hair in a pageboy, a style I hadn't seen for a while. She turned the subject to the bedroom, where we could go to say good night to her children.

Tod was not a sculptor you read about much, but he always had enough commissions to get by. Molly didn't help his career any, according to Alice, because she wasn't expansive, couldn't give one of those casual but tasteful dinner parties that made patrons feel they were really at the table of an artist and an artist's wife. Music and Art High School aside, she wasn't exotic or bohemian or even interested. I'd say that being teen-agers was probably the most coordinated thing the Goldsteins had done together. She certainly didn't have much to say at the table. And when Doug talked with her after dinner — I guess it must have been the wine — she closed her eyes.

At the end of the evening, Alice was talking with Tod, and I could hear him say, "Come on, Alice, like old times. You know you're welcome."

I couldn't tell: Was it she who hinted they stay with him? Or had she floundered under his insistence? She was not one for a definite no. "Well, Tod, I don't know . . ."

A while later she came into the kitchen. Molly and I were putting things away. "Tod seems to think Leo and I should stay with you, Molly." She piled up some scraped dishes where she knew Molly left them for the au pair the next day.

Molly didn't answer right away. In the short pause that ensued, Tod would have had time to go through don't be silly, the kids love making believe they're camping out, there's more than enough room, it's no trouble at all, why don't you stay a month, would you be more comfortable in our room, we can use the couch, what's wrong, is it something I did last year, are you mad at me?

Molly said finally, "It's okay."

"What's okay?" Alice asked sharply. She had little patience with Molly.

"It's okay. Whatever you want to do. It's okay."

I don't know what possessed Alice. "Well, I'm not sure about Leo. Last time he enjoyed being with the children so much. But now . . ." I felt she should have at least picked up the clue of Molly's blank stare.

I butted in. "It's ridiculous for you to stay here when we have so much room."

"Is it, dear?"

"Absolutely."

"Wouldn't you like your privacy?"

"We'll have plenty of privacy."

"Well, then, whatever you say."

The second day at Pietrasanta I went swimming with Leo while Alice went along with Doug to the foundry. We had rented bikes and cycled there along the flat road. We yelled comments to each other, we raced, we had fun.

It was still early when we got to the beach. The sun was not too strong. We locked up our bikes, untied our towels, and headed to the water. The dirt-colored sand was damp on our feet. I could smell the breeze. Leo put his hand on my shoulder. I felt part of the day.

We walked to the Goldsteins' cabina. We had our suits on under our clothes and went into the small wooden room to undress. I watched Leo take off his jersey; turned away as he unbuttoned his fly. With my back to him I took off my sundress with its flowing skirt and hung it on a peg.

The attendant had set up two beach chairs and an umbrella for us by the time we came out. Leo was wearing old black bathing trunks and I was wearing a new black bikini. I watched him as he reached up to adjust the umbrella so that we could get the sun. He was strong and muscular. His stretched-out old bathing suit did not disguise his stomach. When I talked of Leo's looks, Doug always said he had a gut. Well, he did. A solid gut, but nevertheless, as Doug said, a gut. It certainly didn't bother me that he no longer had the ideal body of a Yanoff melted nude. I was relieved that he wasn't perfect. I was looking at the man.

I stretched out on the beach chair, which was now in the full sun.

"This feels good," I said.

Satisfied with his adjustment, Leo set his chair parallel to mine and stretched out too.

"Peace," he said.

But I didn't feel peaceful. I stood up after a short time. "Come on," I said, "let's swim."

He opened his eyes slowly and looked up at me, mocking incomprehension. I took his hands. We both made a show of me pulling him out of his chair. "Come on, I'll race you to the beach," I said.

I won.

"You coming in?" I asked as he sauntered to the waterline.

"Later. I'll watch you."

"Oh? Okay."

Maybe Alice had been right. "A day at the beach? Swimming? Leo, be serious. You know you're afraid of the water."

Afraid? As I swam, I felt I could swim forever. The tang of salt, the sting of the sun, the strength in my arms and legs, the ocean on my body. There was more tow than I had realized. When I turned toward the shore, I saw I was quite far out. Leo was waving me in.

By the time I made it back, Leo had waded knee-deep out to me.

"Remember Gaeta," he said.

"The water's fine," I gasped.

"I can see that."

"Give me a minute."

But he didn't wait for me to catch my breath. He picked me up like a plastic float and carried me down the beach over his shoulder. "Leo! Leo! Come on!" I pounded the small of his back.

He dumped me on my beach chair.

"Now stay here!" he ordered.

I was dizzy. I was laughing.

He pushed my wet hair off my face. He took my towel and put it over my shoulder. I bit the end of it to stop laughing.

"You went out too far."

"I know."

"Do you want to end up like Bev's secretary, drowned?"

"Not until I write 'My Life in Italy.'"

He smiled. He liked that.

After I dried off, I put on my sun lotion.

"Roll over," he said. "I'll do your back."

"What about yours?"

"Don't worry about me."

He crouched in front of my beach chair, squeezed the lotion

into his hand. "It's warm," he said, touching it with his fingers. "That sun is hot."

I stretched out on my stomach.

He untied my bikini strap and rubbed the oil on my back.

At noontime, when we were eating ice cream and talking under the shade of the umbrella, I saw two figures coming toward us.

"Oh, no."

"What is it?" Leo mumbled.

"We have visitors."

Alice and Doug came across the sand, shoes in hand. Alice carried wine, and Doug carried the picnic basket she had prepared.

Sitting under the umbrella, flushed from the walk, she said, "I thought we'd have lunch here. There's time."

"Time, Alice? I thought we had the whole day."

"Well, dear, part of Tod's work is going to be cast this afternoon. It would be a shame to have come this far and not see it. Tod can get Leo and me in. And Doug tells me you've a standing invitation at the foundry."

"Doug, I told you I wanted a day at the beach."

"And I told Alice."

"We can have lunch together, at least," Alice said.

"At least," Leo repeated in Italian. He winked at me and laughed. Flicked the stick from his ice cream in the sand. He got up and slapped Doug on the back and took him over to the cabina to change.

Alice watched them go. "I guess he's gotten beyond being interested in an old friend."

They came back from the cabina. Doug was tanned from a week at La Spezia. Tall and trim. He was careful of his body, and he looked more manicured than Leo. His arms were longer and thinner. Looking at them, as he walked with Leo, I realized that they irritated me. This is crazy, I thought.

"What's bothering you, Betsy?" Doug asked, coming over. "What's that look on your face?"

Well, Doug, to be honest, it's your arms. But I wasn't honest.

"Nothing," I answered. "I don't know what's wrong with me."

I guess I didn't. On the scale of human values, what were arms? And why should I suddenly take exception to my husband's?

Doug wouldn't press any further. "You want to go for a swim?" he asked me.

"Sure."

At the water's edge I said, "You knew I didn't want to spend the afternoon at the foundry!" Suddenly, I felt relieved. That must be what was really bothering me. "Anyway, how come they're casting Tod's work in the heat of the day?"

"They're backlogged because of the big piece. Lipchitz, you know."

"I wish I didn't."

Tod was so happy to see us that I forgot my annoyance. And it was an opportunity to see a piece cast. The workers in the foundry were in their bathing suits; their streaming sweat made them appear just as molten as the fiery red bronze they poured. Rather than watching the process, I found myself staring at them. Alice said beaches exist all over the world. To have missed seeing Tod's work cast would have been a waste.

Leo hugged me. He sighed. "Ah, me," he said. "Betsy, let's try again tomorrow."

But tomorrow was a Sunday, and Tod had arranged for us to go to Carrara and to have lunch at a mountain inn with a group of his friends. And I ended up in the wrong car — Brenda Gorewitz's two-seater. Brenda was a sturdy, trimly put-together woman of forty. She was a tight-lipped loner and had a lot of money. Five years earlier she had enrolled in Tod's class at the university out of curiosity. She'd never sculpted before. Now she was getting ready for a group show in The Hague.

I'd been introduced to her at the foundry and had taken a look at her pieces. She said, "This is a skier." Very competent stuff, Doug thought. I thought she had no imagination at all and less humor. "This is a clown," she said, in a noncommittal, vaguely familiar way.

I wanted to tell Brenda there had been a mistake; that I really didn't want to ride with her in her new Porsche, as Tod had led her to believe. At that moment Doug waved and called out, "See you there."

"No!"

"No what?" Brenda asked.

I was stymied.

I saw Leo in the front seat next to Doug. Alice was in the back seat, already in earnest conversation with Rienzo, an Italian-American sculptor. The car passed by.

"Want to catch up to them?" Brenda asked.

"Why not."

"I'll give them a chance."

We let the other cars pass, then we started up. On the outskirts of Pietrasanta, Brenda picked up speed. She went barreling along, passing one car and then the next on the narrow road. We got close behind Doug's car, beeped, and passed it. I turned in my seat, caught Leo's broad smile, and waved. Damn, why wasn't I with them? She overtook Tod's car. Molly must have told Tod to slow down, because Doug overtook him too.

Brenda meant to keep her lead at the head of the caravan. The road to Carrara became progressively more steep and tortuous, and Brenda kept accelerating. I rolled the window all the way down; my heart was beating fast.

"Enjoying the view?" she asked me in her deep voice.

The voice, which made no concessions to the heart, reminded me of Salmanda's friend from Greenwich Village — Duke.

"I'm enjoying the blur."

"Are you?" She went even faster.

When we slowed down to pass through mountain towns, the grim-looking, inbred people who lived on these peaks would stop to stare at us. What must it be like to live at inaccessible heights? Their fate seemed sealed. Born on mountaintops, they could never come down.

"God, those people are closed in."

"It's tough," Brenda agreed and revved up. "Having a good time, kid?"

I looked at the set of Brenda's jaw in her nondescript face. She didn't blink an eye as she sped, as she screeched around hairpin turns. What scared me about Brenda behind the wheel was what annoyed me about Doug day by day — she seemed inoculated against danger. Suddenly, as she sped along, faster, faster, the mountain people reminded me of me.

She was daring me, Brenda, because I was a dare to her. Away from her teacher, Tod, and all the people she hardly knew, behind the wheel and in control, she used all the considerable logic at her command to drive like a maniac.

"Too fast for you?"

"No."

Let her do her damnedest. Could her car reach the velocity of my crazy thoughts? Leo's oiled hands on my back. Alice's free, rich life. Doug's thin arms. If I told Doug, Brenda's making a pass at me, he'd look at me as if my imagination were making a mountain out of life. If I told him I could feel Leo's hands on my back, shoulders, spine, on the top of my buttocks — would he hear me?

I shivered.

"Are you cold?"

I rolled the window up a bit and made the mistake of looking down. We were zipping along the curved roads. The panorama below seemed peacefully waiting for our tumble. I looked behind me. I made out Doug's car for a moment in a pass below us. I saw Leo's bulk.

"What's so great down there?"

God, was she watching me or watching the road? I closed my eyes. I saw Leo's face, his gray eyes, his irregular teeth when he smiled. He lifted me over his shoulder. Stop! With my eyes closed I lost control. I had a dizzying sense that the car was vertical. It would have to overcome gravity not to topple, though velocity was on its side.

"Open your eyes, scaredy cat."

Scaredy cat did it. I opened them, all right. "What are you watching, Brenda, me or the road? The joke's over, okay? What the hell are you smiling about? Goddamn you, slow down!" Oh,

God, I was getting nauseated. I was going to scream, I was going to puke all over this car. "I said slow down!"

Brenda laughed.

"It's not funny. I feel sick!"

"Don't move around so much in your seat. Hold on."

She pushed the pedal to the floor going up the hill.

"Stop this goddamn car, goddamn you!" I was beginning to shake. I couldn't control anything, my gut, my tears. I was hysterical. "Who the hell do you think you are?"

My loss of control dampened her confidence. She did slow down. And I didn't think. She must have seen me opening the door. Maybe that's why she slowed down. I jumped out. I landed on my feet and cut across to the side of the cliff way before Doug's car came near.

"But we're here!" Brenda called to me from the car, as if that was all that mattered. We were, in fact, close to the town. I had almost made it.

"Leo!" I called.

Leo got out of Doug's car and came over to me. He put his arms around me and turned me from the onlookers. I was shaking in his arms. I could not talk.

"What's wrong, Betsy?" he asked. "What happened?" he asked Brenda.

She didn't understand a word of Italian and replied, "What the hell's going on?"

Leo motioned her to start up. The other cars began to follow. We were being left on the road. He used his head. He took me over to a crevice in the mountain, as if I had to throw up or pee. He held me in his arms. I kept saying, "Hold me, hold me." Finally I broke away. "I wish we were back on the beach," I said shakily.

"We could be," he said sharply. "You see? This is Alice's fault."

"Couldn't wait, kiddo?" one of the patrons of the arts in the party said as Leo and I walked into the restaurant. "When you gotta go, you gotta go."

"I went," I said.

Doug was very concerned. "Are you okay?"

"I could be better."

I tried to forget I had just done a Freud 101 on the mountain-top. I tried to forget by drinking too much wine with lunch. Sunday dinner, I should say. A rustic Sunday dinner. Special rabbits killed for us, fresh pasta, local Chianti, the whole bit. Even the day-old Sabbath bread tasted fresh. An authentic rustic dinner in the mountains, where the proprietor and his wife rushed around, making familiar warm jokes with Tod. There must have been sixteen of us, and we sat at one long makeshift table.

Almost everyone there was American except Leo. He sat next to Alice, doing what he always did in these artistic circles. He made things come alive with his irrepressible jokes and kidding. The rabbits were one thing; Leo was another. He convinced us we were where we were. Through him we had a stake in Italy.

Alice, at these parties, always seemed flushed from food and wine and Leo. She always seemed to enjoy his jokes as if it were the first time she heard them. She listened to him talk about Italy as if most of his information hadn't originated in her files. The information itself didn't matter. Her lover, with his irony and good humor, was Exhibit A, the spirit of the place.

This afternoon, the atmosphere turned. Suddenly Leo and Alice were talking about politics, and they were not laughing. In these crowds, Leo usually spoke a magical Italian that was somehow translated through face and gesture, even to those who knew just a modicum of the language. Now he was talking fast. Of course, Tod's Italian was good, and Rienzo — one of Alice's favorites — had been born in the vicinity. I think they found him drawing on a rock like Cimabue. Or was he chiseling it? Anyway, he got to art school in America and then came back again summers to cut. There were many important people there that day. Even Brenda's done okay since then. Sometimes when I pick up the *Times* and look at the exhibit ads, I am cast back to Carrara and that table. Sometimes I see one of those faces on TV. But I didn't have time for them then. It's all or nothing for you, Betsy, Doug would one day say. At that table it was all Alice and Leo.

"The workers are fed shit!" Leo yelled. It seemed to fall on Alice's shoulders. It was her country, the country of capitalist pigs, that supported the Christian Democrats, who were the backbone that kept the Pope going strong. It was American consumerism that infected Italian youth, made them want everything money could buy, including lavish, expensive, priest-ridden weddings. She thought she was liberal. It was she and her kind who kept the pigs in power. Who brought the Mafia back to Italy after the Second World War? America! Alice! Alice was America.

His attack was so outrageous, so virulent, that he must have been kidding. Or was he saying something?

All Alice did was say "Oh, Leo," and "Oh, Leo," again and again, as he piled up his accusations.

"You know who killed your dear Martin Luther King, don't you? You did! All Americans did. It's a racist society."

"Oh, Leo. You say that after fascism?"

"What fascism? You find me an Italian who's a fascist now, and I'll show you someone who's been contaminated by capitalism."

"*You* can say that."

Then he said, "You kill your blacks."

"We do," I cut in. I began to talk as fast as Leo, perhaps as wildly. I talked about Martin Luther King, Jr. I talked about my friend Salmanda. I went through everything that had happened to her in America because she was black. The wine got in the way of my diction, taking me from scene to scene without much connection. As in most of the heated political arguments I've heard in my life, I was not only talking about the world; I was sticking daggers into somebody else's heart.

"Hear your friend?" Leo interrupted, turning on Alice. "Listen to dear Betsy, dear. Look what America did to her Salmanda. You see how they treat blacks there. Martin Luther King was killed by all of you. She knows you're a fascist too!"

"Oh, no, Leo," I murmured. "We're all guilty, but I didn't mean it that way."

"Why don't you go back to America?" he shouted at Alice. "Do something for your country, the way I'm doing something for mine. Organize a march!"

I forced myself to focus on Alice then. She was blurry, and her neck tilted downward. Her face folded like an unwatered flower. She looked the way a well-mannered little girl does when she's hurt. "That's not what I meant," I told her.

"Oh, yes it is," Leo insisted. "She's a fascist."

Then I was sure I hadn't meant anything dark at all. In those days I was sure that, by marrying Doug and settling down to work, I had shed my shadow. I tried to explain to Alice that I had had a tough ride, that I was talking about Salmanda, that it had come out wrong.

But what I had done, I now see clearly. Leo, at a table of Alice's friends, had berated his lover mercilessly. And I, with absolutely no provocation, had jumped in on his side.

The next day I woke up with a hangover and the feeling of having done something monstrous. I guess that is what happens when you don't take responsibility for your own meanness. I had exaggerated it into something especially awful; at the same time I didn't remember my exact words and didn't think I had said anything wrong.

It was hard to face Alice midmorning in the garden. She was sitting out there, writing one of her letters home. We were alone. When she looked up at me, she smiled. She doesn't hate me, I thought. It proves I haven't done anything wrong. But there was something so heavy in me, a confusion so deep, that even as I apologized once more for my outbreak, I felt I had to get away.

Of course, Alice was totally preoccupied with Leo's behavior. Goodness knows whether she had paid attention to my words or whether she was just sitting there, trying to adjust to his sting.

She put down her pad. "He doesn't know himself, Betsy," she told me. "Or perhaps, after all these years, I find I don't know him. He can talk about capitalism lately as if he's just discovered it. But tell me, Betsy, who is it who wants a big wedding for his son?"

That was the first time I heard about Cosimo's wedding plans. Leo's son was nineteen and he was engaged. But in Italian fashion, the wedding date was not set. Money had to be saved, and Leo had to secure his son a position. In the meantime Cosimo and Franca would watch television each night under Flora's eyes. Alice and I had spent a fair amount of time analyzing the mating habits of young Italians.

"And do you know why he wants a big wedding, Betsy? I mean why Leo wants one as well as his son? In order to impress Franca's parents. Do you know why he has fascists on his mind? Because his son is marrying into a fascist family.

"Well, I'm not going to save for Cosimo's wedding. I've made that clear. I'm not going to save for foolishness. He'll have to figure out a way."

What she meant was, she was not going to pay. It was like her to figure out costs in advance. But to worry Leo about it, that was new.

I was sitting next to her. My head didn't feel very good, and I was trying to get my tongue to taste.

"Fascists, Alice?"

"Yes. Sly, small-minded fascists. They have money, but they are not going to put down one cent to see their daughter marry a Conti. They don't approve of the family, you see. The only reason they've consented to have their daughter engaged to Cosimo is the status Leo has gained by having an American 'wife.'" Alice put her hand up in despair. "Leo has to justify his family to the fascists. So much for the newly elected head of the communist union."

"He was elected?"

"Yes."

"He didn't tell me! Why didn't you tell me?"

"We declared a moratorium on politics, until yesterday it would seem."

"So he won. I'll be."

She didn't answer. She went on to talk of her mother. Maple's ruthlessness and beauty and lack of conscience were a staple of our conversation. Now the desires that had been Maple's birthright were transplanted into the heart of every little bourgeois girl. The wedding will cost millions, Alice said. Their millions were our thousands, but they amounted to the same thing. "Millions," she repeated, "so that his son can marry into that awful fascist family. He'll have to find the money. I'm not going to save for Cosimo's wedding. No matter what he told Franca's family. I've made that clear. I'm not going to be part of that foolishness. He'll have to figure out a way."

They had another fight that night. I know because it woke me out of a bad dream. Doug had wanted to make love to me that night. But when he put his arms around me, "They'll hear!" I whispered, and moved away.

"And last night you were too drunk."

I felt nothing at all, so I felt bad.

In my dream, Leo and I were in the wooden cabina. It was very cramped. It was like the cubicle in the record store on Eighth Street where Salmanda and I used to listen to records we weren't going to buy. I asked Leo what he was doing in Greenwich Village and he said he had heard it was a good place to learn how to swim. Don't be silly, I said. It's too hot to be silly. It was so hot in that dream and in that closed little cabina. I took off my dress and put it on a peg. Then I was wearing it once more and had to try to get out of it again. Dress, bra, underpants. Everything I took off came back to dress me. I was in a sweat of frustration.

Leo was standing there, naked. Can't you help me? I cried. I was tangled in those reappearing clothes. Trapped in the struggle. Leo, like his big penis, stood stiff.

I tried again and again, but it was futile, boring, endless, this attempt to undress. At the same time it was painfully frustrating.

Why could he undress? Why couldn't I? He was so close. I was so tangled. I saw the heavy sacs of his balls. They felt cool, like a velvet shadow.

Behhtsy, whatever are you getting yourself into now? I knew that voice. The amusement in it was laconic, though the words were drawled. It was Salmanda talking. All that mattered then was answering. But I didn't say a word. I couldn't. An ominous being was approaching. I made thrashing efforts to lift myself out of my tangle of clothes and called out again for Leo's help. But the more I thrashed, the more enmeshed I became.

A door opened. Alice was there. She wore a black skirt and a white blouse and the room was suddenly very big and very light. "I'm sorry!" I cried. "Forgive me. I'm sorry."

"Sorry about what, dear? You're not the first one. He's like that, you know. See?" Alice pointed to the opposite wall. On it was one of Yanoff's melted Leos. It was part paint and part Leo. Leo's back was toward us and his ass bulged as magnificently as in one of Doug's master drawings. He was on the run. He'd been trying to get away when he got trapped in the painting. His head was back, and there was a grimace on his face, though I could see only the chalk outline of his flattened profile.

I began to laugh and laugh and laugh.

Bang!

I shot up in bed. Doug didn't move. I was short of breath and dizzy. I staggered out into the hall.

"Oh, Betsy," Alice said. "Why, then, I'll leave on the light." She meant the bathroom light, which she was about to turn off.

She was naked, covered only by a flimsy short piece of pink net. Her ample pink body stood out against the light. She seemed shockingly, blatantly, naked. Perhaps because when she was dressed, she often seemed demure.

She didn't say anything else. She didn't apologize for being soft and pink or for being in the light. She just turned her back and walked down the hall.

Back in bed myself, I could hear Alice and Leo whispering. After a while there was silence. Then I heard rustling and more whispering. Silence. Then I heard Alice moan. She moaned and moaned. She moaned until, under her voice, I heard Leo cry out and come.

"What's wrong?" Doug asked me the next morning. I was propped up in bed. I hadn't slept all night. Overwork, I told him. Getting so upset about Brenda's driving was absurd. I had to get away. I needed privacy. I needed time to come to myself. I hated to leave him and to leave him with Alice and Leo, but I had to; I had to get away.

He looked at me irritably. Anita Garibaldi, I said. I began to talk about my work. I began to talk about Pius the Ninth having to flee from Rome. He went to Gaeta. I had to go to Gaeta too. It wasn't my relatives; it was my work. The more I talked to Doug, the more I believed what I said. I wove the nineteenth century around us like a net.

Doug was very understanding then and didn't hold me to our earlier compromise. He said he'd go back to La Spezia to wind up some business for the Kaufmanns and return to Rome. He wasn't having much fun, anyway. He was doing Pietrasanta for me.

It was up to me to tell Alice and Leo we were leaving. The four of us were sitting around the kitchen table, drinking our morning coffee. I made light of the whole thing. "You and Leo can have the place alone, and have it for free."

Leo looked amused. I was speaking in English; I doubt he understood exactly what I had to say. But he knew I was turning things over to Alice so that she could make plans. I think he probably thought she was getting her way. "Gaeta," she said wistfully. "How I wish I were going with you, Betsy." When I saw how sad she looked, I almost invited her. I didn't look at Leo, and I didn't listen to his talk. I just prayed to God to get out of there quickly. I loved Alice. She was my friend.

PART II

GENIUS ON THE NIGHT SHIFT

ॐ 5 ॐ

My life began to make sense again during the train ride to Gaeta, standing in the aisle by an open window, feeling a breeze. I was alone. No Leo, head back, across the way from me. No Alice reading me my paper. I went into my compartment. I flipped through *Il Messaggero*, then put it down.

Behhtsy.

I've been to the mountaintop, Martin Luther King had preached. I'd been there too and gone hysterical. Salmanda would have appreciated that. Where was she? On the train to Gaeta, in the full blaze of the late sixties, I wondered once more if Salmanda had been careful. I wondered if she was alive. All the way to Gaeta I thought of her. She swept Leo away as she had in my dream. She blended into the Italian landscape somehow, bringing back my past, soothing the mistakes of the present. Making me feel I could start out all over, and this time feel free.

The first time I saw Salmanda Blake, she was sitting on the long table in the cafeteria of Horace High. The proctor had not yet shooed her off. She was a very tall girl, even thinner than she was tall, and even blacker than she was thin and tall. Her skirt and blouse made desperate attempts to meet at her middle to cover her. One knee sock had given up and hung limply at her ankle, as if waiting around without much hope of being pulled up.

She was an exceptional person, extremely complex and full of life. Her mother was down south. Salmanda had come north to go to an integrated high school with the same spirit of adventure that brought my grandfather Gaetano to the land of opportunity years before. My grandfather crossed an ocean. He disembarked Lupis and became Lewis. Vintage Ellis Isle.

Salmanda lived with her aunt. Auntie had a house off Grant Avenue, the colored thoroughfare of Passaic, New Jersey. Through high school we spent many late afternoons at Auntie's. The kitchen was in the basement and always had the sickly sweet smell of evaporated milk. We did algebra down there. Then we went up to the living room, gossiped endlessly, and watched "Amos and Andy" on TV.

The day I met Salmanda, she was perched on a table surrounded by white kids and black kids. She was carrying on as if the cafeteria of Horace High, and the table on which she sat, dangling one long razor-thin leg, was the world. One look at her, and you knew everything was possible. She'd better be careful, I thought.

"Behhtsy," Salmanda said, squeezing everything she could out of my name after my platonic friend Paul D'Amato introduced us. "You're a good-looking girl. Why don't you make Mr. D'Amato happy and go out with him?"

She was not a good-looking girl. Not only was she too tall, too thin, and too awkward, but over each cheekbone her black skin was bumpy. And her hair hung in greasy patches above her ears. These were the years before naturals.

But she could be transformed. I remember the first time I saw this. She was practicing basketball during gym period. The dumb one-piece blue gym suit with its man-shirt front fitted her.

She had the blue belt tied tight around her waist, and her pitch-black limbs shone with perspiration. She held the basketball in one hand as if it were an apple she could bite. But instead, after a moment fraught with concentration, she dribbled it down the court, her long, thin body making perfect sense. When she got close to the rim of the basket, she jumped. Her body became what it needed to be to allow her to flip the ball with one hand. Hardly touching the rim, the ball streamed through the net.

This view of her was intensified a few years later — the summer of Salmanda's troubles. She was at her friend Duke's stifling apartment in Greenwich Village. She'd come in after seeing her lawyer in Passaic. Her dress was soaked. Her stockings sagged, and her black pumps, which she walked out of, gaped. I could hear the shower covering the unfriendly silence between Duke and me. When Salmanda returned, she was wearing a freshly laundered man's white shirt, open at the neck. She concentrated on zipping the fly of her skintight jeans. Her acne was gone, her hair slicked back. All zippered, she looked up. "That's better," she said. Her almond-shaped eyes took over. I thought, Salmanda Blake's an ugly girl, but she makes a beautiful boy.

"Hey, the proctor sees you!" I warned Salmanda on the day we met. She slid off the table.

"You're doing a *fine* job," she told the proctor as we passed him on our way to the lunch line.

"You're lucky he's not," I said.

That's how we became friends.

We were fast friends all through high school. I knew how brilliant she was. It surprised me that in high school the teachers didn't. They always assumed she was getting away with something. Like A plus. So how did she cheat?

Salmanda was born with a lust for scientific inquiry. She was aflame with curiosity. She could fly as high as a theory took her, then bring it back to earth. She really understood how electricity was harnessed; she understood the closed circuit that ended in a light plug in the wall. For me, H_2O was a foreign word for water. For Salmanda, water was H_2O.

She was a whiz in the sciences and math. What was it the teachers disliked? The abandonment with which she understood? They probably wouldn't have liked that even if she'd been white.

One day in trig we had a hell of a problem on a test. She yelled out, "That's it!" I turned around. She was oblivious of the class, the test, the teacher. She was holding her trig textbook open, finding the one link she needed. Her outburst was one of sheer mental integrity. The problem led her on. I understood this. Immediately. I guess in the long run it didn't matter that her high school teachers didn't realize what they had in her. I just think they should have. People like Salmanda don't come along every day. I'd never met anyone like her, this wild girl who could think. Her uniqueness, intelligence, and free spirit were A-bombs. I cautioned her to watch out. "Oh, Behhtsy, don't you be a scaredy cat!"

She blew her credentials in chemistry the day Mr. Misch walked in and found her in his closet. I don't recall the joke she was preparing. It may have been just the way his face jumped when he heard a scratching, turned around, opened the closet door, and found her in there. She was facing the class, smiling. Her knee socks made wiggly lines around her thin calves. He sent her to her seat with a wary comment that seemed to erase her from his consciousness. He was a meek man and didn't want any trouble. But he knew she'd been in there to steal.

Try to tell her. I tried. During our senior year, Miss Fat and Fearsome, our "guidance counselor," told Salmanda she should switch out of the college prep program, take a commercial course, and, if she wanted to do something "dignified," learn to type.

I tried to tell her one afternoon at Auntie's. Auntie was downstairs in the kitchen with us, making us hot chocolate. Auntie was as petite as Salmanda was long and lanky, but both had the same fine small bones. She wasn't black like Salmanda. She was brown, and it was as if street knowledge itself cast over that brown an aura of white ash. She didn't waste words. She was in touch with who she was, vitally connected to what it meant to be black in America. She was middle-aged then, her face weathered, and her grayish-black hair, to which she took an iron, was straight enough to be pulled back in a bun. Her steady eyes intrigued me. They held secrets about our country, because they were blue. I sensed in her the strength of the immigrant.

Salmanda, with all the aplomb of Don Quixote fighting the windmill, told Auntie of her meeting with Miss Fat and Fearsome. She thought it was funny. "I bring her my application to Englehurst College, and she doesn't even hear a thing I say, Auntie. She looks me square in the eyes and asks me if I can type."

"I don't think that's so funny, Salmanda," I said.

"Betsy here's right, girl." Auntie had lost her suspicion of me early on. If her niece had to hang around with white people, I think I was the one she'd have chosen to feed her a spoonful of sense.

"I mean, I know she's an awful person," I continued. "She hates everyone who's stuck in Horace High the way she is. She's a frustrated old maid. But she has power."

"Well, if she has power, good. 'Cause she's going to fill in my scholarship form and write a letter."

"But what's she going to say, Salmanda?"

"What does she say about anyone, Betsy? You think she's going to spend time making up something special? I told her to say I need a scholarship in order to go to college."

"And she told you you wouldn't get in."

"And I told her I had to get in. What else could I do? After all, she signed my college prep cards all these years without calling me in once. It's her fault I never took typing."

"You said that, child?"

Salmanda looked at Auntie's astonishment and laughed.

"Salmanda," I cut in, "I'm not so sure this is funny."

But it turned out all right. Two months later, there's Salmanda, sweeping into my home room, right in the middle of the Pledge of Allegiance. "Behhtsy, I got it! I got it!" She's waving a letter in the air and her skirt is hitched up in pursuit of it while we're saluting the flag.

I think Salmanda was the first Negro girl from Horace High to win a scholarship to college. That did nothing to calm her high spirits. Until then, the legend of the school had been Randall Jones. He was a Negro who many years ago was accepted at Princeton. He drowned his first year there and they named a statewide scholarship for him. "I'm glad you're not signing up for swimming," I said to Salmanda our first week at Englehurst. Englehurst College. A new school put up on a pretty Jersey meadow. Its catalogue said it emphasized science and fellowship.

Naturally, Salmanda signed up for basketball. She made varsity her freshman year. I stayed late after classes to watch her practice — once.

"You're always clowning," I said. I was driving her home. "Those girls are there to practice, not to clown. You're better than all of them and they don't like it one bit!"

"They don't? They don't like to win?"

"Salmanda, be serious. My impression is that they need you to win, but some of them don't like the color of your skin."

"Behhtsy! This is the North."

"Yeah, you don't have to sit in the back of the bus. It's great, isn't it? Anywhere you want in the bus, a lap away from a white person. You have all the luck."

"You're just jealous of me fooling around with all those girls."

"Jesus, Salmanda, where do you find these things to come up with? Now I've heard everything."

Whatever I said about prejudice didn't penetrate. I kept trying. That spring we applied for summer jobs in the chem lab of a chicken-rendering plant in the Jersey flatlands. We had heard about the openings one Friday at Englehurst, and Monday we were there.

Our applications were taken in the main office. I filled mine out in the employment section and was told I would be contacted, if I was going to be contacted, within a week. As I waited for Salmanda, a guy passing by the desk I was sitting at asked me if I'd like coffee and a doughnut. Later on, Monty told me that it had been he. Though I said no thank you, when I looked up from my calculus text, coffee and doughnut were there.

Salmanda's interview took a long time. "Wow! You must have done well. Here, want this doughnut? What did he say?"

"Oh, he didn't have that much to say."

"*You* were talking all that time?"

"No. Come on, let's get out of here." She took a bite of the doughnut, then gave it back. "It was filling the forms that took so long," she said once we were outside and walking along the gravel path to my car.

"More than one, hah? I only had to fill out one. You're going to get that job, no sweat."

"Oh, I got a job, all right. But not yours."

"What do you mean?"

"Well, he looked over that form after I filled it out and then, real slow like, he looked up at me. 'Miss Blake, do you really want a job for the summer?'"

"'Not only do I want one,' I said, 'but I have to have one.'"

"'Then I'd fill out these if I were you.' That was nice of him, wasn't it, Betsy? He said I shouldn't have any trouble at all. With summer vacations and all, they always need people in the plant."

"The plant? You're going to work in the factory?"

"The night shift. I got it right away."

I looked at her. She did not seem to be bitter or upset. She was smiling as she got into the car, as if already contemplating the fringe benefits of this new absurdity. I did not know whether she was faking. It seemed to me that one sentence hung between us: Salmanda, you were not even considered for the chem lab because you're a Negro. I knew she did not want to hear this. But I assumed she realized that's what had happened. It was obvious.

"Look, Salmanda, you deserve a chance for the job in the chem lab, and you're not getting it."

"Betsy, that's your job. They're already serving you coffee and doughnuts. That job's got your face written all over it."

White? Is that what she meant? Were her high spirits a front? Was she faking the insult away?

"Come on! Everything's cool," she continued. "Let's celebrate. Let's go to the Village. One day won't matter. Let's not go to school."

Greenwich Village is thirty-five minutes and forty light years away from Passaic. One day that spring Salmanda had taken the bus, gone to Washington Square Park, and sat on a bench. After that, all she talked about were the characters she met. Particularly her new friends Duke and Pam. She always wanted me to go over there with her on a Saturday, and I always said no. But that Monday I said sure.

We had already missed calculus, and I didn't think I could take an hour of dictionary study. That's what English composition had degenerated to at Englehurst. Maybe it was the emphasis on science and fellowship. Salmanda got a charge out of it. She was always raising her hand to ask questions about syllabic consonants or superscript numbers, flagging minutiae. She had an appetite for the absurd. Once she spotted a possibility for it, she couldn't get enough. She'd often stand up, thin, black, blazing, asking her question.

I wanted to be with her that Monday. I wanted to find the right words. I wanted to warn her about something. About what? About being Salmanda.

She talked my ear off through the Lincoln Tunnel about her Village friends. It was Pam this and Duke that. All the bars they drank at. Seven and Seven. Seagram's 7 and 7-Up. That was the big drink. It was pleasantly esoteric and in the know to flash your doctored ID, look the bartender in the face, and coolly say, "Seven and Seven."

I parked the car in a lot on Sixth Avenue to propitiate the gods of chance. A ticket or an accident, and my parents would know I'd been there. I was careful; I thought ahead. I rushed after Salmanda down Eighth Street.

Washington Square Park is one of the great places. Great places have salient characteristics. They set a mood. They stay the same. Certain people gravitate toward them at certain points of their lives. Later they say, "I went to Washington Square Park the other day. You wouldn't recognize it. I wouldn't even dare to sit on a bench. God, has it changed." They've changed.

That Monday we had our lunches with us and we ate them on a bench among the many office workers who were out on such a beautiful day. I looked like them, and Salmanda almost looked like them. For we were dressed to interview. I was so clean I squeaked and every nail was immaculate and lightly polished. In order to get a job you had to conform to the image you imagined in a boss's mind. Salmanda tried to. But in her pumps and the dark checkered dress Auntie made for her, she looked so black, gangly, and uncoordinated. Her high spirits burst through her disguise.

"Duke!" Salmanda called out. She stood up and waved. "Duke!" Someone turned around and, without much of an acknowledgment, walked toward us. The figure was clad in jeans and a loose Hawaiian shirt. Polyester blue waters and yellow leis slid along the chest, which was that of a plump, emasculated boy. The hair was thin, dirty blond, and hung in strands below the ears. The face was blandly amorphous, like the body gasp of a dying blowfish.

The figure stood in front of us and lowered its eyes in recognition.

"Duke, I want you to meet my friend, Betsy Lewis."

Duke nodded at me noncommitally and then took out a hip flask and handed it to Salmanda. Salmanda took a swig and passed it to me. I gulped. It was harsh stuff. Pure rye.

I looked at the park through my whiskey tears. It was saturated with molecules of light. The grass was so new that the green had not solidified, field after field of soft, wet lime, shadow and hue. Washington's white arch, its mammoth white stone, stood in substantial contrast to it. Later, when I saw Monet's dissolving cathedrals, I was thankful that he was French, that he had never had a chance to break up Washington Square Arch.

It has to stand out against the sun, against the vivid colors of people's clothes, their dogs, their balls, their bikes, their skates, their guitars, their chess games. It has to stand out against the variegated blur of movement, the pointillistic pantomime of generation after generation.

"You and Duke have a lot in common, Behhtsy. Duke here's Eyetalian too."

I looked at Duke. She was Italian too. I'm Italian and proud of it. My parents never wanted to go back. My grandmother taught me a few words and how to count.

Salmanda had told me Duke's father was a doctor in Philadelphia and paid her each month to stay away. My father owned a lumberyard in Passaic. What would he do if I had stray whiskers running down the sides of my face and hanging under my chin?

(On the train to Gaeta, I tried to match Duke's type. Venetian? Abruzzese? No. Duke here's Eyetalian too.)

Pam was a bit more reassuring at first glance. We went to her walk-up off St. Mark's Place. When we got to her floor, there was a big black guy taking a leak — door open — in the toilet in the hall. Salmanda had already reported on him, his equipment, and the outside toilet. I was too polite to stare as we walked by and rang Pam's bell. Pam was reassuring because she was feminine, intense, and took voice lessons. She aspired to the stage. No matter how boho she was, she was systematically striving for something, she was aiming to achieve. She had an oval face, dark hair and eyes. She wore an off-the-shoulder peasant blouse, a sweeping full Gypsy skirt, and no shoes. She was one of those Jewish girls who look Italian. She had a tiny gold star of David on a delicate gold chain around her neck.

"What's that drag you're wearing?" she asked, pointing at Salmanda's checkered dress. I was immediately warned. She had a real smart-ass raspy voice. And she spoke directly to Salmanda, as if I weren't there.

We went out in the street together. Salmanda and I in our interview outfits, Duke with her replenished hip flask, and Pam in her bare feet. I remember Salmanda whooping it up, talking with strangers, and in her high heels racing the barefoot Pam to the park. Greenwich Village is not the easiest place to upstage others, but Salmanda got people to stare. The race gave Duke and me a chance to be silent together, an opportunity we would always take when we were alone. "Salmanda talks about you a lot," I tried. Duke turned and looked at me as if to say, What else is new?

Later that day I was back on a bench in the park, alone with Salmanda, worrying whether I was going to get caught in a traffic jam in the Lincoln Tunnel. My clothes were killing me. The short, stiff sleeves of my linen dress were making rashes under my arms.

"What do you think of Duke and Pam?" she asked me.

"Pam's okay, I guess."

"You guess?"

"Well, she thinks she's hot stuff."

"She is. What do you think of Duke?"

"Why didn't you tell me Duke's a homo?"

"I did too tell you! I most certainly did. I told you she was butch."

"Butch?"

"Butch. Don't you know what butch means, girl? You acted like you did."

"Well, if I didn't, I know now."

"What about dyke?" she challenged. "Do you know what a dyke is?"

"Well, if I didn't, I'd sure as hell know how to look it up in the dictionary."

"Come on, Behhtsy. What's a dyke?"

Nonchalantly as I could manage, I ventured forth. "You mean to say it means something other than what the little Dutch boy put his finger in?"

She laughed so hard that people turned around again to look.

"Take it easy!" I told her. "See? Everyone's looking. It's as if you go out purposely to find weird people. It's like being happy about the night shift. You're trying to ignore society, but you can't." Here were the words I had spent the day trying to formulate. "Open your eyes, Salmanda. Look around. You've got to see what's up if you want to make a life for yourself. Look at Pam. She may have a bathtub in the kitchen now, but she's aiming for something big. She can go barefoot in the Village. But I bet you a million she wears shoes to Scarsdale. She looks reckless. You *are* reckless. You've got your future in front of you, but you've got to see who and where you are. When you run around the Village the way you do, people stare. And you can't afford it. You don't have parents in Scarsdale. You've got an aunt in Passaic and a scholarship. Once you graduate, no one will be able to keep you down. But you've got to be careful now. Duke's flaunting what she is. Duke's weird. That's what I think of Duke."

Salmanda invited me in when I dropped her off. We went downstairs, where Auntie was fixing a meal for her two little foster children, Salmanda, and a man named Ralph, who popped in to eat and sleep.

"How'd it go, child?" she asked Salmanda. She was so proud of this wild and gangly niece. But you could see her trying not to show it.

"Behhtsy here's gonna get the lab job."

"Come off it, Salmanda!"

"But the man was real nice to me, Auntie. I got a job in the plant."

"You speaking true?"

"Would I lie to you?"

"Well, that's something."

Auntie had expected nothing and was once more astonished by her intelligent niece, who had got her hands on something. Auntie took a leap of faith in educating her sister's child. Maybe what she knew deep down in her bones wasn't in every single case true.

"Come on up, Betsy," Salmanda said. "I want you to hear one thing before you go."

She had a record player in the living room. "Here, just listen to this while I change. Pam got it for me. It's really neat."

She put on a record of Odetta's and handed me the jacket to read. I had never heard of Odetta before, though I loved folk music. I listened to a lot of Pete Seeger. I felt an affinity with his lyrics. I was not interested in politics then. I lived in my parents' country. It was the only country in the world where everyone was free to make something of himself. It was a vast and omniscient state with its own set of inalienable rules. Live by them and you'll be fine. Ignore them and you'll find out. It's up to you. Still, when Pete Seeger exhorted the coal miners to break down the halls of marble, I felt the thrill. It was an apocalyptic vision. I had one too. I believed all the underdogs all over this land didn't have to break down a thing. All they had to do was learn to fit in.

So Pam liked Odetta and gave Salmanda this gift. I looked at the cover. I liked Odetta's strong and interesting face, the drama of her short-cropped hair. Then the voice came out from under the static of the needle. It was as rich and powerful as Mother Earth, in throat contact with the wisdom of the ages. It didn't matter whether the song was light or sad; the overwhelming intelligence and sensuality shone through. It was like taking your first look at Washington Square Park.

Salmanda came back into the living room and her entry startled me. I was deep in Odetta's songs. But it was good that she disturbed me. I had to go.

"Just hear this next one, Betsy. Just one more."

Salmanda, in her jeans and shirt, sat on the windowsill looking out on the street, relaxed and confident, herself, the interview paraphernalia peeled off. I sat in a deep upholstered chair that was too deep because the springs were no good.

Odetta sang a song called "Maybe She Go." It was about a girl on the precipice of life.

> Maybe she go
> Maybe she don' go

> Many a time she afraid to go
> Many she do go.

The passion of Odetta's voice added all the nuances to that simple refrain; she was singing to our guts. What was going to happen to Salmanda? What was going to happen to me?

> Sometime she sit on the ol' front porch
> Sayin' nothin' makes no sense
> What is the use of making a change
> What is there the difference?

What is there the difference? Didn't there have to be a difference?

> There's somethin' that say she stay where she be
> Somethin' say go
> But nothin' that say what somethin' will be best
> Nothin' she know of.

But something *had* to be best. This was a dangerous song. I watched Salmanda looking out the window as Odetta sang the refrain for the last time.

> Maybe she go
> Maybe she don' go . . .

Not only did Salmanda have to go, but she had to go with great strength and great conviction. In a world full of prejudice and hate she had to shine like a star. She was the exceptional person. The Jackie Robinson of science. By studying hard and pretending to fit in, she'd make it in the white world. She'd be an example.

When the song was over, she took the record off and came over to me for the cover. As she put it on, she said to me, "Betsy, I want to tell you something." I knew she was serious, because she didn't play at elongating my name. She stopped fussing with the record and sat back down on the windowsill.

"What if I tell you I'm weird like Duke?"

"You?"

She was a genius, that's what she was. A genius on the night shift. She was peculiar, because there was so much to her. But she wasn't weird.

"Me." She straightened up and looked in my eyes. Her neck was long and her chin was firm. "I want you to know I'm butch, I'm a dyke." She turned sideways and stared out the window as if she saw all the way down the street.

"Well," I said finally. "The most important thing for you right now, Salmanda, is to keep up your grades."

On the train platform in Formia, I shook off my memories. I rented a car from a dealer by the station and drove the five miles to Gaeta. At first the road was flat and unimpressive. I could have been going through small towns along the Jersey shore. I was driving along this dusty road to the place my grandmother had left. Why did you leave Gaeta, Nonna, I once asked her. Because she dreamed that in America she'd wear a hat. A lady's hat. She'd be a signora. Her oldest son, Tommaso, hadn't shared her enthusiasm. He stayed, came over when my mother was a grown woman, and after a while went back.

When any of our relatives waxed nostalgic about Italy, my father would say, "Why don't you do what Tommaso did and go back to Gaeta?" That proved his point. Tommaso had gone back to deprivation, World War II, and Mussolini. I remember my mother getting letters from him when I was small. She'd look at the envelope as I admired the thin, thin paper. "I wonder what he wants?" she'd say while I stood waiting for her to open the letter. I would send my mother a postcard from Gaeta. She would look at the picture, then ask my father, "What's she stirring up now? Why'd she go see that phony baloney?"

At Gaeta, I followed the signs to the old section and drove up a very long and curvy road, the Street of Pope Pius the Ninth. The street of the nineteenth-century Pope. Recalling him cleared my head. All contemporary accounts said that Pius the Ninth had a beautiful voice, and from the many descriptions I had unearthed, I knew that on his elevation he was as handsome as Leo. Leo . . .

Can beauty get you in trouble? The Pope began his reign in a sweep of liberal reforms — because of the admiration he saw in men's eyes. He proclaimed freedom of the press in Italy; he pardoned all political prisoners. Everyone loved him. Then he became enraged, his vanity mortally wounded, when, after all he did for them, the people wanted MORE. He had to sneak out of Rome and rethink his strategy in Gaeta. When he returned to Rome, his liberal days were over. He no longer looked in men's eyes for a mirror. The power of office became his cudgel. Was Leo riding on his popularity in the union? Would he change? Alice thought he already had.

The librarian at the Risorgimento museum in Rome had told me of a woman in Gaeta who rented rooms in her apartment to scholars. The building was right on the top of the hill. It was a big restored nineteenth-century palazzo. Had the Pope slept there? The woman looked at me in the doorway, paused, and then, though her rooms were filled, offered to clear out a tiny back room for me. This little room suited me. From it I could look down into an overgrown garden where children were playing. I watched them for a while, under the startling reds of the bougainvillea. Then I went for a walk.

The old section of Gaeta was a painfully beautiful ruin, a maze of small roads winding up and down along the hill, leading into courtyards and out again to other small streets and alleys. Worn-out paths, stone steps. So much war damage had been done to this area since the nineteenth century that most of its houses were skeletons among vegetation. Amid the ruins I could hear the clatter of workmen. The Romans were just beginning to rediscover one of their ancient summer places. The restoration had started on the "dachas," as Leo would have called them. Just a little place in the country, comrade, where my wife can collect fresh eggs, where the air is pure.

Returning from my walk, I went into the garden across the street from the palazzo where I was staying. I passed the open gate and crossed the large green lawn, which ended at a stone wall. From the stone wall I looked far down a rocky cliff to the open sea and to the few small boats on it. My grandfathers had been fishermen. They had fished this sea.

Then I walked down the hilly street to the caffè I had spotted earlier from my car. The outdoor tables were shaded by crimson bougainvillea, lush and gorgeous. From my table I had a view not of open sea, but of the wide, calm crescent of Gaeta's bay. I could see the NATO ship at anchor farther out. The American flag was up against the blue sky. The heat, the flag, the strangeness, the familiarity . . .

I took out my notebook. I was thinking of Doug. I wanted to share with him the impressions married people share. He'd be amused that the woman who rented me a room apologized for its being in the back! Noise bothered Doug, so we often trudged from pensione to pensione, looking not for a room with a view, but one over the airshaft in the back. No airshaft with this one though; children, noise. I wanted to give him my impressions of my walk. Now that I was alone, I felt we could really talk. But I didn't write to him. I wrote: "This is the place I can't come back to. This was once my real home. I'm here among the pink-purple bougainvillea, but this is not my home."

I put my pen down. Drank my coffee. Stared at the bay some more.

My uncle lived on the other side of the bay's crescent, in the new part of town, Elena. Since the late nineteenth century, that's where the Gaetani had moved. After all, only the rich can afford ruins and only the poorest of the poor are stuck in them. That afternoon I got as far as Tommaso's address. The newish three-story building stood in front of me, on a little square with a church. Beroni, my mother's maiden name, was on the second bell. The minute I saw it, I knew I wasn't going to ring. I decided to write Tommaso a note rather than call, and then I decided to mail it rather than stick it under his door. The Italian mail was worse than ours in those days. I was leaving everything in the hands of fate.

Three afternoons later, I returned from the archives to find a letter that had been hand-delivered. "My dear niece," it said. "What a grand surprise to hear from you and what a miracle that we received your notice. The mails are not to be trusted. Nothing works anymore . . ." I was expected for Sunday dinner.

Tommaso had for so long been a warning in my life that I was almost embarrassed to meet him. I half-suspected that his first words to me would be "I'm sorry."

He had left America before I was born, with his wife, who was pregnant. She lost that child on the boat. They had not been back in Gaeta a year before the war began. Tommaso's wife was pregnant again when she was killed outside Monte Cassino. I was a history major before I realized that it was either the Americans or the British who had dropped the bombs that made a disaster of Tommaso's foolishness. The next time my father shouted at me (before I married, we had some royal battles), "If you're too good for it here, why don't you go back to Italy like Tommaso?" I told him it was the American bombs that had destroyed Tommaso's life. He told me I always had an answer.

I expected to find Tommaso's life in shambles, somewhat like Salmanda's if I saw her again. I arrived on Sunday with a very big box of candy, a bottle of Sambuca (shades of Signor Sordi), and a desire to turn around and run.

"Betsy, welcome!" my uncle bellowed, spitting out his English. He opened his arms wide, then he crushed me. Luckily, I hadn't brought flowers.

"Let the poor girl catch her breath," said Margherita, Tommaso's second wife. I handed her my offerings. "Come in! Come in!"

"Meet your cousin," my uncle said. I turned to the young man in the vestibule. "I'm sorry I missed you when you brought the letter, Angelo."

"We were worried you would not find your way, Signora."

"It was no problem at all."

"Your Italian is very good," Margherita said. "Your parents speak Italian in America?"

"No. I learned Italian in school."

"In school," Margherita repeated, as if to remember. "Your husband isn't with you, Signora?"

"I told you!" my uncle told her, then turned to me and confided, "She's never been to America. Come, sit down, sit down!" I was led straight into the dining room.

I sat on the daybed there. Margherita poured cordials into little hand-painted glasses she had taken out of her china closet.

I looked at my uncle, who sat next to me, pressing my hand. His bald head seemed chiseled out of tough, eroded stone. He had high, defined cheekbones that glinted. Blood pulsed through arteries at his temples and up and down his thick neck. His white shirt was open at the neck. His blue Sunday slacks rode up his ankles and tugged at his stomach.

He was close to seventy by then; his wife was much younger. Margherita, short and plump, came over with her tray. After serving us, she sat down next to her son. Angelo was taller than his parents, slim, dark-haired, good-looking. Polite. Formal as his suit. He seemed quite mature for fifteen. Margherita doted on him; he was her accomplishment. She wanted us to get to know each other. But my uncle cut in. He was talking so exuberantly that it was an effort for me to catch each word at first. He spoke in a dialect I remembered from childhood. I was often told to ignore it. My grandparents were old and couldn't change their ways, my mother had explained. One day when she was minding me, my grandmother taught me how to count. "Uno-due-tre," she crooned her numbers with relish. "Uno-due-tray," I remembered.

"Talk to your cousin," Margherita coaxed her son while my uncle stopped to take a drink.

"How do you like your stay in Italy?" he asked in good Italian.

But my uncle didn't wait for me to answer his son's question. He simply started up again.

Well, he wasn't an easy man, Tommaso. My mother was right there. King of his castle. Old cock of the walk.

Margherita looked perturbed. When the doorbell rang, she

was startled. "Who can that be?" she asked sharply. "Excuse me."

A woman and her son entered. It was as if they brought heat and dust into the carefully shaded and immaculately clean room.

"What are you doing here?" I could hear Margherita admonish. "I should have known!"

"Have I committed a crime?"

The woman was fair, trim, nervous-looking. Quite big-breasted. Her heavily clad tits pointed her toward me and she ran after them. She was a quick woman. "So here you are! I am Clara, Signora," and she went on to explain how she was related to me. I made out that she was a distant cousin on my father's side, as well as being Margherita's cousin too. Margherita looked less than delighted. She rolled her eyes as Clara introduced her son, Rinaldo. Rinaldo was shorter than Angelo and didn't have his refined bearing. He had a tough, sullen face and a peculiar smile. It was his mother's, yet it covered only his lips. His mother said, "Say hello to the signora."

"Please, not signora. My name is Betsy. Call me Betsy, please."

"Beatrice," my uncle supplied. Bay-a-tree-chay. Only he, who had been in America, could pronounce Betsy. Bay-a-tree-chay. My Italian name put me back on my grandmother's lap. "Call her Betsy!" my mother would demand.

"Beatrice," Clara repeated.

Because Clara was so fair, I said, "You look more like my mother's side than my father's."

Clara beamed. "I wouldn't be surprised if I'm related to her too. We are all relatives here."

My aunt moaned. She clapped her hands to her lap, got up, and went toward the kitchen. "We've just come to say hello," Clara called after her. "Don't bother about us."

Margherita returned with two more place settings. Evidently she didn't believe her.

Everyone became merrier at the table. My uncle poured the wine. Margherita served a first course of prosciutto and salami that had to be rearranged in the kitchen in order to stretch two portions more. I looked at the three choice cuts of prosciutto on my own plate. There's something intimidating about the Italian laws of hospitality: I had to be offered more, though I certainly could have done with less. Not that there wasn't enough for everybody. Soup, pasta, rolled beef, chicken, potatoes roasted in chicken fat, salad, fruit, pastry, chocolate, coffee, liqueur . . .

As the courses progressed, my physical discomfort seemed to be an emblem of my uncle and aunt's generosity. "You are too thin! You are too thin!" I heard each time I tried to demur. As I forced the food in, I fantasized that I heard the *aaaaaaaaaaahs!* of their satisfaction. I felt I had swallowed a beach ball. It began jutting from my stomach, touching the very tops of my thighs. I felt uncomfortable too with the family situation. While my aunt was determined to feed me, Clara was determined to engage me.

"You have no children, Beatrice?" Clara asked.

"No, I don't."

"How long have you been married?"

"Almost five years."

"Ah, well, it's the moon. The moon has to be right. I was a lucky woman; I did not have to wait for my Rinaldo."

"Not even five months," my uncle interjected, and everyone laughed except Clara.

"He'd like to make a joke of mother's love, Beatrice. Better five months than five years, I'm sure you'd agree."

"Well, no. My husband and I are not ready for children yet. We each have a lot we want to do."

"Ready? What does it have to do with being ready?"

"I know, I know, Clara," my uncle agreed. He was a big drinker and, like Bev, despised an empty glass. Filled hers up. Filled his own. "You are an innocent. You never heard of *birth control.*"

"What?" Clara asked.

My uncle had said "birth control" in English.

Rinaldo caught on and repeated for his mother.

"I want him to learn English, Beatrice," Clara said, turning to me again. "He has a good head. If he learns more English, he'll go far."

"Angelo could learn English like this!" My aunt snapped her fingers. "I want him to take lessons."

"English!" my uncle spoofed. Then he said to me, in English, "How you think I speak?"

"Very well."

"And that's almost thirty years ago, don't forget," he said in Italian to his son. "Thirty years. You hear what your cousin Beatrice says, Angelo? I still speak very well."

"Yes, Father."

"See, Angelo, you don't need lessons for these things. I learned English from the school of life. Didn't I, Betsy?"

"You certainly did, Uncle, but that doesn't mean Angelo has to as well."

"Ah," he said.

"Ah," my aunt mocked.

Tommaso turned his slurred attention to both the boys. "You're young. America's for the young."

"Uncle, why did you leave America?" I asked hesitantly.

"It's their turn," he said. "It's their world now, God help them. If they want America, let them go."

"You're so smart!" Clara snapped. "Why didn't you stay in America, Tommaso? Why didn't you come back a rich man?"

"I had my reasons!"

"You're so smart! You don't believe in God. You talk like a heathen about sacred things."

"Enough, Clara!" my aunt cut in. "Shut your big mouth!"

Clara went back to the moon. "Don't listen to this nonsense, Beatrice. And don't worry. Someday the moon will shine on you."

"That's not — " I stopped myself. The moon. I remembered Monty at the plant in the flatlands. Monty. The summer of Salmanda's troubles. The heat.

"You look sad, Signora — "

"Beatrice!" My uncle corrected his wife.

"Are you missing your husband?" Clara asked.

"Oh, I'll be seeing him soon."

"Doesn't he mind that you travel without him?" my aunt got in.

"Well, we each have separate things we have to do."

"But a woman without a man — "

"In America there are lots of women without men," my uncle interposed. "The men die. The women live long. In America it's the women who wear the pants. It's the women who have the money."

"Do they really wear pants?" Clara asked. "Or is that just in the movies and on television?"

"They do wear pants."

"Do you?"

"There I do."

"Well, I don't care!" Clara said triumphantly. "Even if they do wear pants, I'm like an American woman. I have no husband anymore to protect me. He died so young, Beatrice. But do you know what I have? I have a son!" She put her arm around Rinaldo and fixed his hair with her free hand. I thought she'd take her napkin, wet it, and wipe grease from his chin. "I could be an American woman. With my Rinaldo, I could travel anywhere." She patted his cheek.

"So could I!" Margherita interposed with a bit of fire, clasping the hand of her son.

"Children are wonderful," I said.

"They are a comfort," Clara said and tried to pat her son's cheek again. "I should send you to America to take care of your cousin Beatrice!"

"I'm not going to America, Clara. I'm going back to Rome." My God, I thought, what am I getting into?

"Rome?" The consensus of the table: Rome was crazy. Who in his right mind would go to Rome?

"I was there once," Angelo said. "It's corrupt. It's even worse than here."

"Why don't you give it another chance, Angelo? Come visit my husband and me. Any time."

"Thank you, Signora. But there is nothing there for me."

"Oh, Angelo. There is so much there if you just give yourself the opportunity to see it. There is history and art and tradition. Wonderful people. I have some friends I'm sure you'd get along with, who'd love to meet you and show you the sights."

"It's all politicians there. You're nothing there without the right connections. One hand feeds the other. Believe me, I don't need people to show me what there is to see."

"Well, it's funny, isn't it? Here you are two hours from Rome and you won't even take the trip. And I had to cross an ocean to get there."

Rinaldo said, "Rome's not so bad, Angelo. They have lots of things for the tourists to see. Maybe someday I'll buy a big car and go there and take rich Americans around and make lots of money." Thug-faced Rinaldo revved up his future car, put his arms in front of him, and *ruhhhhruhhhruhhh*, he steered it as his mother watched in delight.

She pointed to her son's head and said to me, "He has something up there, doesn't he."

Through the noise of Rinaldo's revving, my uncle whispered, "His ass."

"Not all Americans are rich, Rinaldo," I said.

"Stop!" his mother told him instantly. "Listen to the signora. She's speaking to you."

Rinaldo let his engine die. Then he took his hands off the wheel.

"Not all Americans are rich, Rinaldo."

"But they have a chance," Angelo said.

"A chance as well for other things than money."

"Are you rich?" Rinaldo asked me.

There was a long pause.

Like any other animal sensing danger, I suddenly forgot my bloated body, bolted up straight, sniffed the air. I had felt uneasy about this overabundant dinner that my relatives could ill afford. As Clara talked, I had been daydreaming about taking them to a restaurant tomorrow, of sending them some fine gift to thank them once I was back in Rome. Of sending Angelo some expensive books and pocket money. Of Angelo visiting Rome for a few weeks. A boy like that, with Doug's connections, maybe we could find him something. I had grown high on my generosity and the surprise and gratitude I imagined it would provoke. My feelings changed radically when I saw that these people wanted something from me.

I told you so, my mother was whispering in my ear while with one nervous hand she was taking a big squeeze at my heart. He always wants something, that one.

The silence encouraged Angelo. "Is it true, Signora," he asked me, "that in America electricians make a lot of money?"

"Don't bother your cousin!" my aunt admonished Angelo. "Don't you see she needs a rest!"

"Electricians make good money, Angelo," I told him. "They make good money even if they're not that good."

"Here I'll be an electrician's assistant for another seven years. Then, even then . . . *puff!*" Angelo blew away his future.

"Then go to America!" Uncle Tommaso yelled. "You'll see what you make!" He was on an entirely different wavelength from his wife and son, from Clara and her son. He was unconscious of the fact that they were all building a house of daydreams. A rich, childless cousin comes and carries a manchild to the United States.

"America? Is it America you want? Go there, smart one! Go there! You'll see!" My uncle turned to me. "Hey, wop!" he yelled in my face, startling me. "I no forget my English, see. Hey, Betsy, you wanna know why I no stay there?"

I nodded.

"There you work like a nigger," he told me. "Sonna bitch boss. You wop, boss say. Wops make wine. You bring me wine. Sure boss. But I no bring. Five dollars a week. Work like a nigger. Fuck them. Sonna bitch, bastard boss. America? Streets gold? Shit! My wife, she wanna go home. I take my fist. I tell sonna bitch boss, this wop no give no wine. POW! Understand, Betsy? POW! Sonna bitch." Tommaso laughed. His red face perspired as he socked the air.

"You hear, Angelo? Rinaldo, are you listening?" my uncle asked in his graceful Italian. "You understand any of this at all? I didn't have to learn my English in school. I haven't forgotten a word of it. Ask Betsy."

"You haven't forgotten a word, Uncle," I said.

"POW!" Tommaso yelled in delight, hitting the son of a bitch again. "Shove job. Up yours. I go home."

6

I went back to my room and slept way past the siesta. I woke in the middle of the night, hot, confused, reaching after the fragments of dreams. Leo? No. Monty? It was Monty. Clara had brought him back with her talk of the moon.

Awake, in the dark, I saw Monty again. Monty as he had been when I met him, when I had the job in the lab that summer, the job Salmanda should have had. I was walking up the gravel path to the lab, the stink from rendered chickens mixing with the heat once more. I was opening the door and feeling the air-conditioned air greet me . . .

My first duty of each day was to collect coffee orders from the seven technicians and phone them in to Monty. He was the book-keeper in the main office assigned to coordinating the orders. He'd call me after the delivery was received and I'd walk over to the main office to pick up. So this was work.

Monty was tall and well built. A Canadian. He told me he had once almost played hockey professionally. The skin of his face was as white as the country he came from, crepe-paper white.

He looked up from his work when I walked in, and the skin of his face creased at the jowls. This gave a serious look to his long face, his small green eyes, and his short, straight nose. He'd hold that pose of seriousness for a moment, as if he were making a transition from his figures. I say "as if," because I began to realize he was expecting me, waiting for me. Then he'd smile. He had a nice smile that did something sexy to his fleshy face. He looked me up and down.

"Here comes the sugar in my coffee."

Dopey.

"You like him, don't you, Behhtsy? Don't make the poor man suffer. Go out with him."

That was Salmanda on the phone at night. During her break at the rendering plant. She too was learning work. She would have absorbed much more organic chemistry than I, had she gotten the job at the lab. She wouldn't have settled for filing reports, smiling, and running for coffee. How could she sound so happy after the deal she got? Factory work. Genius on the night shift.

"You're just chicken," Salmanda said over the phone. "And believe me, I'm getting real familiar with chickens. Give the guy a break. Go out with him. Don't be a scaredy cat. It'll be good for you. I know."

"How do you know?"

"Hey, don't get on a high horse with me. I've been with my share of men."

"You have? But then why — "

"I don't know why, Betsy. I honestly don't. All I can tell you is, when it's over, something's missing. It never means much, that's all."

It never means much? For years I had sat in the movies and watched close-ups of lovers' faces. The music, the intense looks, the way the lips opened slightly as they kissed, would stab at my stomach and then ripple up to my heart.

Monty picked me up at my house and took me out to the movies. When I got home, my mother was waiting up for me, although she had worked all day. My mother. The strain of tension in her eyes. She could not rest until she raised her daughter.

"Do you do it deliberately?" my mother asked me.

"Do what?"

"Find losers."

The next week I went to see him at his place. Monty had a basement room in a boardinghouse. It was a big rambling building in a sleazy area. Because he was in the basement, he had a separate entrance.

"Welcome to my palace, sweetheart," he said. "Come on in. It won't bite you. Take a look around."

It was a small room with a narrow bed. There was a little fridge he used for beer. On the windowsill over his bed was an old round fan stirring Jersey dust. It was a hot weekend in August. Monty was wearing chinos, but his feet were bare and his shirt was off. "A beer?"

"We'll miss the movie."

"We have plenty of time."

"It starts at two, Monty."

"We'll make the next one. Come on. Sit down."

We sat on his bed and drank beer and talked about the people we knew from work. Our conversation centered on Lois Percy. Lois had been in my home room in Horace High and was now working full time in the business office of the plant. She was a very prim girl. She was even pretty in a good-girl way. She was tall, blond, and much too thin. Her back was elongated and very stiff. The gold cross that she flaunted around her neck looked capable of warding off werewolves.

"Lois came over here once," Monty said. "Now she won't."

"Why?"

"I tried to kiss her. You'd think it was attempted rape."

I laughed. He put his arm around me. We looked at each other. Very slowly, he moved his face toward me, tilted my chin with his free hand, and kissed me.

I moved away.

"You going to call the police?"

"It's just time to go, Monty."

"Sure, Lois."

"You take that back," I said, pushing him.

"You make me." He grabbed my arms.

"Let me go! You *are* a rapist."

We started a mock battle on the bed. "Lois," I called out. "Lois, where are you when I need you. I've sinned against you, Lois. You were right!"

We were cuffing each other pretty hard. "Come on, Monty. It's no joke anymore. You're hurting me."

"You have to kiss me first. Kiss me and we'll make up."

"Over my dead body!"

"There, there. That's a girl." He was on top of me and had my hands pinned up over my head on his pillow. "Come on, now, be nice to me."

Suddenly we stopped joking. We were looking very seriously at each other. He waited. He held me there and he waited, knowingly.

"I give up," I said softly and kissed him on the lips.

We kept on kissing. "Let's get rid of this." He unbuttoned my blouse. Then he unhooked my bra and raised it. "You're beautiful," he said. "Look at yourself," he said as he touched me. Then he had his teeth around my nipple, hurting me. "Look at these, just look at these," he whispered. I opened my eyes. I saw him sucking at my exposed breasts.

"What's wrong with Monty?" I asked my mother. "He's a good friend."

"Then keep it that way. See him at work."

"But we're just going to the movies."

"You're headed for trouble."

"What the hell have I done now?"

"Don't you dare curse in this house. You're just lucky your father's not home to hear you."

"What crime am I committing?"

"If you don't know in your heart of hearts, then I can't tell you."

That fall, back at college, I began to meet Monty outside the house. Every Saturday afternoon and most Tuesday nights I went to his room.

His little room. None of the charm of the little room on the Street of Pius the Ninth. I got out of bed, wide awake by then, and went to the window. Work like a nigger. I opened the shutters and took a deep breath. I looked up at the pale moon. Light was evaporating around it. I couldn't see a face.

I thought of my parents. My father ran his lumberyard and my mother worked as a typist three days a week in a law office. She didn't have to; she just couldn't sit still. She just had to work. Her own parents hadn't understood it. They were old-fashioned. A woman's place. Old-fashioned and lax. She told me her own mother and father hadn't wanted her to finish high school. But they were immigrants and didn't know. She was born out of ignorance when her mother was almost fifty. I don't know if she ever forgave her mother for the superstitions that had abetted her birth.

My mother wanted to have her own family young. But it took her a long time to carry a child to term. There was going to be only me. That's why my parents were so critical, so strict. Because they loved me. They were doing it for me. I was too young to know what I really felt or really wanted, my mother explained to me. As I grew up, *no* was their favorite word. It built character.

I could be quietly rebellious. But in my heart of hearts their values supplied me. I knew I was wrong. I knew I was wrong seeing Monty on the side. Salmanda encouraged me. I knew she was wrong. "Go on, girl, you're only human," she'd say. "Have fun." Salmanda was not raised by my mother. I was very excited and very guilty about petting with Monty. I knew it was life. But as I tried to convince Salmanda, life was alien and dangerous. It was something to be done, if at all, on the side.

When I saw Italy for the first time, I was knocked out by the accepted sensuality of the streets. People accepted their bodies. Women accepted hair under their arms and on their legs. Men in business suits accepted their balls, gave them a tug as they walked. The woman in the fruit store openly nursed her baby. Her husband didn't wait on the me behind my eyes, but the me that came in a body. There's a cadence of flesh in Italy, an earthiness. It didn't travel well to New Jersey. If at all, I'd glimpse it fleetingly, at one of the weddings my parents and I had to go to, when one of the old-timers did a dance. "They're still doing *that*," my mother would say. When I came back from my first trip to Italy, I felt like ripping the country out of my father's *National Geographic*, exhibiting it to my parents, and saying, "See!"

"See what?" I'm sure my mother would have answered. Just as she said, "I have no idea why you want to go there. It's dirty."

Well, I was dirty about Monty. I'll never forget that Tuesday night. My father was watching television. My mother was sitting farther back, where it was better for your eyes. She had a cigarette going in the ashtray, she was watching the set, and she was knitting. She often seemed intent on catching up with her hands.

I walked downstairs with my notebook. "Where are you going?" my father asked without veering from the set. He was dark like me and had the rather prominent Roman nose I have. He was a big guy, with a gut. He looked really handsome when he dressed up. My mother was blond and big-breasted, short and slightly plump, like Clara. Everyone said we had the same brown eyes. Only hers were really vulnerable. She always looked at me as if she were going to cry. "Don't upset your mother."

Where was I going? On Tuesday nights I said I was going to the library. The library wasn't that far away from Monty. I could go to the library as well . . . For some reason, that night I broke it up with another excuse. "I'm going over to Salmanda's to study."

"Salmanda?"

"You know her, Papa."

"You mean the colored girl?"

He turned down the set. "Did I hear you right? The colored girl?"

"She happens to be a specific color — Negro."

"You're talking to your father," my mother said.

My father's tone had set me off. But I must have been imagining it. Neither of my parents was prejudiced and they were proud of it. America was the greatest country in the world because everyone had inalienable rights. I mean, my parents had a reason for not wanting to see Italy. Mussolini and his pal Hitler, they never fooled my father.

And they didn't send me to parochial schools. It wasn't the money. They wanted me to take advantage of the science courses once I got to high school. I remember my mother shouting to her deaf mother, "It's not Italy. Here, the best education is free." She was always ready to teach my old nonna something about the New World. My father defended the public schools too. "She's got to learn to get along with all kinds; that's what this country's about."

"Betsy, let me get this straight," my father said. "You're going to take my car and drive to Grant Avenue at night?"

"Oh, I can take the bus." I could also see what he meant. Going to the Negro section of town at night was more complicated than saying I was going. "Don't worry, Papa. I'll be careful. Salmanda's block is safe."

He reached over and turned the sound of the commercial off completely. "You drive her to school, don't you? We've never said a word. But do me a favor, study with her there, at the school."

I was impatient by then. I was almost eighteen and they still treated me like a kid. Monty was in his room. Maybe he was sucking on a bottle of beer, propped up on his narrow bed. Shirt off. Waiting for me.

"I said not to worry, Papa. Salmanda's block's as safe as can be."

"And I said see your friend at school, that's enough."

"How can it be enough? Salmanda is my best friend."

He turned all of his attention to me. "Your best friend? A nigger for a best friend?"

"Papa!"

"Don't you 'Papa' me! How do you like this, Camilla? First you tell me she's been acting like the cat that's swallowed the canary, and now she has a spear-chucker for a best friend."

"Don't talk like that, Papa!"

"Now you're teaching me how to talk?"

"You're saying terrible things. It's not like you."

"I'm not saying nothing wrong, Betsy. Listen, it's okay to go to school with them. We're the melting pot. Your colored friend, she's got the opportunity to get an education and make something of herself. Where else in the world could she get a deal like that? I say good for her. They should all be like her. But you draw a line. Believe me, Betsy, they like it better that way. That way they know just where they stand."

"Salmanda's aunt would agree with you."

"See?"

"But whether you say it or she acts like it, it's wrong."

"No, it's not, Betsy. It's the way things are. It's common sense."

"Listen to your father," my mother said. I think she married him for moments like this. Don't be fooled, she often told me. Sex is something that disappears quick. Find yourself a decent man.

"It's not the way things are," I said. "It's not like that in Paris."

"This ain't Paris. It's Passaic."

"Well, if it's Passaic, Papa, I'm late for a date. I've got to get going."

"Not so fast. You got cotton in your ears? You're going nowhere. You're staying right here."

"I am not!"

"Camilla — "

"Betsy!" my mother said. "What's gotten into you?"

"There's nothing wrong with me going over to see Salmanda!

You're not going to make me think there's anything wrong with that!"

"I'm surprised you didn't invite her here," my mother said sweetly.

"I will. But it's too late tonight. I've got to go there."

My parents looked at each other. "Maybe I could cook something for her," my mother said. She faced me. "For a smart girl, Betsy — "

"Why don't she sleep over?" my father started yelling. "Why don't you have a pajama party. Put your heads on the same pillow."

"Why not? What's wrong with that. Just tell me. Why not?"

"They smell!" my father screamed. "They come to the lumberyard. They wanna work. You think I'd ever hire one? They stink!"

"Papa! That's prejudice!"

"Just one minute, young lady," my mother said. "Your father knows what he's talking about." She put her needles back in her bag.

"It's prejudice. Salmanda doesn't smell."

"Let me talk! Make believe I'm one of those professors your father is paying for. You have that notebook. Open it up. Write this down. I used to sit next to one in shorthand. It was night school, in the summer. My parents didn't know where I was. You know where I was? Learning something. Anyway, I had to sit right next to one. It would have looked funny if I tried to change my seat. That would have been prejudice, like in the South. After all, it was public school. Everyone has the right to be there. But, Betsy, the first few minutes of that class, I felt I was being punished for taking things in my own hands. For learning something. That girl would sit down, on a hot summer night, why — "

"The stink'd take the wind right out of your sails. That's what your mother means!"

"Shut up! Shut up!" I forgot about my notebook. Let papers tumble all over as I put my hands to my ears.

"Betsy — "

I didn't listen to them. I ran out the door.

"Door's open," Monty called out. He was on his bed, sucking his beer. "After this one, I was going to give up on you." He held up the bottle.

I exploded into my story right in the middle of the room.

"How come you're so concerned about them letting you see your girlfriend in the open when you don't give a damn that they don't like me? Not that I'm complaining. Come on over here."

"That's not the point. It's so unfair. It's prejudice. It's nothing but prejudice. Both of them. Salmanda doesn't smell."

"Depends how close you get."

"Don't be filthy."

"Come over here, sweetheart. Please, baby. I'm just trying to cheer you up. Come here. I'm gonna calm you down."

Monty and I had gone pretty far by then. Lately he'd been saying that when a man and woman loved each other, she would kiss him below the waist and he would kiss her below the waist too.

"Do you believe that?" I asked, incredulously.

"I know it."

"Have you done it?"

"That's mine to know and yours to find out."

I remember Salmanda telling me that one night, coming from a basketball game, she heard this in the college parking lot. "Suck, honey, suck!" the guy had pleaded. "Blow's only an expression."

Is the number 59?

That is not the number.

69.

Blow job.

Cock-sucking.

People did it.

That night Monty was very insistent. And once we started, I was very hot. He didn't tell me to look, the way he usually did.

He turned out the light. In the dark he took my underpants off. He went down on me. I could feel his hands, then his face, in between my legs. His soft tongue was inside me. After a while he moved his body so that my mouth had access to his genitals, his hip bone, his thighs. The hardest parts of a man's body while he was being so soft down on me.

So this was 69. It was no worse than prejudice.

In fact, I forgot about prejudice, about everything except what I was feeling. Rushes of pleasure scared me, felt more and more like pain, until they reached high up inside me and broke. "Well," Monty murmured. "Well, well." He came up from my legs. His face was over mine, pungent and wet like a brook. "Should I?" he whispered as he mounted me. I was already opening to him. He entered me. He came quickly the first time, before he could pull out.

Walking down my street late that night from where Monty dropped me off, I wondered if the house would still be standing.

My mother was standing. Her face was rigid and white with cold cream. Her eyes were red and wet. "Thank God your father's asleep. But I'm a mother. I'm a mother," she said angrily. "Even when you walk out, I wait up until you're home."

I walked by her before she could see what she had to cry for. I was sore and throbbing, and I was scared to death.

That night I prayed to the Madonna. I hadn't done that for years. Dear Mary, Mother of God, if I get my period, I'll believe in you always. If I get my period, I'll never, never do it again.

I got my period.

Actually, it never was the same again. Monty's putting on a rubber always signaled the risk I was taking. "Don't worry, darlin'," he'd say as he made love to me. While he made love he liked to make up little stories. One was about the future and the house we'd buy. He'd come home every night, take me in his arms, unbutton my blouse, take down my underpants, feel me warm and wet under my skirt. Don't worry, he told me. The rubber's safe. And if not? Why, then, he'd come home not only to his beautiful wife but to his little son.

As he talked, as he made love to me, I saw the tract house in the subdivision (he didn't want to stay in the city), I saw the ironing board out, a kid by my side. I saw Monty coming home from the plant. Is this what I wanted from life? As Monty built the house of our erotic pleasure, I felt my pleasure go.

"I don't know," I said to Salmanda one spring day. We were eating our lunch under a tree at the college. "Maybe my mother's right about Monty."

"There are more guys in the world than the Royal Mounty Monty, Behhtsy, that's for sure."

"Now you sound like my mother."

"I sure don't mean it like her."

"Then you sound like you want me to take on the navy."

"Or someone who'd take you to a basketball game."

"Monty and I keep talking about going. I want him to meet you. But something always comes up."

"And I know what it is."

"Now, now, Salmanda, that's not nice."

"Maybe I'm not nice."

"That's because you're a star." I was referring to basketball. I leaned back against the tree and closed my eyes. The school year was promising to end, was whispering that after exams time would accelerate, exhilarate, offer more. For me the more included a summer job away from science. I had a job in a bookstore in Greenwich Village. I hadn't even tried to go back to the chem lab. Monty said I'd be too distracting. The weather was balmy and I breathed in deeply.

"Maybe I'm falling out of love," I said finally.

"Why, you sound like that's a tragedy."

"Well, given how far I've gone, it would be."

"Behhtsy, are you going to be with only one man the rest of your life? Are you going to marry the Mounty and be faithful and true forever and ever? Damn it, girl."

"I don't know if I want to get married."

"You don't have to get married."

"I've got to get married some time."

"Why?"

"Why? Salmanda, I'm not a virgin anymore."

"So?"

"So? You think I can just go on like this. Monty now. Someone else later. On and on. What'll happen to me?"

"Well, I'm never getting married, and I think I'll live."

"That's different, Salmanda. You know it's different. Why, if you liked men, you'd be in the same boat I'm in now."

"Maybe."

"Maybe. Maybe, my ass." I looked up at the leaves. From the time I was a kid I liked to watch them against the sky. "You'd have to. That's the way things are. A woman just can't go from one man to another. It's not right."

No answer. I waited. "Sal——" I began and looked over. She had stood up. She was walking away.

The next time I was to pick her up for school, Auntie came out and told me she was staying with a friend. After that, she began to miss classes.

And I missed my period. At first I thought it was the strain of final exams and tried not to panic. But school ended, my job began, and I spent a week looking for stains every time I went to the bathroom. Then I panicked. But after a few more days of wondering what I was going to do, I suddenly felt peaceful. After months of fogginess and confusion about Salmanda's being gay, about my parents' prejudice, about my going to bed with Monty and deceiving my parents, my body was formulating a solution for me. Biology itself formed a plan.

I remember Monty walking into the Chinese restaurant, wearing khakis and a shirt open at the neck. The blue of it accented his pale skin. In shoes he seemed extra tall. And in clothes he seemed a stranger. Suddenly biology wasn't a rational subject that my parents encouraged me to take. Someone I didn't know at all could put a baby in my stomach.

"Hi, there." Monty sat across from me in the booth on the worn red damask banquette.

"Hi," I said, and lowered my eyes.

"What's this meeting called for?"

"Nothing special," I said. "It's just that we can't live in your room."

He ordered beer. "We don't live there. You come there when you feel like it. I'm surprised we're sitting here now. What if your father walks in? What if your mother sees you?"

"Monty, I told you about my parents. They have a way of wearing me down. My mother especially. I was afraid if you came around too much they'd both find a way of breaking us up."

"Your father's got money. Maybe he could have paid me off."

"That's nice."

"Well, I'm not good enough for you. I hope your other boyfriends are."

"I have no boyfriends except for you. You know that."

His eyes said, I'll bet. They made him look second rate.

The conversation was much different from when we were in bed. I switched to the menu. He didn't know how to order. I asked him if there were a lot of Chinese restaurants in Canada. He began to talk of Ottawa. He got into his own conversation and we both began to relax and drink. I changed to Seven and Seven.

By the time the subgum came, I looked at him happily, then devoured my meal. "You certainly have developed an appetite," he said. "You want more?" He'd been playing with his food.

In the fullness of the moment I said, "I have something to tell you, Monty. It's a confession of sorts. All the times you've talked of our future, especially about the house you want to buy for us, I've been scared. Scared to death."

"How come?"

"I've lived in a house all my life. And in that house, I've never been able to do what I want to do. I want something else, Monty."

"You sure didn't let on at the time. I could have sworn you liked houses."

"I think it's the way you presented them to me."

"So you remember? Why are we here? Is it something else or somebody else you want to tell me about, Betsy?"

"Oh, Monty, don't get the wrong idea. There's no one else. Honest. I want you. You know, when I was little I asked my grandmother why she came to America. You know what she told me? She came to America so that she could wear a hat. There were hats in her America. For her. In America she'd be a lady. Imagine. I guess I'm like her. I figure America's got to have an apartment in it for me. My America. I know it sounds silly, but I've really let this build up in my mind. It's made me distant. I see that now. But if we love each other, it's a small matter, isn't it? We can live in an apartment as well as a house, can't we?"

He smiled at me indulgently. "So I'm getting a free meal for this? Betsy, baby, don't worry. An apartment first. Whatever you want." His legs caught one of mine under the table. "As long as I have you to come home to. But I'll be jealous of every guy who gets in an elevator with you. I'll ask about every one of them when I get home. I'll want to know who's been brushing up against you like it's an accident, who's after your ass."

"I'll be getting home the same time as you. We can ride the elevator together. I'll just keep my job at the bookstore. I'll find a sitter for the baby."

"No, sweetheart, you won't work. When I walk in the door, I want to see my son with you."

"Or daughter."

"It'll be a boy. Honey, get the bill and let's get out of here. If we don't go soon, I'm going to embarrass you when I stand up."

"I don't care if it's a boy or a girl as long as it's healthy. My mother had problems carrying. That's why there's only me. And about the job, Monty; I have to work. I never planned to just sit home with a baby. I'd go berserk."

"Come on, sweetheart, we have time enough for that."

"About seven and a half months, I'd say. Oh, Monty, I'm pretty sure I'm pregnant."

"What?"

"I've missed my period, and I've been regular all my life. I didn't think it would be like this, Monty. But everything else fades. I feel so happy. Isn't it wonderful?"

"Wonderful."

"Are you okay?"

"I'm just surprised."

"Don't you want the baby? Don't you want me?"

"Now, darlin', don't get upset. Have you been to a doctor?"

"Not yet."

"You get to the doctor first, then we'll talk about babies."

"This is something a woman knows."

"Are you feeling okay?"

"I never felt better. Only don't tease me about other boyfriends." I sat back, put my hands on my stomach, and smiled. There was no more indecision for me. Life had just rendered complexity speechless.

We didn't wait to open our fortune cookies.

We went back to his place and made love like crazy. Without rubbers.

Then we made a "date" for Saturday. I told my parents I was going out with him. He was going to pick me up at home.

> Sometime she sit on the ol' front porch
> Sayin' nothin' makes no sense
> What is the use of making a change
> What is there the difference?

That Saturday night I sat on my ol' front porch. I waited. Monty didn't show. I waited and waited. I called and there was no answer. I called and I called.

"A steady fellow, this Monty," my mother said.

Sunday I walked over to his room early, praying he'd be in bed. Nothing. Monday I drove to the flatlands. The stink of rendered chickens inflamed the past. I walked into the office where Monty used to have my coffee order waiting for me. Lois Percy saw me. She was wearing a diamond as substantial as the cross around her neck. "Betsy," she called out in a friendly manner.

"It's nice to see you. Are you going to work here again?"

"Where's Monty?" I asked, cutting through her good nature.

"His mother is very sick," she said. She was amused. She couldn't get my grades in high school. But she sure as hell knew how to stay afloat on the ship of life. "He had to go back to Canada immediately. He doesn't know when he'll be back. He told us to hold his last week's pay."

"Oh, my God."

"It's tough," she said.

"You don't know how tough."

But maybe she did.

I tried to catch Salmanda at home. She had started working the night shift at the plant again, right after her last exam. When I got to her house, a distracted Auntie said she wasn't there. So I figured she was off somewhere in New York.

I went all over the Village, looking for her. Climbed up the stairs to Pam's place on that unusually hot June day. Then to Duke's place. "Come in," a hostile voice called out, even after I said, "Salmanda! You're there! It's me."

Duke's room in the heat. Roach powder and ward-green paint. Smelling the way it looked. Salmanda slugging rye.

"Have a seat," Salmanda said, motioning to the naked mattress. Through the closet door that didn't shut I could see Duke's junk shoved in. Duke lived like I felt.

"You on your lunch hour?" she mumbled, meaning from the bookstore.

"I don't work on Mondays. I've been all over looking for you."

"You got me."

Then she realized I wasn't in any better mood than she was. "What's wrong with you?" she asked.

"Everything. Monty left."

"So the Royal Mounty skedaddled."

"Yes. He ran like hell when he found out I'm pregnant."

"Pregnant?!"

My mother couldn't have done it better. I almost said, I'm sorry.

"Let me at him," she continued. "I'll show that bastard what to do with his cock."

"Try Ottawa."

"The motherfucker! You sure he left?"

"According to Lois Percy."

"Lois Percy." Salmanda stood up and did a tipsy, mincing imitation of Lois' good-girl walk.

"I need help, Salmanda."

"You need an abortion."

I burst out crying.

Then Salmanda had her arms around me. "Don't cry, Behhtsy. Please, baby, don't cry."

I knew I needed an abortion. I hadn't the courage to be an unwed mother or a Carmelite.

"Duke can arrange it, Betsy. It'll be all right."

"Duke?"

"She knows good people. She'll be back in town by Wednesday. She'll know what you can do. So hush now, Behhtsy."

"I don't want her to know it's for me," I sobbed.

"I'll tell her it's for Lois Percy."

That Saturday night Salmanda met me in New York and we traveled uptown together. Duke had arranged to meet us in a very genteel East Side gay bar.

"Forget it!" I said as soon as I saw Duke, malevolent and alone at a table. But I didn't mean it. Salmanda brought me over.

Duke didn't say a word. She was smoking a cigarette and looking as if the world was a fool not to dance with her. She eyed me. We sat down and ordered drinks.

I watched the girls dancing. Many of the pants-clad dykes with short hair looked like good-natured tomboys. The fems in dresses sure looked fem. The only man in the place was the swish bartender. It was a tony place, and every once in a while, even when the music played, you could hear a hush, as though everyone were participating in a secret.

"Want to dance?" Salmanda asked.

"I'm in no dancing mood," I managed nonchalantly.

Salmanda got up and went over to another table. She spoke
to a very pretty girl, who seemed pleased to see her. The girl got
up and Salmanda led her to the floor. They danced, Salmanda
moving as gracefully and confidently as she did on the basketball court.

"You've been out of town?" I asked Duke.

"Yeah."

I think Duke got her reputation for being in the know by saying little and saying that little with an air of ennui. Reputations
fulfill themselves. People tripped over their words, keeping her
in the know.

She was dressed neatly for the occasion and had her thin hair
newly washed. Clusters of blond whiskers rose from the sides of
her chin and under it, reminding me that her father paid to keep
her away. I tried to keep my eyes off Duke's whiskers, and she
excluded me from her range of vision, as if I were not yet
born.

We both watched Salmanda dance. She was the only Negro in
the bar, but it wasn't her color alone that made people watch
her on the floor. It was the rightness of her stance as she led the
pretty girl in the dance. Drag became her. She didn't look like a
tomboy; she looked like a long-limbed, athletic, and virile boy.
I thought our own friendship had a current of electricity running through it. And a vision of destiny. As the music swelled, I
thought it was a great friendship. What we didn't share in bed
sent sparks flying. Maybe that's what Duke and Pam didn't like.
I believed that if Salmanda was careful, she could lead her people on.

Times change, my father was first to acknowledge. Slowly, my
mother would add. They believed everything would be different
between the races a hundred years from then. And they ap-
proved. In 2059 I could meet Salmanda on Grant Avenue at
night. No sweat. I too believed it would take forever to smite
discrimination. But I saw Salmanda in the forefront of the effort. Helping her people, just as she was helping me. That's what
a hero is, what a saint is. Someone we expect to go against

self-interest until he accomplishes for us what we believe is right.

But here we were, a hundred years too early, in a gay bar, about to ask Duke where someone I knew could get an abortion. I understood why I never wanted to look at the world of spite in Duke's small and avaricious eyes. She was Salmanda; she was me too, sunk low.

"Your girlfriend's got troubles," Duke said, finally.

"How'd you know?"

"She told me."

"Well, let's cut the shit," I said suddenly. "It's not my girl-friend, it's me."

Duke was caught off guard. She almost said something. Her mouth opened before she clammed up.

Salmanda came back to the table, sat down, and slugged her melting Seven and Seven. "Behhtsy here has a girlfriend in trou-ble. Can you do something for her?"

"I told her it's me."

"Everyone's got troubles, it seems," Duke said and then she looked into my eyes. "For your kind of trouble, I can set it up with a real doctor for six hundred. There's a student who'll do it for three."

"How good's the doctor?"

"He's a doctor."

"Thanks. Six."

"You get what you pay for. Hey, Salmanda, how come you didn't tell Betsy about *your* troubles?"

Salmanda looked sheepish. "She has her own."

"What troubles, Salmanda? What's wrong?"

"Let's get out of here, okay? Duke, you wanna come?"

"I'll be in touch. It's eight-fifty so far."

It dawned on me why Duke had picked this elegant place. I left her ten toward the bill.

"What is it, Salmanda?" I asked at a Village bar.

"Duke has a big mouth."

"*Duke* has a big mouth?"

"Betsy, I was about to tell you when you came round on Monday, really I was. I've been busted."

Busted?!

Vinny's, 1959. I bet the cop's ordering veal parmigian' with a side of spaghetti and his wife's having stuffed shells with salad on the side. He's big, not bad-looking, with a bit of a pot. His wife's face is trampled by make-up. They're paying a baby sitter for every minute they're there. You never take me out anymore — maybe this meal was to show her he did. He's looking anywhere he can. She's thinking, How can I order a cannol' for dessert without him tellin' me I'm gettin' fat?

Cops see everything. But not off duty, at a place you take your wife. He glares at the spade with the white girl. And this is supposed to be a nice place.

"Come on, hon, you're off duty, let them be."

He's just gonna do Vinny a favor. He goes to their table.

"What's that you're drinking?" he asks the blond girl.

"What's that to you?" the nigger answers.

By God, he's a she.

The cop takes out his badge. "Here's what it means to me," he says to the white girl. "How old are you, honey?"

"Old enough to know better and young enough to try." Toad out of that pretty mouth.

"You'd better be able to prove it."

"Offff-icer," Salmanda says, "I'm going to answer your question. She's drinking cream soda. Me too. Want a taste?"

"You said *that*?" I asked Salmanda at the bar.

"Sure."

"Oh, God."

And the cop said, "I'll tell you what. You get out of here by the time I'm back to my table and it's Pepsi-Cola. I won't ask for her ID or you for proof you got tits. My wife and I just want a better view of the premises than the two of you. So just pay up and get lost. Clear?"

Vinny himself came over, and when he "Miked" the cop and

Mike "Vinnyed" him, Salmanda knew no one was going to start trouble.

"Not at that very moment, not there," I said.

"Anything wrong, Mike?"

"Nah, Vinny, just give these *ladies* — I use the term advisedly — their bill."

Vinny made out the bill, the cop went back to his table, and Salmanda didn't budge.

"You should have gotten out of there quick!"

But this was the old Salmanda, Salmanda before her troubles, when life still had a home room and Mr. Misch could find her in his closet. So the cop had dirty-mouthed her with that tits stuff and didn't like her being with a white girl. She could locate her anger in high-spiritedness and she could call staring-down a cop lots of fun. In fact, that night at Vinny's, Salmanda could excuse the cop or not care, because freakish behavior, outbursts, weird people, appealed to her. If she could have free run of the circus, she'd be darting between the trapezes in motion and discussing relativity with the geek.

"The cop weird? Damn it, Salmanda, he's society, he's what we're up against. You should have done what he said. You should have run like hell, disappeared!"

The cop and his wife left before dessert. When he passed her table, Salmanda smiled wide at him, as if she had just sunk a basket.

That night she was arrested. She was at an all-girls party with that blonde from the night shift — Gail. They found her "fooling around," as she put it. When a cop tried to get a feel in on Gail, Salmanda lunged at him. So the charges were not only disturbing the peace and contributing to the delinquency of a minor, but also resisting arrest.

Auntie bailed her out. She didn't have to deal with the fact that her niece was gay. Salmanda had been with white people. That's what you get.

"Oh, my God, Salmanda. And you didn't tell me."

"You have your own troubles, Betsy."

"And you've spent your time helping me."

We ordered another round. She looked me straight in the eyes. We had gotten to the pus point. "If they find out at Englehurst, Betsy, they may suspend me from the basketball team."

"Oh, Salmanda!" I cried out. "Don't you worry about that!"

I still remember how relieved she looked, as if I were saying, Don't worry, they won't throw you off the team. What I meant was, Basketball is the least of your worries. If you don't get a good enough lawyer, if they frame you into jail, you'll end up somebody's maid. A Negro woman with a record. Gay, to boot. You'll scrub floors. Only through cunning, exile, and isolation can we outsiders survive. Look who was talking. I was feeling sick to my stomach. I wondered when Duke would make the arrangements. I'd been too cool to press her.

I watched Salmanda stretch, relax, feel better. She had spent the week since the arrest worrying about basketball. One mistake. An A-bomb. Boom! A ruined life. Look at her. Look at me. And she's worried about losing a chance to play ball. Then the nausea passed, my stomach settled, and I felt an overwhelming tenderness for my friend.

"I don't think they'll find out at Englehurst, Salmanda. After all, it happened in a different town. It didn't hit the papers, thank God. School's out. Just keep your mouth shut. Don't tell anyone else. No one. Get a really good lawyer, that's the main thing. Auntie will help you. Why, I bet you this whole mess can be cleared up over the summer."

"It looks like we both got our share of troubles, Behhtsy," Salmanda said to me and smiled.

We drank like crazy then. We went from bar to bar, alternating between finding funny things in our situations and feeling despair.

I was too woozy to go home. I called my mother and in a slurred voice said I was staying with an old high school friend, Lois Percy. I refused to stay at Duke's. So at three in the morning we rolled into Pam's. Salmanda had a key, got in, and made herself at home. She joined the sound-asleep Pam in the bedroom.

I stripped to my underwear and slept on the couch.

A few hours later I felt something intruding on my uneasy dreams. I fought it off till dawn. My head was sore and I did not want to open my eyes. Finally, I put my hand between my slippery thighs. I was startled awake. My hand, my thighs, Pam's couch, were slapped with blood.

"Salmanda!" I screamed. "Help me!"

She jumped into the room, following my voice in her sleep.

"What?" she asked plaintively, her hands on her eyes. She was struggling to wake up.

"Look!"

"Behhtsy! Lord, I don't believe this, girl."

Half-naked herself, her chest glowing, Salmanda put her strong wiry arms around me and got me into the hall and to the toilet. I thought I was going to vomit in the sink. I stood over it, gagging. The blood was rushing down my legs. It looked like a hemorrhage from the space between the porcelain and me.

"I'm losing my baby," I moaned. "I'm like my mother."

"Calm yourself, girl. We got to get you cleaned up. Your period's come down."

Had I been pregnant? In that room in Gaeta I wondered once more. Enough of the moon! I left the window and lay back on the bed. I closed my eyes. Remembered the summer of Salmanda's troubles. Monty gone. Auntie on the telephone. "I don't know what's gotten into that child," she said. She was worried enough about Salmanda to call me. I told her I'd come over. "You're going over there?" my mother asked me. She'd been listening. I said, "I'm going for a walk."

"She's sleeping," Auntie said when I got to the door. "She'll wake right up when I tell her it's you."

I sat in the living room. I saw the hat Auntie had worn to church. It had primroses and cornflowers around it. Its spring made me sad.

"Hey, what you doing here?" Salmanda asked in greeting. She'd thrown on a pair of jeans and was zipping its fly over her shirt.

"I came to say hello. Surprise!"

"Well, hello." Salmanda sat down. Auntie sat down too.

"What's new?" I asked Salmanda awkwardly.

"Hey, Auntie. Go make Betsy and me something to drink, will you?" Auntie didn't budge.

"Why you just sitting there?"

"Come on, Salmanda. Auntie's worried about you. Talk with us. You seem upset. What's wrong?"

"What's right?" She took a long breath. "Okay. The dean called me in."

"In July? What happened?"

Salmanda looked at me and smiled. I didn't know that smile.

"I thought he was going to suspend me from basketball. Even though you told me not to worry, that's what I thought. But then, I walk into his office, and I think, Betsy is right. He was as nice as can be.

"He told me he called me in so that we could go over my transcript together. 'Ex-emp-lary, Miss Blake.' For a minute I think, Heck, I'm going to make captain of the team next semester. You ever see the dean, Betsy? He's a little man. All buttoned up, neat as can be. He just about made a mustache. But he sure looked good to me. Like all my worries vanished."

They seemed to as she talked.

"So, I say, 'You know, Dean, sir, I want to apologize to you about the police. They had no right to come to campus just to check out if I'm really a student here.'"

"The police?"

"That's right, Betsy. They came to Englehurst in a squad car."

"How could they? It's not even the same county. It's intimidation!"

"That's what I told the dean. They could have called the registrar for what they needed. They had no business bursting in on the dean. They were discriminating against me, or trying to; that's just what I told him."

"You could have waited for him to bring up the subject. And 'Dean, sir.' I don't know."

"Well, right away I felt I could talk to him. Tell him anything.

I guess I needed you there. Because you're right. He said, 'I understand, Miss Blake. There's no need for you to explain. I want you to know I understand. That's ex-actly why I called you in personally today.' And I'm so dumb, Betsy, that I was about to thank him. Thanks, Dean, sir. Something like that. You know what he said next?"

"Maybe I don't want to know."

Salmanda looked at Auntie. "He pushed my transcript aside. 'Wherever you apply to next, Miss Blake, you'll have a recommendation from Englehurst College.' I say, Dean sir, I'm staying at Englehurst. I'm happy right here! Like I was reassuring him. He looked in my eyes. I don't know how he had the guts. He said, real slow, 'I'll repeat, Miss Blake, you're a smart girl. We want to do the best for you and the school. Let's make this as pleasant as possible under the circumstances. I'm sure you wouldn't want a black mark on your record. As it stands now, without altercation, wherever you apply to continue your education, you'll get a recommendation from us. If I were you, Miss Blake, I wouldn't tamper with that.'"

Salmanda's eyes shone. The old mischief was replaced by something new that also burned. "You understand what I'm telling you, Auntie? They threw me out of school."

What Auntie always knew came back to her. "I hear," she said. She got up. "I hear." She left the room.

"I've disappointed her."

"Salmanda," I asked, "what reason did the dean give you?"

"Reason?" Salmanda returned her attention to me.

"I mean, this isn't Siberia and it's not *1984*. What grounds did he give for suspending you?"

"Grounds? He said I'd be happier elsewhere."

"Then there's got to be recourse, Salmanda. This is still America. A person is presumed innocent until proven otherwise. You can't give up. You've got to speak to your lawyer. Something has to be done."

"Recourse, Behhtsy? Why, I'm surprised at you. I thought you'd know right away. Those cops told him I'm gay."

7

I think we each have an experience in our lives that molds us. It usually happens when we're young. Though not always. Its hallmark is that it hits us face first. Everyone else may see it coming. To others it may be as plain as it can be. But we don't expect it. Its full force sends us reeling. We go over it endlessly after it happens, and in future years a drink too many, a smell, a sound, or someone new to tell brings it back.

For Salmanda it was the arrest. We had a theme now, a cause, Salmanda's troubles. I pushed Monty to the back of my mind. I'd meet Salmanda whenever I could. On lunch hour from the bookstore, after work, we'd sit on our bench in Washington Square Park and Salmanda would talk. The night of the arrest, the wild party, the cops arresting her for resisting arrest . . . Like a friend of mine who later died of lung cancer and who would discuss the disease in any other part of his body but the lungs, Salmanda concentrated on that one charge against her. It was the most benign.

There should be a word for hope after hope is gone. I know it's braver and takes more energy than "delusion." Salmanda's lawyer advised her to get character references along Grant Avenue. She asked me to come along. She needed help, and I as well as she believed I could be helpful. Seeing us together, the merchants would know she was a credit to her race. I took off a day from the bookstore. Salmanda didn't have to take a day. Shortly after she was called in to Englehurst, she lost her job on the night shift. She was laid off.

This is the Grant Avenue where Auntie, who owned her own house and two others, was known. This is Grant Avenue before it was burned and sacked, before it was renamed Martin Luther King, Jr., Boulevard in honor of the man whose assassination precipitated its ruin.

Martin Luther King, Jr. Alice and I had mourned his assassination the first day we met in the Center's back gardens. For him to have come up between her and Leo in such an ugly way. For me to have backed Leo . . . But it's difficult for Americans to understand how Europeans see us. To them, we are capable of being cowboys, outlaws, bloodthirsty and effective rednecks, one and all. Isn't that what Leo had been trying to say to Alice during that dreadful lunch in Carrara? He forgot what happened to Socrates, Christ, forgot the Crusades, the Borgias, the concentration camps. He took up JFK, Martin Luther King, Jr., Robert Kennedy, random rapes, savage snipers. Europeans think we're savages. I think they're disappointed. We left them when we were humble, poor, confused — unconscious of the murder in our hearts.

That's what I had been trying to say at Carrara when I brought up Salmanda. Hadn't I seen Auntie's neighborhood burned and sacked right on the front pages of the Italian papers?

Inner cities, ghettos, these were places where people lived. The Grant Avenues before the fires charred them. The streets teemed with life, the storefronts were not boarded up, the people were black, and the merchants were white.

Mr. Wiley, a fat man, sat on a chair in his furniture store. He sold the type of cheap, flashy stuff that looks as if it's never paid off. He sat on a simple well-made rocking chair. He didn't sit on the junk he sold by installment.

"This is my dear friend Behhtsy Lewis, Mr. Wiley."

He was very pleased to meet me. "How's your aunt, Salmanda?"

"She says hello."

"A fine lady. A credit to you all."

His bulging neck swelled. His small eyes kept secrets. Dirty secrets. He looked me up and down.

"Mr. Wiley, I don't know if you've heard, but I've gotten myself in a mess of trouble." Her smile was girlish, as if her troubles were still pranks.

"She's done nothing wrong," I said, as if to explain her silly grin.

"You were there?"

"Oh, no!" How could he think that? Maybe it wasn't so good for Salmanda that I'd come along. "I've known Salmanda since high school, and we go to college together." I said *go* not *went*. We were both good girls. We both attend college. We study. There's an authority stalking the world, and to achieve one must pretend to obey it.

"You've got yourself a good woman for an aunt. She's proud of you and you should want to do her proud."

"I do, Mr. Wiley. Honest. That's why I'm here talking with you. She's done business with you all these years. She said, Go see Mr. Wiley, see what he can do."

"Do about what, Salmanda? You put yourself in places you have no business, and now you're going to cost that woman to get you out of trouble."

"I didn't do anything!"

"I didn't say you did anything."

That's when the scene turned lush and Southern. Mr. Wiley, born in Hackensack, rocked back and forth on his veranda. "What I heard, I don't believe. I know your aunt. I know you. I wish I could help you for her."

"You *can* help, Mr. Wiley. All you have to do is sign here."

She took her paper from her sloppy notebook. "It says you know my family, you know me, and that I'm of good character. That's all."

"Of course you're of good character," he replied. "Have I ever said different?"

"Then you'll sign?"

"Give me some room to breathe!" In her sudden burst of enthusiasm she was hovering over him, her petition too close to his face.

"That's better. I'm a businessman, Salmanda. I don't sign things. I stay out of things on principle. You tell your aunt I say hello, hear?" Hear?

"But you said you wanted to help me for her. Others will sign if you do. That's why I came to you first."

"If I can do something constructive now or in the future, you come right back and let me know. Don't you stand on ceremony with me, Salmanda. Hear?" Again.

Then he looked us both over. I thought of the old one about white-skinned people coming out of the oven before they're fully baked. Mr. Wiley seemed incomplete. He said, "You tell your aunt not to fret. I'll do what I can."

"Nothing! He'll do nothing! He'll do exactly what all the others did when they didn't sign." I said this to Auntie back at the house after that long, disappointing day. I was rarely so forthright and rude.

"Don't you mind," she replied. "He told me not to fret, didn't he? Mark my words, he had his reasons for not signing. He has his ways."

And she believed it. Until the day a stroke uprooted her sturdy unwhimsical brain and made Auntie a stranger and a captive in her own home, she believed Mr. Wiley was of some help. Be it God or Mr. Wiley, Auntie needed to touch white in order to hope.

After that, Salmanda's in the Village all the time. She can't sleep, and though she answers every ad, she can't find another job. Liquor brings out the bitterness in both of us. She picks me up at the bookstore after work. We prowl at night and drink.

"Hey, what are you doing with white pussy?" a guy yells after us late one night.

"Say that again!" Salmanda turns sharply and calls after him and his two friends.

"We can eat her better than you . . . Yeah, sure . . . Give us a chance." They weave down the street, away from us.

Salmanda seems stuck in a slice of time. I think she may run after them. I'm ready to hold on to her, to keep her back. She's sweating like hell, and when she turns back to me her eyes make her look crazy. "You hear? You hear?" she keeps asking me.

"Don't pay attention — "

She tears away from me. Garbage cans are lined along the street, adding the stench of moldy food to dog shit and human piss. She goes down the street, kicking cans over. One after another, down they go. Spilling out kitchen rot. Making a hell of a racket. When I catch up with her, she grabs me.

"Do you hear?"

"Yes, I hear! Yes! Yes!"

That night was so hot. As hot as it was the day I bumped into Leo at the Spanish Steps. Poor people hot. Old ladies fanning themselves awake on folding chairs hot. Puerto Ricans playing cards and drinking beer from paper bags, gorgeous black whores with aimlessly aimed walks hot. Whoever is on that street dissolves into the humidity, avoiding us as we pass.

Salmanda looks around at the mess she's made. Puzzled. As if she doesn't know where she's been. There's a garbage can cover near us. She kicks it. It rolls off the curb into traffic. A car brakes to avoid it. Steaming curses from the guys in the car. The lid is rolling, the car's stopping short, the voices of abuse are following us. They are Salmanda screaming.

"We'll write, Salmanda. I'll come back. You'll come to Boston. You'll see."

"Boston's a swell place," she says, gulping her rye. "You're going to like it there. You'll meet some guy that'll make you forget Mr. Royal Canadian Monty."

"I've got a lot to forget there. What an idiot I was!"

"You don't love him anymore?"

"I don't know if I ever loved him. I loved the excitement and the room and . . ."

"And?"

"For a while I loved the thought of the baby. Oh, how I wish I had gone to a doctor first."

"So you wouldn't have scared the bastard away?"

"So I'd know if I'd been pregnant or not. So I'd know if anything *had* happened to me. Sometimes I think nothing's ever going to happen to me. It's strange, as if I'm made to be part of someone else's story."

"Some dark, handsome stranger who'll sweep you off your feet."

We were in Duke's cruddy room. She crouched over Duke's expensive hi fi, which tried to look like nothing on the floor, and put the Odetta record on. Then she poured us two stiff glasses of rye.

"I bought this one today," she said as Odetta began to sing. "It's for you to take to school with you."

"Oh, thanks, Salmanda."

"Maybe when you play it, you'll remember me."

"We'll write, Salmanda. I'll come back. You'll come to Boston. You'll see."

Salmanda shrugged.

I continued. "I'll tell you one thing, I'm going to stay away from men. I mean, nothing serious. I'm not going to repeat Monty over and over."

Odetta was singing. We listened for a while.

"You want to dance with me, Betsy?"

"It's awfully hot."

"Oh?"

"But sure, sure I'll dance."

She took me in her arms.

There's somethin' that say she stay where she be
Somethin' say go
But nothin' that say what somethin' will be best
Nothin' she know of.

"This isn't exactly a fox trot," I said. Always joking.

She had both her arms around my waist and I had my arms around her neck. We swayed back and forth, French dancing. Her head was above mine, but leaning against it. She was dancing and she was crying.

"Don't cry, Salmanda. Things will work out. Remember once you told me not to cry. Remember?"

She held me tight. I held her. I closed my eyes.

"You want to lie down for a while?" she whispered.

I could feel a thrill go through me. I pushed against it. I pushed away. "I have to go, Salmanda."

"Why are you leaving me, Betsy?"

"I've got to, Salmanda. I've got to go somewhere else, do something else, before it's too late."

"Too late? Like it is for me?"

"Don't talk like that."

"How the hell should I talk, girl?" She grabbed me by the shoulders and brought her face close to mine. "You're going away, but I'm staying here."

"Here?" I said. "Why here, Salmanda? You shouldn't even be in New York. But no, you don't stay put in Jersey till it's over. Can't you see, being here, in this shithole of a room, isn't any help to yourself? Being here makes everything inescapable, makes everything worse."

"If you don't like Duke or Duke's place, maybe it's 'cause she got your number, girl."

"Quit that jive talk, will you? What's Duke saying about me? She has no right to talk against me. I haven't done anything to her."

"Oh, no? What about defiling her blessed sanctuary here with bahhd words, Behhtsy?"

We gave each other a look, and then we cracked up. We laughed so hard, tears came to our eyes and our sides hurt. We were back to mimicking creeps and watching "Amos and Andy" on TV. Then Salmanda poured us more to drink and put the record on again on the same side. She sat on the windowsill and listened for a while.

"Salmanda, come on, what does Duke say about me?"

"I don't give it much mind."

"Come on, stop teasing me."

"Maybe Duke says you're teasing me."

"That bitch! She's just jealous that we're friends. Leave it to her to try to turn that into something dirty."

"Would it be dirty, Betsy? How dirty? For a while you sure seemed to like dancing with me."

I didn't answer.

"Shit!" she said. "Goddamn shit!" From the sill, she kicked the mattress.

"You're the best friend I've ever had, Salmanda."

"Then why are you going away?"

"I told you. I'd never go back to Englehurst after what they've done to you. I've got to get away. I've got to do something new. I'm sick of pretending I can do science."

"But you're good."

"No, I'm not. Sure I can study and memorize. But I'm not good. I'm not like you." *And you blew it!* Those unspoken words hung between us. There was an undercurrent of recrimination in the air.

"I thought you said you were going to keep your job and get a room in the Village."

"I changed my mind."

"You can afford to."

I didn't answer. We let Odetta's voice seep through our anger. "I've got to get going," I said finally.

"And I've got to get drunk."

"Walk me to the bus, Salmanda, come on."

"Have a drink first."

"Come on, Salmanda. Walk me."

She took the Odetta record off and put on its cover. "Take this with you. It's yours."

"I hate to leave you like this, Salmanda."

"Bye, Betsy."

"Won't you come out with me?" I waited. No answer.

Then I left her there with a drink in her hand, sitting on the windowsill, her last mumbled goodbye smudging the half-opened window.

When I got outside, I found Duke sitting on the stoop. Her sitting there hit me like the heat.

"I won't be around for a while. I'm going to Boston."

Duke nodded.

"Duke, I've never seen Salmanda so low."

"She's got her reasons," she said in her flat voice.

"I know. But she can't drink them away. Duke, watch out for her, will you?"

Duke looked up from one step below. "Watch out for her?" she asked with authentic interest.

"You're her friend."

"Salmanda better do her own watching out. We watch out for ourselves in this world, baby."

Salmanda better do her own watching out.

"Behhtsy, I bet you never heard of the Black Muslims." She said that to me the last time I saw her. It was a few years later. I was home from college and we met in a bar in the Village.

Black Muslims? She was whispering something as alien and spooky as butch and dyke had once been.

"They're a secret now, but just you wait. They're going to come out of Chicago and fix this country up good, once and for all."

I didn't believe her. I thought the Black Muslims were her imagination going a new route. Well, I certainly did get to hear about the Black Muslims. In English, in Italian.

The last time I tried to contact her was when I was about to get married. I wanted to let her know about Doug. I called Grant Avenue.

"Salmanda?" a voice that sounded like Auntie's replied. "Salmanda?"

"Salmanda Blake."

"No Salmanda live here."

"Auntie?"

Click.

I let that click stand final. It was like a chalky eraser over a garbled blackboard, muddying a confused message.

Where was Auntie now? Had her houses on Grant Avenue burned down? There was no Grant Avenue anymore. There was Martin Luther King, Jr., Boulevard. It would parallel the gracious John F. Kennedy Avenue on the white side of town. That dawn in Gaeta I saw the sixties recede into history, leaving what history leaves. A name on a street. A statue in the square.

I stood in the vestibule of my uncle's apartment. He and Margherita would not let me take them out for the midday meal.

"I don't know how to thank you for your hospitality," I said.

"Stay," he answered.

"I wish I could. I have to get back to Rome."

"Rome." He sneered. "When will you come back here?"

I shrugged.

"Stay, eat with us, you can go later," my aunt said.

"No, thank you. If you're not going to come out with me, I'm going to drive the car to Formia and get an early start."

"But the restaurants feed you poison. Eat with us. Angelo will see you off later."

"I'm sure Angelo has better things to do."

"Oh, no, Signora!"

"Beatrice!" my uncle admonished. She had slipped again.

She turned marriage-deaf and continued: "At least wait until Angelo gets home. He will be so sorry not to say goodbye."

"Oh, Aunt Margherita, I wish I could. But if you won't come out with me, I'm going to rush for the two o'clock train."

"You'll be seeing your husband soon. I understand." She took her two index fingers and brought them together.

"No, it's not that."

"Oh, it's not that, is it?" Margherita laughed. Her face turned red as a bawd's. "At least you'll take a cheese."

"Oh, no."

"But you liked the cheese. Wait!"

"Mmmm. It's good," Doug said. We were on the terrace of our apartment on Via della Buona Fortuna. The sky was unpierced blue.

"It's a goat cheese. I think I'll bring Alice some of it. I begged my aunt not to give me a whole one, but she said I can use it as grating cheese once it dries."

"Italians always get the last word. You should know that by now."

"I'm Italian too."

Doug was lounging in his chair. One long leg was stretched out and the other one crossed it at the knee. He seemed amused. "Did you think I was implying that you don't get the last word? If you did, I apologize."

"Don't be cute. I mean, I'm Italian and I'm not Italian. I really am from Gaeta, and I'm not from Gaeta at all. My aunt and uncle wined me and dined me and spent money they can't afford, because I'm blood."

"Well, you can send them something. Come here. Have some cheese. We have time," he said expansively. "We have all the time in the world."

"Have you been drinking?"

He poured us some wine. "I'm drunk on having you home."

"You want to know the only thing I could send them?"

"Sit down and tell me."

"Okay. Thanks." I tasted the wine he offered. "I could send them a ticket to America for Angelo. Not only am I their flesh and blood, I'm their pipe dream."

Doug took my hand and kissed it. I watched him.

"You'd like Angelo," I told him. "Without his zits he'd look like a Caravaggio."

"Sounds more like your type."

"What do you mean?"

"Nothing."

"What do you mean, nothing? You must mean something."

"I don't know. Come on, Betsy. You've just been home a few minutes. Do you want to pick a fight?"

"No, I want to tell you about Angelo. I want to tell you how warmly my aunt and uncle treated me and how overwhelming it was at first. I mean, I didn't come from a demonstrative family, if you remember."

"They mean well."

"I guess. Anyway, it was all touching and kissing and too much food and a lot of conversation, until suddenly I realize I'm being rubbed for luck. I'm like a big lottery ticket coming their way, and they love me."

"What do you want them to love you for, your curly, curly hair?"

"What do you love me for?"

"For all that you can be," he said. "For all your possibilities."

I felt awkward, as if I should atone for all that I was not.

"What about my exaggerations?"

"I've grown accustomed to your exaggerations," he sang, parodying the popular song.

He got up and put the cork in the wine bottle. He cleared the table and put the cheese away while I went inside and took a shower. Then we went into the bedroom and made love. As we made love I heard Alice moan, I heard Leo cry out.

The next day I went to see Alice. The late afternoon light that has no favorites came in from the window behind her. It immortalized the stove between the window and Alice's back. There were just the two of us in the kitchen. We were going to eat supper together. The table we sat at was a wooden plank Leo had attached to the wall; it rested on two brackets and two legs.

It was Alice's working counter as well, and it was long and narrow, like the kitchen itself. Above it were wooden shelves that housed the anchovies in oil and artichokes in oil that Alice prepared for him, and the pickled eggplant and the pickled mushrooms that his sister Flora sent over. I imagined Leo coming home from work late at night, cutting a piece of bread, and letting the liquid from one of these condiments soak in.

I was sitting at the opposite end of the table, near the door. In between us were green beans and green salad, cold meats, and the wedge of cheese I had brought over. Resting on the stovetop, behind Alice, was a bowl of ripe fruit for later. Alice ate slowly, picking her way through the small feast as if held more by interest than appetite. This approach was deceiving. As she often said, she was capable of eating more lettuce than a goat. She put down her fork to postpone that pleasure after I said to her, "I feel I owe you an apology."

"About what, dear?" She looked puzzled.

"About leaving Pietrasanta so abruptly. About being so vindictive during the lunch at Carrara. About a lot of things."

"You seemed upset."

"I was. I needed some time alone to sort things out."

Alice looked at me carefully. "Have you done that?"

"More or less. Yes. I feel much better. Much clearer!" I exclaimed optimistically.

"Well, I'm glad. For you. And your uncle? What was he like? Oh, Betsy, tell me about Gaeta, do!"

I told her about my relatives and she listened. Her empathy was as deep and still and persistent as the dying light. She didn't break in with reminiscences of Nick visiting the hilltop in the Abruzzi that he had come from. No old stories about him and her and Leo. Instead, she entered into my discoveries. I talked with her the way I had the first time at the American Center.

After a while I found myself talking about my mother. My mother had cut Tommaso off, just as she and my father had cut off any interest in Italy. Except for the little I had gleaned from my grandmother, I discovered my heritage on the sly in college. But my mother didn't want to hear about my courses, though she and my father assumed an attitude of respect for the drawings of the Italian masters when Doug was around. "You people know what you gotta do," my mother said when we told her we were going to Italy. She thought Doug did.

They were not affectionate people, my parents. I couldn't imagine them in Gaeta. They got over things like that. For them, my growing up was a succession of emotions to overcome. They tried to wash me clean. And maybe they've succeeded, I said to Alice in a lowered voice. I was thinking, Leo is an emotion to overcome. Did it really matter last night that when Doug embraced me, I had to force myself until I thought of Leo? After all, sex goes quick. My mother.

Alice was not one for head-on collisions. But when it came to mothers — she evoked hers. Maple Blanders came into the room and stamped on our hearts. After all, wasn't my mother simply instilling common sense? Maple Blanders allowed her daughter's tonsils to be removed on shipboard by a drunken doctor; she watched in her evening gown. Maple lay in bed with her dead husband while rigor mortis set in. Maple dressed her daughter like a doll. All my own mother did was teach me that my own emotions would spoil me rotten if I allowed them to.

"She loved power, Betsy. She was a monster of egoism. I'm not Catholic, dear, but isn't that original sin? There's no stopping a person who's drunk on power. No controlling the evil it produces. That's why I'm afraid for Leo. For him. I remember the sweet, dear person he has always been. I see him now grown ruthless, relentless, impervious to the things of the heart. Quite like my mother."

"But, Alice, Leo's not Maple Blanders. He cares about people. He wants to help."

"No doubt. And now that he's head of the union, he's been able to accomplish things he wants."

"See? What's he done?"

She smiled. "He's done quite a few things quickly. There's no stopping him, it would appear. He's spoken to Fenzi and the committee. He's been able to get the workers extra money they actually are entitled to under the existing contract."

"Really!"

"And Fenzi's invited him to dinner in the country."

"Well, it's a good sign that management is treating him as an equal, isn't it?"

"I'm not sure it's an honor to be Fenzi's equal. Power is a dangerous game. Leo's up to his cusps in it, it would seem."

In the last daylight I watched Alice's deep eyes and full lips. Under her low-cut blouse and the pleated skirt that hid her hips, I saw her ample body. As she talked I heard her moan. I felt that she was being unfair to Leo, and I couldn't understand why. Why shouldn't Leo rise? He had been a worker for year after year. Why shouldn't he improve himself? Wasn't I proud of Doug, supportive of each find, each sale, of each step upward he took in the firm? Wasn't that love too?

"He's so busy being a communist, he hasn't time to work," Alice continued. "'What do you have against clean hands?' That's what he snapped when I insulted him by asking about his job."

"Alice, aren't you in the least bit happy that Leo's fighting for his own rights now and those of all the workers? Aren't you the first to say they've all been kept down in the most shameless way?"

"Don't you think Leo is accommodating himself?"

"I think he's standing up and letting his voice be heard by the bosses."

"Leo doesn't have a well-defined sense of limits, Betsy. He doesn't understand moderation. He doesn't see that one wrong battle won can lose the war."

"Alice, that's what people said in America when the Negroes began to march. They were going too fast. My parents believed it would take another hundred years for them to integrate. They were all for integration in the twenty-first century. What about now? I look at what's going on in Italy and I get a feeling of change with every crane I see standing up against the sky. Leo's on the move, and that's good. I don't know, maybe it's an instinct, but I think he's at the right place at the right time."

"Things changing? What I see is waste all around me. I see Leo's son waiting for his father to procure him a position he doesn't deserve so that he can marry that dreadful little girl. I see Leo at work, the Leo who used to mock the entire system of favors, jockeying there for his favorites, just as he's jockeying for his son! Well, you'll see, Betsy. Do you want to see *Tosca* next Thursday? Leo can get you tickets if you wish."

I smiled. "Do you remember the day we met you told me Leo could get me tickets? Sure we want to go. I can't wait."

"Good, I'll tell Leo."

"You'll come too?"

"I've had enough of *Tosca* this season," she said tersely.

National television had finished filming *Tosca* the previous week, so I was not surprised, though disappointed, that, arriving at the ruins that housed the outdoor summer opera, we found our tickets waiting for us at the box office, not in Leo's hands. Our tickets were for the fancy seats with the pillows on them in the front. "Leave it to Leo," I whispered as the lights dimmed, nighttime took over, and the music began. Then I was in the music's spell. There's nothing in *Tosca* that isn't Rome, every note a souvenir of that eternal, human city.

Toward the end of the first act, when the Roman police chief, Scarpia, enters the church and vows to have Tosca, the lust in his voice sinister and thrilling, I felt a big hand on my shoulder. I put my hand over it; I did not have to turn around. Leo had slipped into the empty seat behind us. While he and Doug whispered, I listened to the music and held on.

When the act was over, Leo stood up quickly. "I see Gaeta has treated you well." I was wearing my favorite sheer, light blue summer dress, and I was still quite tanned. Before I could answer, he said, "Come. Come with me."

Leo had the connections to go back stage to the makeshift bar. He greeted workers and singers and scene changers. I could see he was well known even there. We were drinking the espresso he had ordered for us when —

"Oh, there you are!" A tall, redheaded woman rushed toward him. He held her arm as if to keep her from crashing into us. "Marcella, I want you to meet my friends."

She was Marcella Sarti, a young singer in the chorus of the company whom Alice knew. Alice had mentioned her and her French husband, what lively people they were, and how she'd like to get us all together. That had been some months ago, and the words were on the tip of my tongue. They stayed there. The way Leo held her arm; the way Marcella said, "Conti, two seconds please!" The way he looked at us, mocking a helpless shrug. "Duty calls. I'll be right back." He put his coffee down. It was even the way he put his coffee down, damn it! Leo's heart was strutting.

I watched them. He had an arm over her shoulder as they moved from us. I could see her gesturing and talking quickly at the end of the bar. I could see the amusement with which he let her go on. She seemed as tightly wound up as he was relaxed. She was tall, taller than I, and had something I'd noticed in other redheads — big bony hands, too long for the rest of her arms. Well, she didn't hide them in her pockets. She waved them in the air, threw them to the side, played with them under Leo's chin.

"Oh, boy," I said to Doug. "No wonder Alice didn't want to come."

"What?"

"Can't you see?" I was so irritated that I pointed to them. Leo saw that. He took her arm and led her back to us. He was no fool.

"I am sorry, I am not able to talk with you right now," Marcella said in English, and ran by.

"Ah!" Leo involuntarily raised his hands at her exit.

"Problems?" I asked cryptically.

"When you get to know Marcella, you'll learn how to make them even when you don't have them. You'll see."

"She seems angry," I said.

"Women! Doug, how do you manage to stay so calm among them? Give me lessons."

"I practice," Doug said.

"He doesn't need to practice. He was born reasonable."

"What's that supposed to mean?" Doug asked.

"Practice, Doug. Practice," Leo quipped.

Doug shrugged. "Tell me, Leo, do you know anyone who can give us permission to take a look at the mosaics they're restoring, as long as we're here?"

"Permission, dottore? What we need is a flashlight! Just one minute."

So we took a walk in the extensive Roman ruins behind the giant pillars that housed the summer stage. In the cool night air, with Leo for a guide, I kept thinking that perhaps I'd been too quick to suspect his relationship with Marcella. Finally we got to the roped-off area being restored. The sign read: IT IS FORBIDDEN TO ENTER. Leo entered and shone his flashlight on the ancient mosaic floor, which now sparkled like a cluster of uneven stars. Doug put his arm around me, and we followed the trail of Leo's light. We both marveled.

Leo accompanied us back to our seats with the aid of his flashlight, then slipped away. The second act had already begun. Scarpia was in his apartment in the Palazzo Farnese, waiting for Tosca, his lust propelling him toward his death at Tosca's hand. What an act! I kept being brought back from it because Doug was cold. Well, I was cold too. No matter how hot the day, in the damp ruins, at the edge of the city, it seems the night sends fog through your flesh and makes you shiver. "We should have brought sweaters," Doug whispered, cutting through my mood.

After the act was over, I asked, "You want to go?"

"It's freezing."

"Let's go."

"You don't want to go, Betsy."

"Sure I want to go. I've seen the mosaics. That's what the evening's about."

"No, it's about love triangles. Melodrama al fresco." He shivered.

"If you're so uncomfortable, Doug, let's get out of here."

"It's your opera."

"You don't like it, do you?"

"It has its place. I've seen it done better."

"So have I."

"At its best it's limited."

"As limited as passion, as limited as Rome?"

"Don't exaggerate."

"Doug, why the hell don't you go back stage before it's too late and tell Tosca not to exaggerate!"

He laughed.

"I'm not joking. She's not a sensible person; she needs some advice." Then I managed to smile too. "Listen, Doug. Seriously. Take the car. Go home. I'll take the bus."

"You'll freeze. I can't leave you here."

"I want you to, honestly, sweetheart. If you're shivering beside me, it'll ruin the third act."

"I'm worried about your being cold, and you're worried about my ruining the third act! Okay, I'll go!"

"No, I'll come too."

He got up. "No, stay. Enjoy your opera!"

I was about to get up, I was about to insist, but . . . "Okay," I said. "I'll see you home later. I'll stay. Don't be — "

"See you later, Betsy."

"Wait, I'll — " He was burning mad. I stayed.

No sooner was I alone and the lights down when something happened. As the music began, Leo was crouching next to me. "Here, I thought you —" In his hands he held a shawl. "Where's Doug?"

"He decided to go."

"What a shame. He'll miss . . . Well, move over and let me sit next to you."

He put the shawl around my shoulders.

A lone shepherd is heard from off stage. The plaintive voice announces dawn. Tosca's lover, Mario, hears the music as his jailers wind up an all-night card game. They have work to do. Unwittingly, the shepherd is singing Mario's execution song.

"What do you think?" Leo whispered as the offstage song dies. "What do you think of that voice?"

"It's Marcella, isn't it?"

He patted my shoulder tenderly, then hugged me. "Well, what do you think?"

"She's very good."

"It's her first solo. You cannot imagine the opposition in the chorus. It almost upset the shooting schedule last week. The jealousy! This has taken all my attention for two weeks! Ask Alice! I have hardly been home. I have had no rest. When union members — not party members, mind you — went against Marcella, I had to do what I could to get her the part."

"*You* had to? Why did you have to do what you could?"

"She's a good communist."

"A good communist? Leo, you're impossible!"

He hugged me again, affectionately, the Leo who still told jokes. We sat holding hands and listening to the music like two teen-agers at the movies. I felt we needed each other very much.

Then he slipped away. I pulled the shawl — was it Marcella's? — tight around me and watched the stage. The Italian patriot, Mario, was sitting down to write his last words to Tosca. Instead of writing, he remembers. He sings an aria about the first night they made love. The stars, the moon, the garden. Tosca abandoning herself in his arms. Mario, himself, trembling as he undresses her. The hour is gone, he sings from the dawn on stage out into the cold. L'ora è fuggita.

Is it possible that we remember a night of love before we die?

"He's terrified of her," Alice said. I had met her in the late afternoon on the Pincio for a drink. I had spent the day distancing myself from thoughts of Leo and Marcella. I thought I was doing okay. For I loved Rome at the end of August, when you could really see the nineteenth-century city. That's because the cars clear out, most of the Italians go to the beach and leave the city to an earlier pace. There are tourists, but they go only to certain places. And for me they fit into the serenity that falls on the depleted city. Even in a group they seem no longer like a crowd, but more like pilgrims, slightly crazed, sadly making their rounds to the anointed places.

Since it's Ferragosto, the Assumption of the Virgin, the big holiday time, the produce is not as plentiful and fresh, and a number of restaurants you might expect to stay open for tourists, close. Still, you can walk all over Rome without getting run over and see all sorts of monuments and squares from new perspectives. That's what I'd been doing, and peacefully. Maybe it's the lack of carbon monoxide and Latin lovers and car doors opening that makes the heat of late August seem not so hot. Until Alice brought up Marcella, that is.

"She's very rude," I said.

"Leo's afraid of her," Alice insisted.

"Afraid of her?"

"Yes. Terrified. There's a woman who gets what she wants. And she's an ideological communist, the real stuff, a cold fish, as tough as nails."

"Well, I can understand your not liking her anymore."

"I was fooled by her. Just as Leo is now. Imagine him getting her that role! The shepherd boy!"

"Well, to give the devil his due, it really didn't come off too badly. She has some sort of presence, Marcella. She really did sound as if she were the personification of what had to happen, the day."

"She's talented. But you see how destructive she is? She had her chance to take over a part because of Leo, but even that was not enough for her. She actually wanted the shepherd to be *on* stage for the TV cameras. Well, she infuriated everybody. Now she's blaming the Christian Democrats for trying to take the part away. She wanted a strike! Leo had his hands full, keeping her in the role. Did she care that *Tosca* was being filmed for TV?

For the people? Not one bit, unless she kept her part. She's very much like my mother. Nothing is worthwhile unless it causes everyone trouble. And my mother . . . she certainly did have talent too."

"Talent," Alice said, as if it were a suspicious property. For me it had always been the highest good. A way of entering the world. A way of bartering the present for the future. Salmanda had had talent, more than she used. I couldn't afford to be so wasteful. Neither could Doug. Maybe Alice disdained talent because she originally came from where the talented end up.

I remember Alice sitting there at the outdoor table, sipping the aperitivo I had offered her. My eyes went beyond her to a row of pillars, on top of which were busts of Garibaldi's troups. I was finishing up the first draft of my study of Anita Garibaldi. Staking my own claim on the world. Thoughts of Leo came back to me, of how we had held on to each other like children at the outdoor opera. Both of us so venal. He, because he had pushed an absurdity to a conclusion. He was using his newly gained power to promote a woman, just like any other big shot acting big. Just like any other big shot he had joked about in the past. I, because I had let my husband go home by himself, not only for the love of *Tosca*, but because Doug shivered in the dark. He got cold while Leo listened to the red-haired Marcella.

I asked Alice, quietly, "Don't you think your mother, at least through her talent, gave something good to the world?"

I thought the look in Alice's eyes was surprise or amusement. "Maple Blanders? Ask that of anyone who ever worked with her." And Alice went on with tales of Maple's ruthlessness, of the corrosive effects of her beauty on others. I watched that cold star shine as Alice talked on in her clear voice. That voice was never shrill or demanding. When contentious, it cloaked its own firm grasp of reality under soft-sounding questions. I could understand that the stage was out of the question for Alice from the beginning. She would never project that voice, let it ring in her ears, while she pretended to communicate to people she could not see. And I wondered what magnificent powers would always be muted in her, for to forgo balance and to demand would be to open her little compact and see her mother in its mirror.

I envied her her balance, her compassion, her maturity, that day. I wished I had a modicum of it to erase Leo from my heart, to be worthy of her. Doug loved me for my potential. What was I if I didn't develop the talent Alice discounted? On the Pincio that day, swimming in my own venality, everything rested on my having something to say.

Then Alice surprised me. She told me she was going to take a trip. In two weeks, she'd go to France to visit dear friends, then to America and her son's place, then stop over in England on her way back. She wouldn't return until the middle of October. As always, when Alice discussed travel plans, she talked of how economical the proposal was. She had a very good deal on her ticket and lots of friends waiting to see her, inviting her to stay. These were not arrangements one makes overnight, and I could imagine the months of tentative planning, the letters back and forth, while she waited to see. Had Leo not been elected head of the union, it might have been the perfect time for both of them to go. "Now, who knows, Betsy. The union is one thing. But if Leo's propelled into the party . . . I can't delude myself into thinking that he'll ever see America again."

I sat there admiring her. Why, to leave at this moment took courage. To leave Leo. She couldn't want to. I thought, She knows men, she must have a plan.

"What do you think, Betsy?"

"How I wish I had your wisdom."

She looked at me quizzically — puzzled, actually — and said, "Well, I have quite an opportunity. It was Bev who found these marvelous tickets for me, *with* stopovers, and I had already put aside money for two. Then my old friend Soren Boxer — have I mentioned him to you, Betsy? — has been pleading with me to come stay with him in Paris . . ."

At the time I didn't quite hear her out. Now I realized that she had no plan. Alice's talent was, no matter what, to live.

8

It was during the six weeks Alice was away that Leo and I became very close. I was holed up in my apartment, putting the finishing touches on my study of Anita, and Doug was back and forth to London, preparing for the season. Leo appeared late one afternoon as spontaneously as on the night of *Tosca*, when I felt his hand on my shoulder. "I was in the neighborhood. I thought I'd check to see if you have any more gun shots in your door."

"You look hot," I told him. "Give me your jacket." He took off his jacket, which was crumpled. He walked out onto the terrace ahead of me. I told him I'd bring out iced tea. I could see that the back of his shirt was wet, and now, freed from restraint, was peeling away from his spine. Holding his damp jacket, I felt I had offered him the cool breeze.

We sat under the shade of the umbrella, smelling my oleanders and basil, drinking tea laced with mint, and looking out at Michelangelo's white dome. He asked me about my work. It was a great pleasure for me to talk about the Risorgimento in Italian to an Italian. Leo inspired me. He was very interested in the political details.

"So this is what you do all day."

"Day after day."

"What a shame," he said. "A woman who can make such good iced tea."

It *was* good. And that month it got better.

Leo was so handsome. He had a God-struck beauty that seemed possessed of a soul of its own. I couldn't turn away from his vitality, his good looks, his good nature. I tried.

Doug sulked a lot when he was home. I was very preoccupied. But when Leo made one of his visits while Doug was there, the three of us were very friendly. On the terrace Doug would talk about Malatesta and Santo di Tito and other minor masters in that overly precise way he had. I don't know what Leo was thinking. I know I was daydreaming.

Some nights I'd stand naked in front of my mirror, studying my body. I remembered Salmanda's admiration and Monty's. I thought about what the Latin lovers looked at when they opened their car doors or trailed me down a street. I looked at my breasts and remembered Monty's mouth on them. I worried about my stomach. Everyone said I had nice legs. I turned around and glanced backward at my ass. I caught my eyes, and was momentarily stayed by the strain in them. "What are you looking for?" Doug would ask when he was home and saw me at the mirror.

"What do you think of my body?" I would answer.

One day Leo arrived quite late, after I had given up on him. I was at my desk in my work outfit, an oversized man's shirt. I slipped a pair of shorts on under it and greeted him in my bare feet.

"I'm dying," he said. Leo was always dying.

"Go on out. I'll bring you some tea."

When I joined him, he had his jacket off, his shirt unbuttoned, and his sleeves rolled up. He sat there, his gray eyes open, contemplating nothing. He looked as if he'd stopped. Until he saw me. Then he slowly started up again. He turned down his lips in a knowing expression, as though I had witnessed his thoughts.

"What are you upset about?" I asked him.

"I don't think she'll last."

He was talking about his mother. He rarely mentioned his family or his mother's illness. It was Alice who talked about Mamma, the crusty partisan, the strong woman who had led her family on.

"Did you just come from her?"

"I got called from lunch. Ran halfway round town. She's a sack of ashes."

"Is she in much pain?"

"She wouldn't show it any more than a Garibaldista."

"I'm sorry, Leo."

"Some time for the Daughter of the American Revolution to leave Rome." That was Alice. Old as an original daughter of the American Revolution when he was joking.

"What could Alice do?"

"She could have waited."

"Leo, that's unfair. I don't think Alice would have gone, I don't know that she even wanted to go, except that she may have felt the two of you needed what we call 'a breather.'"

"A breather?" he repeated in English, and breathed.

"That's right."

"She went because she wanted to go. Alice does what she wants to do."

"And you, Leo, what do you do?"

He looked at me and smiled so culpably that I smiled too.

"I don't do what I want," he said after the smile faded. "I do what she tells me. I do what I have to do."

He was quiet for a long time. Cooling himself and grieving.

"You're the only American left he feels he can talk to," Alice said when she returned that fall. "Whether it's his mother or his work with the union, he knows you're sympathetic to him, that you'll excuse him, that you'll understand."

"I have nothing to excuse him for, Alice."

"Oh, you're just like me. You excuse him for being Leo. Poor Leo . . ."

Once she returned, all her conversations had a "poor Leo." That Leo was opposed to the "old Leo." The old Leo had arrived at the airport to meet her plane and had waited for hours for her chartered flight. He had rushed her back to their apartment as in the past. He couldn't wait to have her again. "That's his way of dealing with everything, Betsy."

"Are you complaining? It doesn't seem such a bad way to me."

"It has its limitations," Alice said.

"Doesn't everything?"

That week I accompanied Alice to the small apartment in the housing project where the old Leo had once lived. I felt funny, going there while Leo's mother was so ill, but Alice really wanted me along. I think she wanted me to see where Leo came from. I think for her it made a point.

Flora opened the door for us. My first impression was that she was fierce and obstinate. Beauty like Leo's doesn't strike a whole family. The rawboned sister was powerful and handsome. Her thick head of hair didn't sparkle, though, like Leo's, it was speckled with gray.

"Why'd you come?" was the way she greeted Alice. "I could have sent Cosimo with the covers." Flora was a seamstress, and Alice had given her her daybed covers to mend while she had been away. Flora certainly didn't look too pleased to have gotten the business.

"Why, I've come to see Mamma," Alice said in a gentle and reproving manner. "The covers don't matter. But Betsy and I can take them if they are done."

"Of course they're done."

"Did you say Cosimo is at home?"

"Where would he be, at work?"

"Poor Leo" was acting just like a Roman, doing all he could to find the right connections to get his son a city job, despite the waiting list and Cosimo's miserable exam results. Flora's tone announced that she wasn't holding her breath. I wondered, Did Flora bend over a sewing machine and look at what she was mending past the fire in her eyes?

"This is Betsy Lewis, Flora." We were still at the door.

"A pleasure," she grumbled. "Come in. Do you want something to drink?" She led us down the hall and opened the door to the dining room.

"Coffee would be nice, Flora," Alice said before I could get out "Oh, no, we don't want to bother you."

Flora shrugged and opened the blinds that protected the room from sunlight and dust. Just as in my uncle's apartment, the dining room was the only public room. The family rarely used it; they sat where strangers are never taken, the kitchen. "Sit down." Flora directed us to either end of the ornate table.

"I think we've come at a bad moment, Alice," I said, after Flora served us coffee and then went to prepare her mother.

"She's very disorganized, Betsy. I imagine she's finishing up that sewing I gave her. I only gave it to her because she can use the money, though she'll surely spend it. Imagine her buying this." Alice motioned to the table and then further to the set itself. "And now she *needs* a mahogany shoe stand — to keep the dust off shoes, she tells me. Why, the income she could make if she'd just use her head. Ah, here's Cosimo!"

Leo's son walked into the room. He reminded me of my cousin Angelo. Cosimo was tall and thin, and at nineteen his complexion held on to the last traces of adolescence. There was a confused stillness that blunted his gray eyes.

"Cosimo!" Alice repeated, holding out her arms. "It's so nice to see you, dear."

"How was your trip?" he answered. There was something in the awkward manner in which he said that, and in the hesitation before he bent to kiss her, that reminded me of one of Alice's stories about the boy. When he was younger he was talking about his mother, who had deserted him. Alice tried to explain to the child that his mother could have loved him very much and still have felt she had to leave for other reasons. A difficult task, but I'm sure Alice handled it better than most. After the explanation the little boy looked at her and said, "But at least she could have sent a postcard."

"Ah, we're all together," Flora said. She returned with Alice's covers.

"Do have a cup of coffee with Betsy and me," Alice said to the boy.

"No, thank you. A pleasure to meet you, Signora. I must go."

"He must go," Flora repeated, mocking the necessity.

"What do you think of my boy?" she asked me in the same mocking way once he had left.

"He reminds me of my cousin Angelo, who lives in Gaeta."

"Is your cousin engaged to be married?"

"Oh, no. He's much too young."

"Do you think that stops them? Do you think anything stops us when we are young?"

"Some of us are braver than others at any age."

"Brave, hah!" She looked at me less fiercely, sat down, and poured herself a coffee. "Stupid," she said.

She looked at Alice. "He has a head as hard as his father's. He insists on marrying that little girl. So we must do what we must do. Right, Alice?"

"Is Mamma awake?" Alice asked. "Did you tell her I'm here?"

"Of course."

Alice got up. "Excuse me."

"Look at Signora Alice run!" Flora called after her. "She has something against other people's weddings. I don't know why. You want them all to yourself, Alice? Ha!"

After a moment of silence, Flora turned to me and said, knowingly, "Your Italian is good. That's because it's in your blood. Alice, she could be here a hundred years; it doesn't improve."

"Why, Flora, she's fluent."

"Her *o* is terrible. She says 'no' just like an American."

"Well, then, luckily she doesn't say it often."

Flora looked at me with open curiosity. "Your Italian is as good as my brother says."

"Leo speaks of me?"

"My brother," she said. "Of course he speaks of you. He'll never change. He'll always need women to help him. Real women. That one, the Americana, she flies off for six weeks. What does she care? She has Flora to clean her apartment. She has Flora to mend covers that aren't worth ten lire. Why doesn't she throw them away and buy new ones? The things I polish for my brother while she's away, the things I dust. They should all be thrown out."

Flora sat proudly in the formal dining room, which groaned under its heavy table and marble-topped credenza. The style of these big, heavy, immaculately kept wooden pieces could only be called Italianate. They were bought on cambiale, the Italian equivalent of time payments, at exorbitant interest. They were the heart of the public room; they gleamed. Flora sat like a fierce queen at the table amid the spoils Alice often said she didn't need.

Alice returned. She and Flora talked about the mother, Alice in hushed, concerned tones, Flora with a bite of defiance. Flora never tired of pointing out what no one else appeared to take much notice of no matter how often she made it clear. It was she, Flora, who got stuck raising her brother's son, who took care of her dying mother.

It was then that Mamma walked in. I saw the old lady first. Her body was shrunken under her rose-colored housecoat. Standing there all alone and uninvited at the doorway, she seemed suddenly confused and mercilessly exposed.

"Now you've done it," Flora muttered to Alice once she saw her.

"Mamma!" Alice cried.

The old woman walked toward me. Her eyes roved a moment, then they focused once more on earthly things. She looked at me with a curiosity and suspicion verging on delight.

"This is Betsy Lewis, Mamma." Flora pronounced my name better than her brother. "A friend of Leo's."

"Piacere," the old woman said to me.

"Piacere," I replied and went on to tell her what an honor it was to meet her.

"Ah, me," she said dismissively, the old partisan, the fiery socialist who kept her children alive through the days of hell.

She had not been inside a church since she pleased her parents and married, Leo had once told me. He told me the day he explained that he hadn't gone to the baptism of his son. Her practicality, her tough spirit, sustained them all once. Now her very frailty connected her to all the things we cannot see. To watch the strong woman who once lifted them from the dust return to it, her very bones visible and beyond human help under her dried skin, must have haunted her children and her grandchild. Particularly, it must have haunted Leo, an irresponsible son who had never done much for her.

"Here, Mamma!" Flora commanded, sitting her down on one of the shiny chairs after covering its cover with a towel. "Come sit with us, if you must. Here, let me fix this." She straightened the buttons on the old woman's housecoat. "There!"

The commonplaces we exchanged at that table excited the old woman. They seemed to alleviate her pain. For she now lived continually with the boredom children feel in flashes on rainy days. She was never, never ever going out.

I looked from her to Alice, so vivacious, describing her trip. Her full bosom, her blue eyes. Why was it that it was difficult to concentrate on the claw marks running along her long neck? On the lines under her eyes? On time puckering her upper lip?

"My son," the old woman asked at no particular point, cutting in before she returned to her forever. "Is he treating you well, Alice?"

"You know Leo will always be Leo, Mamma."

"He came to see me the other week. Don't rush so to see your mother. It makes me think I'm dead." Her face brightened. For the first time in that family, I saw Leo.

"Mamma, don't excite yourself!" Flora ordered.

"Shut up, Flora! Never mind me, I told him. Take care of Alice. Be as good to her as she has been to us."

The old woman sat straight. Her words were proud and brave.

I saw the Garibaldista Leo had spoken about. I saw the head of the family.

The little changes in Rome began in the next months. Jeans appeared, and not only on the slim-hipped Latin lovers. One morning the women woke up and all of them put on pants. Ice cubes, which had been nonexistent, were suddenly and proudly displayed in many bars. While I drank Sambuca on the new ice cubes or a glass of white wine, still wearing a skirt and jersey, with a scarf tied Roman fashion around my hair, the Italians, in their Levis, were ordering "gin fizz" and "Drambuie." Many a tavola calda, the staple of *Italy on Five Dollars a Day,* had a new sign announcing SNACK BAR. Alice wondered openly if Rome was Rome anymore.

It was Rome, and I watched it pass me by. I felt middle-aged at twenty-eight, stuck in time. My manuscript on Anita Garibaldi had been sent to an academic publisher in America. I was without specific work. I felt raw. Maybe the little changes in Rome had been going on for a while. Maybe it was I, my manuscript completed, who woke up one day and saw them. Doug and I were to return to the States the following summer. What would I return to? I felt I was nowhere.

I was nowhere in Rome until that winter when Mrs. Alston Harrison Peruzzi's will was probated. She was an American expatriate who apparently had found in Rome the health that Keats once looked for. She lived forever. Almost. The American Center was left with an enormous collection of letters and memorabilia from nineteenth-century American artists living abroad. The Center was less than excited by the bequest. But it had to sort things out and see what it had. I was hired for the job.

I'm still impressed by how much Doug knew. He knew those minor nineteenth-century artists and where many of their works were stored and that at the time they did not sell. Forgotten sculptors and painters were part of the catalogue of his mind. He had faith that I would juggle what I learned and come up with something new.

I was not sure I should take the job, because it paid so little, less than the chem lab in the flatlands, years ago. Such a salary was barely a salary. Leo, the champion of labor, agreed. Doug said I should do the job for love and lunch, if it came to that. It seemed to me I should be paid a fair wage for an honest day's work. The money didn't matter, Doug told me. He made enough for both of us. "What's mine is yours, what's yours is mine. Isn't that what makes a true marriage?" he asked me. Is it? I wasn't so sure, but I kept my doubts to myself. I can see now why divorce is so often the rapaciousness of reclaim.

I took the job for love and lunch and spending money. And to celebrate it, Doug and I invited Alice and Leo for dinner. We had to wait for Leo — till he had time.

"Imagine," Alice had said to me. "I suggested to Leo that we should take a weekend away together in January, just the two of us, to celebrate the new year. He looked at me, Betsy, and without a speck of irony yelled, 'No more rooms without baths!'"

Alice's Italy was a bathless double and Leo's hands reaching out to her with a few ettos of pork and a loaf of fresh bread. "He's beyond that now, Betsy. He likes big meals in the country with management. It's nothing for him to be driven halfway to Naples for lunch."

"She'd split a lira," Leo told me a few days later. He had showed up, breathless, at my apartment one overcast afternoon. "You don't know her the way I do, Betsy. She'd split a lira on a waiter's tip."

"Stay out of it," Doug warned me.

The night of the dinner, we went to eat at a trattoria we had never tried, right in our own neighborhood. We'd stayed away because it looked too slick. Leo recommended it — the new Leo; he said we should all eat there, that it was very good. And it was. We sat enjoying our antipasto and wine.

Leo talked about his work with the union. The new types of documentaries he proposed. He had serious things to say. Alice was attentive to every word — almost as if she were eavesdropping. These were stories she hadn't heard before. Leo was proud. He had more than his city and his big hands to hold out to us.

When he had finished, Alice said, "It's truly a good thing you're doing for the people." She looked at him with admiration, and he looked at her with love. The four of us were suddenly a vivid reminder of all our good times together. We were off to a warm and intimate start.

Then the door opened and a woman swept in with a little boy. "Conti!" she cried. "Surprise! No rehearsal. I was waiting for you by the window!" She acknowledged Alice with a nod. "Signora."

"You remember Betsy and Doug?" Leo asked.

"Certainly."

It was Marcella.

She wore an outfit you could sweep in with — a long, flowing white winter coat and a white scarf splattered with orange dots. Those dots should have made no sense with her red hair. "This is my son, Carlo."

Carlo was three. He carried an orange balloon and looked mean. "May we join you?" she asked.

Alice lowered her long neck like a goat, but she wasn't after a plate of greens. It was a particularly young gesture, at once stubborn and shy. She must have used it on her mother. "Oh, no, Leo dear," she said in a little voice. "She can't sit here."

"I didn't realize you lived in the neighborhood, Marcella," I said.

"Across the street from here."

"So we are neighbors," I said, looking at Leo. I could have strangled him. He came to visit me straight from Marcella's bed. Then I looked at her. "We don't have room for two more chairs here," I continued. "We'll have to get together another day."

"We can speak in English," she answered, as if I were stumbling over my words.

"There's no room," I continued in Italian.

"I'll see what I can do," Doug offered.

I looked at him as if he were crazy. "I just told Marcella there's no room."

"I'm sorry," Doug said. "I'm also sorry I missed you in *Tosca* last summer. I left early. I had no idea you were going to sing the shepherd's part. I'd have braved the cold for that."

"So you heard about my performance . . ." The two of them were off. Meanwhile, Alice was swallowing her words to Leo, her head still gazing at the plate.

"We can't let her stand!" he answered to her murmurs. "She has a little boy."

Alice asked him quietly, "Why did you bring me here?"

I wondered the same thing. But that was Leo all the way.

By then, Doug and Marcella were speaking in French. Marcella's hands were gesturing, her open coat was sweeping, but she herself was standing firm.

"Excuse me, maestra," the owner tried. The waiters were making sidesteps around her.

"There's no table for my boy and me. Can you have two chairs brought over among my friends?"

"No, Leo," Alice said. She picked her head up. "No," she said to the owner.

"I'm sorry, maestra," the owner said to Marcella. "How can I, unless I'm requested to?"

"Don't I eat here all the time? Just listen to my boy." Carlo began to cry. The owner knelt down to comfort him. "Carlino," he tried. Carlino picked up his leg and kicked him in the knee. "That's not nice," Marcella said blandly. "You see how he gets when he's hungry."

"Maestra, don't worry. Come with me." He led her to the area around the antipasto display and had a waiter set up a small table. She sat down, looked at us. Then she grabbed Carlo by the hand and stood up. His orange balloon drifted to the ceiling. She didn't retrieve it. Dragging the child after her, she passed our table. "I'm sorry you have to see this," she said to Doug. There were tears in her eyes and she was shaking. "I'm too upset to eat! Good night, Conti." She made a wild exit, that crazy shepherd, followed by one frantic sheep.

"Two more!" Leo said. "One a child! We could have made room for them easily. They're my friends!" He was indignant. I didn't think it worked.

"I told you so. I thought they were having an affair from the

minute I saw them together at the bar back stage at *Tosca*," I
said to Doug as we walked home.

"What are you talking about?"

"Marcella and Leo. That scene at the table!"

"She's a prima donna, that's all. She's used to following her
whims."

"Don't you believe anything ever happens?" I found myself
screaming at him.

I had always had what we now call the "perception" that,
through their years together, Leo may have strayed occasionally
and Alice accepted this in a mature, worldly-wise manner.
For instance, Leo once took English lessons, but he never
learned properly. "You see why," Alice said one day after we
bumped into his flaky and buxom American teacher on the
street.

Alice was amused. A man like Leo, an Italian man, how could
you love him without accepting his foibles? How grateful Leo
must have been to find in Alice a real woman, not one of his
strange girls. Alice could afford to be amused. She was confident
of the sex that bound them, the older woman and the younger
man. She was certainly not amused by Marcella. Still, she often
said, Marcella was a cold fish.

There I was that winter, on one hand concerned about Alice
and Leo, on the other, taking a look at the buxom English
teacher, taking a look at Marcella, and wondering, Why not me?
Did Alice realize that? If she were to, would she even mind?
Sometimes I resented how much, around me, she felt she could
say. Leo too. He blithely walked in on me in the late afternoons,
straight from Marcella's bed, as if my apartment, and my heart,
were a neutral zone. Is that why he didn't want me to take the
job at the Center? So that I could offer him conversation, tea,
peace? Not to mention an alibi. I was quite thankful, the night
of the celebration, after Doug and I had made up and he had
gone to sleep, that I'd be out of the apartment, away from Leo,
away from Leo and Alice's concerns, all my concentration focused on a new job.

But my new job was at an old place. I arrived at the Center early for my appointment with Nano, the librarian. I waited in the loggia for a while; there was a chill in the air. Through a window I could see the workers setting up for breakfast. I went into the salone. No one there yet. I skimmed through yesterday's English-language news. Then I went to the library and down the stairs to the basement office where Nano, Signor Dwarf, sat at his desk, just as he had years ago when he called Alice down to see him, to tell her Leo was innocent, to hint to her that he could expedite Leo's getting out of jail.

Nano greeted me by lifting his eyes from the Peruzzi papers in front of him. "You like work," he said. I answered in colloquial Roman, "Not as much as you do." It was audacious, but because he had always known Leo, I thought I knew him. I won't say he smiled, but he looked as if he wanted to. He got up slowly, hands on the desk, to show me how close he came to having a hump on his back. "This accumulation of craziness would cure even me," he continued in Italian. "Everything must be logged in. Come, what are you waiting for? You're American. Aren't you in a hurry?"

He introduced me to the library procedures; then he took me across the courtyard to one of the unremodeled rooms in the villa, where trunk upon trunk of Mrs. Alston Harrison Peruzzi's memorabilia were being stored. This was where I'd do a lot of my work. I looked at those trunks. They were crammed full of the remains of cultivated people's lives. Then I looked at the desk set up for me by the window. The room, cluttered with yesterday, the desk by the window, the view down to Rome. Was this the room Alice and Nick had lived in years ago? Betsy, I could hear Doug in my head, don't exaggerate.

"Dear me," Alice said, when she visited me there. She looked around the room that she had once shared with Nick. "This brings back everything."

Leo's mother died that spring. Life demanded every breath the tough woman could muster, until finally, when she was completely worn down, one got stuck in her throat. She was aware up to the very end; perhaps she heard the rattle.

I did not go to the funeral, which Alice told me was enormous. Mamma was very well known in her quarter, and her death rounded up old partisans, bringing them back to their source. The television workers turned out en masse. Management and all the syndicates sent great wreaths of flowers, and droves of people Leo knew walked with him. Alice had ample room for observing the whole procession. Leo was so crowded by mourners that she walked and watched from the side.

It's too bad the big-hearted outpouring, the car full of wreaths, and the procession did not lead anywhere. I think there would have been a great comfort in finality: the leftist priest whom Leo called on when no one else would handle her unshriven body, presiding; the coffin being lowered in the grave. Ashes to ashes. The scratch of a handful of dust. The sobs among spring flowers. But Mamma wasn't buried.

It was no less complex in Italy to be dead. The postwar boom, the crane I remember like a cross against the sky, the new apartment building Doug and I lived in, Flora's shoe stand, her self-defrosting refrigerator, the sets of fish plates and other prenuptial finery that Cosimo and the fascist's daughter were piling up, the very fact that they were on a waiting list for their own apartment (a new concept), point out the problem. There was no room. There were plenty of things and few places to put them.

So . . . You wait. Mamma's corpse was moved into a vast warehouse, called an oven, maybe because the coffins are loaves pushed into slots or maybe as a Roman irony against the Church's ban on cremation. It's a game of musical coffins; bodies are moved from storage place to storage place. It's bureaucratic chaos, as the poor people, the little people, form an assembly line of the dead awaiting their fate.

Alice told me Leo was beside himself, trying to find the right people to bribe. Now, if they had paid an exorbitant price for a coffin, which in effect would have greased somebody's palm, why then — perhaps, she'd be buried by now. But who had the money? Flora? Leo? Alice asked me this question a week later as we sat in the Center's back gardens in the early spring light. Mamma had worked all her life and Flora bought dining room sets. Alice was terribly perturbed.

Who could blame her? She had not been treated well the week of Mamma's death. The first night the old woman had been laid out in her own bed, her marriage bed, the bed where she had had her children.

Leo and Flora hardly acknowledged Alice. Cosimo and his fiancée were tired and confused as the night wore on. "Can you imagine, Betsy? They didn't have a word to say. I sat there by myself, at the dining room table, up all night, missing Mamma. I tried to concentrate on the strength of the woman, of what stood out as lessons of love in her life.

"Leo and Flora had their consolation. Most of the night they cloistered themselves in Mamma's room. Each took a turn sleeping next to her while the other sat and looked on. I opened the door. They didn't want me there. I was alone.

"Then, at dawn, Leo came out of the bedroom. Perhaps I had dozed off, because the children were gone. I got up from the table and took one look at him. Why, it was as if he had returned from hell, disheveled and red-eyed. I reached out to him. The way he looked at me! I saw hate, stark hate and anger burning in his eyes. He raised a fist, not at me, certainly; he would not dare. He raised a fist as if he were going to hit God.

"'A coffin!' he screamed. I don't hold him accountable. Really I don't. He was out of his mind with grief, with rage. 'A coffin, Alice! A coffin! Isn't that the least you can do?'"

A few weeks passed before I went to offer my condolences to Leo. He was with a TV crew at Bramante's Tempietto, right below the American Center. The workers were assembling a platform. Leo no longer worked among them. On that bright day, he stood to the side of them, in his white shirt and dark blue pants, scanning the papers on the clipboard he was holding.

"Betsy! What are you doing here?"

"Did you forget I'm working at the Center?"

He kissed me warmly. I said, "Alice told me you'd be here. I wanted to tell you how very sorry I am about the death of your mother."

Then he handed someone else his clipboard. "Come on," he said, "let's go for a walk."

"Did you know Shelley wrote a famous ode right around here?"

"Shelley?" Leo asked. "Ah, yes, Shelley. He's buried near your friend Keats. You foreigners have all the luck. When you die here in Rome, they bury you."

"I'm so sorry, Leo. Alice has been keeping me informed. It must be rough."

"It's Italy." He shrugged.

"I was terribly sorry about your mother. I met her just once, but I've heard so much about her. I somehow felt I knew her."

"There was no one like her."

"And now you feel there is no one?"

"In a way."

"I feel that way, too, a lot."

"Oh?"

"That's why I want to go back to Gaeta soon. I want to visit my uncle again. I want to give it another try. As soon as I can figure out what to bring them, something that won't disappoint them — if that's possible."

"It's not possible."

"What do you mean?"

"Alice told me they want to send their son to America."

"My aunt does. It's a pipe dream. Not that he'll get to America, but that in some magical way I'll take care of it all. It caught me by surprise. This time it won't. This time, when I see them, I'll realize that we don't meet on equal terms. But that doesn't mean we can't meet. They want something from me and I want something from them."

"They want a new life and you want love."

"How'd you guess? It took me some time to figure that one out. I should have come to you right away."

"Of course," he said.

"I love it here," I said, looking at the wild grass and flowers around me. "I love Rome. I love Gaeta. I wish I could find a project that would take me there."

"A project?"

"A new subject to research."

"Why don't you research the beach?"

"I'd do that too. If the Center would pay me more for the Peruzzi papers, perhaps I could stay on. Rome. Gaeta. Oh, I'm dreaming. It's not only leaving the place. It's the friends. You. Alice. Leo, I don't know what I'd do without Alice. She — "

"I saw your black friend."

"What?"

"Your black friend."

"Salmanda?"

"Salmanda. I'm sure I saw her. She came right on the set — not this one. At the Spanish Steps. She was with two white women. I tried to talk with her, but she didn't understand a word I said. I had forgotten her name. If I had called out Salmanda, I bet she'd have stopped."

"So you saw Salmanda, did you? Why didn't you call out my name? That might have slowed her down."

"I tried. Believe me, I tried. I called her comrade because she was black. I wanted to bring her home to one of dear, loving Alice's dinners. Let her talk about America. Let Salmanda say how fair the system is there compared with corrupt Italy. This is a terrible country. Ask Alice. A father tries to get his son a job. Isn't that love? Nothing as terrible happens in America. Right? Alice's grandchildren take merit exams."

"Leo — "

"Isn't that how your friend Salmanda ended up so well? By taking merit exams?"

"Leo, forget what I said about Salmanda. God, I'm so sorry I ever talked about her that day in Carrara. That car ride up the mountain shook me. Then I had too much to drink. Please don't use that as ammunition against Alice. I'm sorry I ever said anything at all."

He shrugged. "Don't be."

"I'm beginning to feel sorry I came here."

"Please don't be," he said and took my hand. "There are not many people who'd go out of their way to see me."

"According to Alice, you're swamped with invitations."

"She complains?"

"Did I say that?"

"Did she send you here?"

"Really, Leo. That's an insult. An insult to her and me and to you too!"

He laughed.

"It's not funny!"

He put his other arm around me and hugged me. He looked at me thoughtfully. He brushed a strand of hair from my face.

"You Americans," he said. "You are all so serious. A funeral or a wedding. It doesn't matter. For example, just this morning I tell Alice there'll be a wedding in August. From her reaction, you'd think somebody died."

"My God, Leo." I was surprised. "Cosimo's getting married this August? Isn't it short notice for a big wedding?"

"See? You're just like her." He kissed me, gently, on the lips. "Smile," he said.

I was flustered by the kiss, so I ignored it. "Where — where did you get the money for the wedding?"

"I won on a horse."

"A horse? Leo."

"A horse." He smiled at me, hugged me, and kissed me again.

I walked back to the Center, thinking, I really don't want to leave Rome.

That night I asked Doug to delay his transfer for another year.

"I've already done that once." He had made us dinner. We had put on sweaters and were eating on the terrace.

"Could you do it again, Doug?"

"You can stay away too long, Betsy."

"I know that. But I feel so in between things. Caught between the old and the new. Out of sync. I could ask the Center for a raise, and in another year I could complete the entire Peruzzi catalogue. That's what I'd like to do."

"Why do you think you're out of sync?" he asked.

I told him of a dream I had had. I was back in college, and my old mentor there, Professor Sotzi, was lecturing in his inspired way. Professor Sotzi was a short man with a wide forehead who wore shiny suits and looked as if he still sold fruit in the North End, as his father had done before him. Western civilization had planted itself somewhere deep inside him, and every class was an intellectual exorcism. Western civilization traveled upward through his warm heart and by the time sheer brain power met it and forced it out of his mouth, he was sweating in all seasons and his words were divine wisdom. He was giving one of those brilliant lectures in my dream and I was enthralled, as I had been since I left Salmanda in Duke's shabby room, left Passaic, and had found old Boston buzzing with its set of ideals and ideas. As I listened to Professor Sotzi's fireworks in my dream, a voice came into my head that struck me as one vivid color. It said, simply, "You are listening to the old. As long as you do, you will never find the new."

"Some dream," Doug said.

"It struck me."

"Are you getting bored with the nineteenth century?" He looked me straight in the eyes.

"No," I said guiltily. "I already told you I'd like to finish the Peruzzi project."

"It's nice to know you still care."

"He told you he won on a horse, too?" Alice said. We were at her apartment. "You see this chair? I bought it a few years after I came back to Rome. I'll never forget Leo rushing in, so flustered and excited. He took my hand and filled it with lire. 'Here,' he said, 'take it! Buy something! Buy something quickly, before I lose it!' And from then on, any time I ever attempted to say anything against gambling, he'd point to the chair as prima facie evidence of the racetrack's benevolence." Alice smiled. "How could I help it? I'd always laugh.

"Poor Flora. I went right over to see her. All that preparation for a big wedding in less than four months. She's depressed. She has a pain in her liver. She hardly talked to me. She can't admit that it's very difficult for her to let Cosimo go. Not that he'll go far. They'll live with her. But that's Leo. 'Take it! Buy something quickly!' Not that I believe for one moment that the money came from the track."

"No?"

"I doubt it, Betsy. It would take too much will power for him not to reinvest it. I think he's borrowed heavily and he's ashamed to admit it. He's a little boy in that way. He has to spend quickly, before he faces the consequences of all that borrowing. Marcella had better get used to pizza."

Late in the spring, Leo called me at the Center. He wanted to see me. No, he'd rather not meet me there. He'd take me to lunch at Romolo's, nearby.

The garden at Romolo's is where Raphael met the miller's daughter, and its small size, old abutting walls, and the clatter of its silence made it a favorite of mine. Too little food for too much money, Alice said. But she'd take visiting Americans there when they were repaying her hospitality, because the atmosphere is historic and the food is very good. I wondered what she'd think of Leo taking me there for lunch, so close to Viale Trastevere, where he once approached her with a few ettos of porchetta and a loaf of bread in his hands.

I arrived first, and since we were eating unfashionably early, about twelve-thirty, there was hardly anyone outside. I ordered white wine in the garden and was drinking a glass of it when Leo appeared. He looked haggard. "I'm dying," he said before I had a chance to finish my thought.

"You're busy," I corrected him.

But he looked as if he had run all the way and was not so sure he had lost his pursuer. He took off his jacket and put it on the back of his chair, undid the top button of his shirt, loosened his tie, and sat down.

"That's better," he said, after a drink of the wine I had poured for him. He seemed to relax. He bantered with the waiter who came over, though it never rose to a joke.

"No, no, let's eat!" he said, insisting I order an antipasto. We ate it slowly and then the pasta dish, which I was glad was not too big. We talked as we had on my terrace, about my work and his work, about what was new in Rome. We had, as always, in my most idiomatic Italian, an immediate rapport. By the time the veal came, Leo was what Alice would have called his old self, relaxed and warm and joking.

"It's always good to see you, Betsy. Have we finished that wine? Waiter," he called. No second carafe for Leo. He ordered a bottle.

Then he began to talk about Cosimo. He had finally secured his son a position. I could see Cosimo, who had never received a postcard from his mother, sorting mail for life. "I'm happy for him," I told Leo. "And the good news comes at the right time."

"Yes, right in time for the wedding."

"Is it true you won on a horse?"

"Doesn't Alice believe me?"

"She's afraid you've borrowed heavily."

"Afraid? Of what is Alice afraid?"

"Of debts. Of your having big debts."

"My debts are none of her business."

"They're not mine, either. But as a friend, I have to say I'm sorry that, for something like a wedding, you have to spend so much money."

"What do you mean, something like a wedding? What kind of wedding did your parents have for you?"

"Doug and I had a very simple wedding. We all felt a big wedding would be a waste of money."

"What isn't a waste of money?"

"An education, an operation — "

"An operation!" He laughed and I laughed too.

"I guess that proves I'm American. I don't know what made me say that."

"You Americans can afford operations. You don't need money to bribe someone to bury your mother."

"In America that would be called a sick joke."

"Poor Italy," poor Leo said.

"Poor Italy. I'm only sorry I have to leave her."

"When do you go?"

"I haven't decided. Doug said he tried for an extension, but my feeling is his heart wasn't in it. He wants to go. So be it. He'll leave and I'll go to Gaeta. Afterward, I may stay in Rome for a while. I don't know . . ."

"Alice told me you're going to Gaeta in August. Betsy — " He stopped. He looked at me unhappily.

"What is it, Leo?"

"It's Alice. She is bored with me."

"Bored?"

"Exactly. So bored that she knows of nothing to do but make trouble. I rush home to her in the middle of work; she is not satisfied. I refuse to have her pay a cent toward my son's wedding; she's not satisfied. I let my mother circle Rome in a coffin; she's not satisfied. What does she want?"

"The old Leo."

"The old Leo who worked for the bosses? This is what makes her happy? I'm not that Leo anymore."

"I know. I think I understand. But you must see, it is difficult for Alice. If you talked with her, she'd understand."

"Talk with her? *She* talks."

"Leo, she also listens."

"To you. She's not bored with you."

"What is this business of her being bored?"

"I'm telling you, she's stirring up trouble. Flora is upset. And Cosimo, who loved her, why now, even if he did know how to tell time, he wouldn't tell her. She still harps on the fact he didn't learn to drive while he was in the army. She says bad things about his fiancée right to his face."

"What bad things?"

"Politics! Politics! My son is lucky he knows his right arm from his left. He wants a ripe girl with, excuse me, big tits to lie in his bed. Alice talks politics. Says bad things about his fiancée's parents, confuses him. He hates her. Cosimo hates her. I can't blame him."

"He has no reason to hate her."

"That's what I tell him. Cosimo's confused. So he hates."

"Perhaps Flora helps confuse him."

"Poor Flora."

"Leo . . . things could get better between you and Alice. Perhaps, uh, Marcella doesn't help."

"You too? Do you know what Alice used to say about such suspicions? Nothing. American women used to be different from Italian women. They knew better than to make scenes. Now look at her! She makes a woman and a child stand through dinner. I'm afraid of what will happen at the wedding. I no longer know what she'll say or do."

"Is Marcella going to be there?"

"Where?"

"At the wedding."

"Why would Marcella be there? The problem is Alice's being there. No one wants her."

"No one wants her? Who is no one?"

"Everyone. I try to tell her and she says I am exaggerating."

"Well, you must be."

"Flora tells her. I tell her. Cosimo won't tell her because he doesn't talk to her! Take her to Gaeta!"

"What?"

"She loves you. She'd love to take a trip with you. You'll be there the day of the wedding. Take her with you if you love her. I'll pay."

I was quiet for a long time.

For dessert the waiter cut a peach for me so that it opened up in sections from the pit, like a flower.

Alice had a slow, concentrated kind of endurance, and she put her mind to her dress for the wedding. I remember her going from store to store, aghast at the prices of readymades, pondering material. I've often thought people pay more for an exaggerated virtue than for an outrageous fault. Take Marcella. She could gesture, cry, stamp, step on people, demand, be hated by many, and yet get by. She was egocentric, on the make, a chameleon, and even Leo, who was enchanted by her antics, saw through her. So did her husband. But he hung around until she threw him out.

Take Alice. She was a very interesting woman, full of compassion, who had lived many interesting lives. Through them all she was thrifty. She always saved. Nick once screamed at her, "Don't you dare turn another collar!" And Leo had given her the ultimatum: "No more rooms without baths!" Maybe it was her self-sufficiency that galled them. She was always able. Or maybe in the midst of all her generosity, the lover felt in her staunch frugality an ultimate unbending.

Doug didn't see it that way. He felt that Leo and his family were blatantly after Alice to pay and that her refusal to contribute to Mamma's funeral or Cosimo's wedding served them right. I just thought there was more to it. After all, it was Alice who had come back to Rome as the giver. Love, dollars, hope. By not giving now, Alice had suddenly withdrawn her support.

Stay out of it, Doug warned me. But it wasn't so easy.

When Alice made the decision to redo an outfit for the wedding, the family insisted she buy new clothes. "Flora came straight out with it, Betsy. As if what I wear is going to embarrass Cosimo and his bride. Well, if I'm not going to pay for the wedding, they expect that I should at least look like a properly well-heeled American wife. Leo saw me mending my good summer suit. 'You can't go to the wedding in *that*. You cannot go.'"

"Would you think of missing the wedding? I mean, they're not exactly being very nice to you. Have you ever thought, The wedding is just too much trouble — I will not go?"

"I'm going to have to buy clothes. I wonder about a hat. Must that be new too? I have to go through this for Cosimo, Betsy. He's still a child. And I'm still his American mother."

Alice found the material for a dress, finally, forsaking the ready-made. I remember looking at the satiny blue material, very pretty, if a little too warm for the season. I eyed the ripples of the blue as she talked about the scoop top, the wide skirt, and the little jacket. "There's plenty," she said.

"I don't think you should ask Flora to sew it," I said.

"Not if I want to go to the wedding!"

"Is that what you think?" I asked Alice, carefully.

"That's what I know. Why, Flora's so slow, she'd never get it done. I'm going to work on it along with a woman in this very building."

Alice held the material up against her. It shone, making the most of her clear blue eyes, her fair skin, and blond hair. Perhaps too much. I had admired the mature confidence of her blacks and whites and muted grays. This material had been on sale, but still I felt there was something desperate in the choice.

I was with her when she decided to put a new veil on her old hat. I bought her a new bag as an early birthday present on the day she picked out new shoes. I was with her when she wondered if the outfit would come together. I knew that on a happier Alice it would have. But I wondered if the strain of the situation and the youth of the blue might conspire against her.

Then there was the wedding gift. She refused to add to the dishes and linens and silverware that had accumulated in Flora's apartment. Alice's gift was going to be a substantial sum. It fluctuated. It depreciated when she speculated on how Cosimo would spend it. When she spoke of the principle behind her not paying for the wedding, the gift rose in value. "Why, I'd give them a milione, Betsy, for something good."

I encouraged her. Yes, I told her, a milione is a good idea. I encouraged her to give it to Cosimo soon. Sixteen hundred dollars would show him that she cared. She looked startled at that, but did not say a thing. I was sorry I had had lunch with Leo, that he had asked me to take her to Gaeta. I was stuck with what I knew and could not say.

Then, one Sunday before the wedding, she called and asked if I could come right over.

"Now it's Sundays," Doug said. "Didn't I tell you to stay out of it?"

Alice had had a terrible fight with Leo, I told him. "I have to go." When I got there, I was glad I'd come. Alice was in a state, nervous — I'd never seen her nervous — standing there in the living room, trying to find her presence of mind. "Look, Alice," I said, "you don't have to talk. Let's take a ride."

"I don't know, Betsy."

"Come on, Alice. Let's go to Castel Gandolfo. I'll buy lunch."

I suggested Castel Gandolfo because it was one hill town the four of us hadn't gone to together. And I did know a good inexpensive, rustic place Alice would like.

"You don't have to buy lunch, Betsy."

"Okay, we'll decide when we're there." And it's true, Alice was always ready to split things with me. Still, I felt I owed her something that day, knowing what I knew.

She was silent on the trip into the country. As we approached Castel Gandolfo, she took her compact out of her pocketbook, opened it, and looked in the mirror. She closed it with a snap. "This is a good idea, dear. I'm glad to be out."

The little restaurant I knew had a terrace in the back that looked down into the valley. The tables were planks of old wood, and the liter of white local wine arrived cool. We hadn't asked; the waiter brought it to greet us. "Trust me," I said and ordered chicken diavolo.

The wine, the bread, the shade, the locals arriving in their Sunday clothes, revived her. I knew how to give her her Italy. She relaxed and smiled slightly. I felt good.

She began to tell me, in her quiet, meandering way, what had happened . . .

Leo had come home late at night. He woke her out of a trou-
bled sleep to make love to her. She was surprised to find him
still next to her when she woke in the early morning. When she
reached for him a half-hour later, he was gone. She found him
in the kitchen, where he was, surprise of surprises, making coffee. "Do you know what he said, Betsy? He said he knew how
many spoonfuls to put in, but how did I add the magic? I said
the magic had always been the both of us being there." They
embraced in the kitchen. They wept in each other's arms. Then
they had a golden hour. She made an American breakfast and
he read aloud to her from the paper he had gone down for. They
ate. Without even realizing it, he made anchovy out of her name.

He told her that now that the wedding was at hand, he realized more and more each day that she had been right. He was
walking a tightrope in his work, in his life, because of Cosimo
and the debts he was incurring for him. It was too late now to
change things. He would if he could. She was right. Everything
was bad. That's why she hadn't seen him for a week. Where did
she think he was, at the track? He hadn't won on a horse; she
was right. The horse was his pride. He was in trouble. He was
deeply in debt. Lend me money, he said. Not for Cosimo, not for
the wedding. Lend me money for us.

Us?

Yes, us. You and me.

What could she do at this late date, after all the pain and damage? There were other factors involved, weren't there? What
about Marcella?

Marcella?

Yes. She told him she didn't want to start any trouble on this
beautiful morning, with the two of them together as it used to
be. But since she hadn't seen him in a week, could he blame her
if she brought up Marcella?

Leo was naked at the table. She was in the nightgown that
turned her body pink. She wasn't like him, never could eat in
the raw. Leo looked at her. There was wry amusement, border-
ing on sadness, in his eyes. "Anchovy," he said, "I haven't been
near Marcella. I swear on my mother's container."

"Oh, Leo, that's not funny."

"I'm hoping Marcella will take her husband back."

Well, then, where had he been this week? I told you, he insisted, I've been in trouble. Alice, if you can lend me money, I'll pay you back. If you can lend me money, this thing will be over. I swear to you.

She wanted to help him. She talked about the wedding. It had been no small strain on her. Flora's tone, Cosimo's quiet, that wretched little bride. She'd been months alone. What would erase those months?

She wanted to help. She left the table. She came back after a while with an envelope. She told him the contents were to have been Cosimo's gift. But what did Leo's son need? He already had . . . Envelope in hand, she recited a Homeric list of his spoils.

Let Cosimo think of his father, she said. His father, who has secured him a position, who has run himself ragged affording this wedding so that a fascist family would approve of his son. His father, who almost ruined his own home life for him. Take the envelope, she told Leo. I'll talk with Cosimo the way I've talked with him before. I'll make him understand. My wedding gift to him, she said tenderly, is to give this to you.

Leo opened the envelope. He spread its contents in front of him on the table. He didn't say a word until he looked once more at Alice's contented face. Is this a joke? he wanted to know. An insult?

She told him she didn't know what he meant; he could not stand her look of noncomprehension. He grabbed the lire in one hand and stood up. With his free hand he took her by the arm and dragged her into the living room. Crumpling the money in his fist, he held it in front of her eyes.

A half milione, he raged like a madman. Do you know what you can do with this pittance? Do you know? He pulled her nightgown up.

She was angry too. You stop that, Leo.

He had the envelope behind her. He was yelling obscenities.

Do you know what you can do with this? Let me show you.

His anger inflamed him. He took the crumpled lire and threw them across the room. He pushed her over to the daybed. He was as violent with her, as beside himself, as on the last night of her trip to Rome with the Keeger girls. Only this time it wasn't love, she told me straight out. It was sodomy.

And when it was all over, it was Leo who was crying. Why don't you love me, Alice? Why don't you have the heart of an Italian woman?

At Castel Gandolfo I didn't know what to say to Alice. I reached across the table and took her hand. I looked at it and at the platter full of chicken bones.

"Why don't I love him? Imagine, Betsy. Then, after I washed and dressed, while I was waiting for you, I remembered the lire. I searched all through the room. I couldn't find them. In the confusion . . . I don't know."

Alice looked at me in puzzlement. "The wedding's next week. You tell me, Betsy. Have I or have I not given Cosimo his present?"

The very next morning Leo called me at the Center. By then, all I wanted to do was stay out of it. I had taken his call in Nano's office. Since Nano was officially on vacation, he didn't appear until midday. No! I said when Leo asked me to lunch. I went back to my carrel, but I couldn't concentrate. It was so silent. The library, the Center itself, was so still in August. What was I doing there? I picked up my papers and went outside. I took a walk to the back gardens, where I had first met Alice. Sat down under a tree, took a long look at Garibaldi's wall. Got up, went to the fountain in the loggia, and watched the goldfish for a while. I could hear the buzz of solitude in the heavy summer air.

Later I sat at my desk by the window in the room Alice and Nick had lived in years ago. I couldn't work. And I was further distracted by the view. Three times a week, with the precision that structures the chaos of Roman life, a little white Cinque-cento would park right at the abutting wall of the villa, two floors below my window. I was at such an angle that I could see in through the windshield of the car. Mine was a telescopic view of a faceless bureaucrat getting a blow job. I saw his cock come out of his pants, I saw the woman's head working away, I saw the tissue (Roman litter) tossed out of the car. I watched in awe and fascination. Other people's assignations, other people's lives.

"So this is what keeps you from lunch."

I turned around, away from the window. Leo was at the door. He put his finger to his lips and shut the door behind him.

"How did you get in?"

He looked at me triumphantly and smiled. He bowed and sat down on the cot. Did he remember the room?

"What are you looking at?" I asked him. He was looking at me. I couldn't tell if he was playing a game or if he was drunk. He seemed high.

"Can't I look at you? Do you have something to hide?"

"Maybe. Is it any of your business if I do?"

"Betsy, you are angry with me?"

"I was working, Leo."

"Why won't you come to lunch with me? Do you hear things? Does Alice fill your ears?"

"With the truth."

He sighed, stood up. He came over to where I was sitting at my desk and put an arm on my shoulder. He looked out the window.

"What's going on there?" he asked, looking down at the lovers in the white Cinquecento. "Ah!" He laughed. "Rome."

"Rome," I repeated. I stood up to get rid of his arm.

"Don't listen to Alice. Let me take you to lunch."

"I'll have lunch with you after Cosimo's wedding."

"How?"

"That's right. After the wedding. I wish I could erase the lunch we had. I see Alice trying to prepare for the wedding, dressing to make you and Flora and Cosimo proud. I see you hurting Alice. In my mind I keep hearing you ask me to take her to Gaeta.

I feel caught. There's nothing I can do. Being a friend to both of you, I feel I'm a friend to neither. It wasn't right of you to come here. You must have been able to tell on the phone that I wanted you to stay away."

"I never come here," he said.

"Leo, did you listen to a word I said?"

"You're Alice's friend."

"And as Alice's friend, I ask you not to listen too carefully to your sister. If you ask me, I think Flora dislikes Alice and is trying to put any obstacle she can in the way."

"Flora?" Leo questioned. "Poor Flora," he said, just as Alice would. Alice also excused Flora's bad temper and curt ways. Flora had no life. She had a life, I thought; she was more a lioness than her brother was a lion. Her femininity stalked the darkest recesses of the den.

"What about poor Alice?" I asked angrily. "She's upset, alone. Why are you hurting her the way you are?"

"That's right. I forget. You are Alice's friend."

"And I'm your friend too. That's why I'm trying to tell you the truth. I don't know what Flora's put you up to, but I'm not going to take Alice away."

"You're my friend *after* the wedding. Now you think you are Alice's friend by not doing me a favor. It would be a favor for Alice too, believe me, if you convinced her to go to Gaeta."

"Certainly, Leo, you know how much I care for you. You can't be blind. This is not easy for me. Doug was right. I should have stayed out of all of this. I don't want to know!"

He stared at me again. "It's not easy for you." He paced.

I sat down on the cot and wiped my eyes with my hands. "That's right, but I've made up my mind."

"That mind of yours," he said huskily. "The mind of Betsy Lewis. I wish I could see that mind of yours." He came over to the cot and squatted down in front of me. He pulled my hair back. "Show me," he said. "Show me that mind of yours. Show me where it is written that you are Alice's friend."

"Leo!"

He brought my head to his and kissed me. I could smell the bite of liquor on his breath. Then he had his big arms around me and was hugging me tightly. He put his head in my skirt. I was smoothing his hair.

"Show me," he whispered.

He looked up at me. I rubbed my hand over his beautiful skin. I was wet with desire.

Then he was lying next to me on the cot. We were kissing. His hands were under my blouse, on my breasts. Everything left me except his touch and his smell, until, suddenly, he stopped. He brought his face from my exposed breasts. He grasped my hands in his and kissed them.

He stood up. His knees cracked as he straightened. "A little cramped," he said. He stood above me, tucking in his shirt. I did not cover myself.

"Leo!"

He looked down at me. "My friend," he said simply. His determined tone was shattering. "Leo Conti is about to do one thing right in his life."

"Don't go!"

He opened the door, looked out, then disappeared.

That afternoon, when I brought the little I had accomplished to his office, Nano looked up from his desk and said, "So you know Leo Conti. He's a phenomenon, that man. A phenomenon."

❧ 9 ❧

I was in Gaeta the weekend of Cosimo's wedding, and Doug was back in America. I had brought my cousin Angelo two perfectly good suits that Doug didn't wear anymore and had left behind. I brought Margherita French perfume, and I gave my uncle a hundred dollars' worth of lire, which I told him I didn't plan to exchange. I was going home. Doug had been delighted when I told him I'd be following shortly. His tone suggested he was very well acquainted with someone I didn't know at all. Me. I was leaving Rome the way I once left Salmanda. Confused. Remorseful.

Everybody seemed happy with the gifts that Sunday in Gaeta, though I guess the perfume was the wrong choice. I wanted to get my aunt something she wouldn't buy for herself. But half-way through the meal, relaxed on the wine and good cheer, she grabbed the bottle in a way that suggested what a silly little thing it was and sprayed across the table at her son. Then he grabbed it from her and sprayed me. "Throw," I said. Angelo did. I sprayed my uncle. That was that. So much for fancy little things.

I spent two weeks at Gaeta. I went to the beach every day. I'd swim, stretch out in the sun, and tan. It was very important to me during those weeks to look good. I stayed in a bigger room in the apartment on Pius the Ninth. I had reservations this time, and the signora greeted me like a long-lost relative. During those weeks I could see that my relationship with my uncle and his family was becoming routine. The last time I had dinner with them, my uncle kept the television on while we ate.

I received two extraordinary letters from Alice about the wedding. And when I got back to Rome, its consequences filled my last days there. I thought about it and its aftermath for years. I remember how it preoccupied me on my plane ride home. I carried the situation aboard, trying to make some sense out of it. My misplaced passion. Leo's mess. Was there a form I could put my feelings in, in order to deal with them? By the time I was in the air, having waved goodbye to Alice, having hugged her and kissed her, and having sworn always to be her friend, I closed my eyes and went over and over the foibles of human nature, what Doug would call exaggerations.

Alice dressed for the wedding and waited in the apartment for Leo to come to take her to the church. By the time she realized Leo was not coming for her, by the time she got to the bus stop — and it took the Sunday bus forever to arrive — by the time that bus made it to the vicinity of the church, why, of course the wedding was over. The reception was in the country. Taking buses there was out of the question this late in the day. A cab? Why, even if she had the lire . . . So she stood outside the church in her blue outfit and her white accessories. The heat and her absorption in her predicament were turning her lightheaded. I can see the kind stranger approaching her in front of the church. She was a lady in distress, just as she had been when her son was little and her first husband in a top hat was confined. Hadn't a gentleman come along? A woman like Alice is a woman like Alice. Why, I've seen her in Italian museums, looking perplexed, and a moment later a knowledgeable guard, unasked, comes along to address her questions.

The man in front of the church looked sadder than she after she told him her story. "Ah, Signora," he said, "che peccato!" He drove her to the country in his car.

She knew the restaurant well. It was one of those rustic inns where, at a wooden table under a tree, you can eat an enormous and hearty meal at a fraction of the price of Rome. Farmers' children had their wedding receptions there, and if you were lucky you'd catch a happy, raucous party and end up with an extra course of pasta on your plate. Leo and she used to make a Sunday outing of it. They took the buses from Rome, and then walked the mile to the place. Then one day she and Leo returned to find it closed for restoration. When it reopened, it was not the same. Not that the outside was altered. But all the weddings began to take place in the enlarged and modernized interior. Eating indoors became something new to do. Prices went up, and the overworked waiters hadn't time for the old jibes and jokes. The local people who got married there were formal and stiff. She and Leo stopped going. When Leo had told her where the wedding dinner would be, she said, "Where?" He had looked surprised and said, "But you always liked it there."

She got out of the car. Not one of the two hundred wedding guests was outside in the woods. She thanked the kind man slowly and profusely, then walked along the path she knew, her pocketbook dangling and her hat slightly askew. She opened the door of the air-conditioned restaurant. The crowd hit her in the face. In the midst of the din, she tried to explain to the owner that she should be at the head table. But she was seated at a table of strangers, at the edge of the confusion, on the bride's side. She felt faint, but she took some bread and water and held on.

She had missed the antipasto and the pasta course, but she was grateful for the lukewarm soup that came her way. By then she had stopped trembling — her nerves wouldn't obey her for a while — and was able to sort the blur of confusion in front of her. She had time. No one at the table said a word to her. Was she there? She began to separate the bride's and groom's sides, and saw faces she knew, Leo's fellow workers, across the room. The head table was far away, but she saw Leo. Flora sat on Leo's right, where Alice should have been. Flora was dressed in blue, as if her intuition taught her how to spite. Her back was straight, her posture proud. She presided. Alice watched Flora and suddenly a timidity overcame her. She felt no confidence at all. Was she Cinderella or the wicked stepmother? Alice Blanders Russo, the uninvited guest.

Leo was having a time for himself. His face was as flushed as Flora's; he was in an animated conversation with his son's father-in-law. Their heads stuck out on either side of the newlyweds. Leo looked aggressive. Was he showing everyone from work that he in no way whatever deferred to fascists? Flora retained a woman's watchfulness even in her glory. But it was Leo who noticed Alice, his bad conscience pointing her out in the crowd. He bent over, said something to Flora that made her laugh, rubbed his hand along her arm, then got to his feet unsteadily.

He motioned to Alice as he walked to the vestibule. She made her way out after him and waited for him in front of the men's room.

"What are you doing here?" he asked, his face slapped cold with water.

"What am I doing here?"

"So late."

"I waited for you."

"You waited too long."

"Well, I'm here now."

"We couldn't save you a place." Leo began to sweat again. "Nine!" he proclaimed. "Nine at the head table. That's the way it should be."

"Tell the waiter to set another place."

"It's impossible. There's no room. Where would you sit? It's your fault."

"Oh, Leo. Do you know what you're doing?"

"Don't cause trouble! Haven't you done enough already?"

"What have I done?"

"Go back to where you were sitting. Discreetly. Stay there. Listen to me!" he shouted. "I'll come for you later," he whispered. He walked away.

"Leo!"

He turned. "By God, let me breathe, Alice. Be quiet. Stay out of this! Don't you dare make a scene!"

He stumbled away more drunkenly than before.

Leo made a scene.

She sat at her table and watched him grow more emphatic. What would the workers think? She could see them clearly, now, across the room. All the old friends were there. Alice hadn't the will to go over to them, to let them see she'd been shoved aside. She picked out the bald heads, the worn faces, the good hearts, of those who had once given Leo and her a party, when she came back to Rome. A celebration, gifts and all, that grew out of warmth and love. That grew out of little. Were they celebrating today? In the midst of so much, they didn't seem to be having fun.

Marcella was not there. That did not comfort Alice.

She turned to study Cosimo, blank-eyed, handsome in his tuxedo, next to his buxom bride. Did he see her? Did he want to? He stared out at his audience as if he were on a podium rather than half the centerpiece of the head table. The bride's father stuck his head past his daughter's breasts to counter whatever it was Leo was shouting. Leo rose suddenly, his chair fell backward, and he left the table, making his way to where his fellow workers sat. Now I should join him, Alice thought, but she stayed.

He wasn't acting like the Leo she knew. The Leo who, when he got flustered on wine, told jokes and elaborate stories. He was talking loudly, motioning abruptly. His tuxedo jacket, the wrong size for his girth, seemed the only thing that held him back. Alice saw Flora appeal to Cosimo's new father-in-law. Of all people! Leave it to Flora to ask favors of a man half her size and to make things worse.

The dapper little fascist went over to Leo. Alice saw Leo put his arm around him and introduce him to his fellow workers in the communist union. They swayed together for a few minutes of conversation. Then she saw Leo — and it wasn't done playfully — push the man away. They exchanged some words, but the little man went back to the head table and sat down with a big smile on his face. Three big men from the bride's side of the family walked over to Leo. It looked like escalating joviality at first, some slaps on the backs and pushes. Alice glanced at Cosimo and his bride, sitting like two dolls on top of a wedding cake. Flora was pretending life was genteel, talking with the bride's mother, who had taken Leo's seat.

Alice had never seen Leo as bad as this, ever. The cruelty that had at one time seemed the remote underside of his cheer, and that had intensified since he'd become a big shot and promoted Marcella, had now emerged. He was very mean. He had been drinking, and he was way beyond himself, out of his own control. No salvation. Why was he standing by that table? What was he saying to his friends in the union as he introduced them to the three big fascists?

Alice felt a rush of fear as clearly as a rush of pleasure. Involuntarily, she searched out Flora, who had her eyes fixed on her brother. Leo was reeling. As he reeled, he shoved one of the fascists. The big man pushed him into the table of his friends. Men from the table stood up. All this money spent, all these relationships battered, for the wedding to end like this. Oh, Leo!

Cosimo stood up and cried, "Papa," like a little boy. The impotency of his voice caught at Alice's throat, where she had a heartful of tears stored up. All she wanted to do was sit at that table where no one knew her, at the wedding where she was not wanted, and cry. But she stood up in her blue dress. Her little blue jacket stayed behind her chair. Her hat fell off as she made her way past the curious to Leo. Her arrival had an immediate effect on the table of old friends. They watched her. The men she knew disentangled themselves from the fascists as she stood in front of Leo. With an aplomb equal to Maple Blanders', she introduced herself to the three fascists. "I'm Cosimo's American mother," she said. She took Leo's hand. "You'll excuse us, please."

Then it happened. At the head table, Flora stood up. Her thick hair was overcurled for the occasion. It gave her the Medusa look. Wrath distorted her face. She thrust her big fleshy arms straight out, pointing at Alice.

"Leo! What is that woman doing here?"

Alice felt Leo's hand tremble in hers.

Then Flora's voice broke and she screamed.

It was Flora who had paid for the wedding.

"Just imagine, Betsy."

Yes, just imagine.

Alice sat on my big trunk in the living room as I packed cartons of books. She was pale, but I could feel her resilience, her energy.

Flora had paid for the wedding. Paid on her mother's soul. For Mamma *had* saved enough to be buried. She was a proud woman. She had had no intention of circling Rome.

"After I'm buried," the ailing woman often told Flora, "there'll be a little something left over for you." So Flora bought the dining room set on time.

"How much did she leave?" I asked Alice.

"Almost six thousand dollars."

"It's gone?"

"Every penny plus for the wedding."

I shook my head. "Poor Flora," I heard myself say.

"They thought it was my fault, Mamma's not being buried."

"Oh?"

"For not paying for the coffin myself."

"I'm not surprised."

"I had no intention of discussing money at the vigil. Flora translated that for Leo. It meant I had no heart."

Isn't that what Flora and her brother had talked about for months? How Alice had no heart. When Leo had visited, worrying about how to pay for a wedding, Flora told him the wedding she'd do if she had a lira to her name. What was one more mouth to feed? She'd welcome Franca to her household. She'd dote on Cosimo's happy face. That was the heart of an Italian woman.

Alice had no heart. Why, she had driven Leo to that tramp Marcella. "Doesn't she mind?" Flora would ask him in a whisper. "American women don't take notice of such things," Leo would explain.

What did Alice take notice of? Why, the night of Mamma's death, sitting out there, acting so sad, would she contribute? Did it matter to her that, without the right palms greased, without a coffin costing four times its worth, there would be no burial place for Mamma? "She won't discuss it." Leo came back to the bedroom the night of the wake. He and Flora looked down at their mother's corpse. "She has no heart!" Flora mourned. "Mamma, tell me, what else can I do?"

What else could Flora do but show her brother the heart of an Italian woman? It was the first time in her life that Flora had money. For Mamma entrusted her, not Leo, with the key to the box in her linen drawer. She looked down at her dead mother. "Forgive me, Mamma, I'm doing what I have to do.

"Leo, I can't let Cosimo suffer any longer. I can't look at the anguish in your eyes. I'm not like her!" She pointed past the closed door to Alice, then she pounded her heart. "I'll pay for Cosimo's wedding. What else can I do? And you, with your new friends, you find a place for Mamma. You take care of that. That's more than I can bear."

"I can't take from Mamma. I can't ask you for this sacrifice."

"Sacrifice?" Flora sobbed. Tears streamed down her face. "You should know what sacrifice is. She should know what it is like to be an Italian woman. To have a heart!"

Leo looked at his sister. "I swear on Mamma," he whispered, "I'll find her a resting place."

"Promise me, on Mamma, that you'll never leave me."

"My dear, dear sister."

Flora looked again at her dead mother. "*She's* left me! All I have is Cosimo and Franca and you." She collapsed, sobbing, into her brother's arms.

"Flora, Flora, ssshh. Here, lie down next to Mamma, rest. I promise, dear, I promise. I'll never leave you."

And in the next few months, Alice told me, promise followed promise.

"Who told you all this?" I asked her.

"Flora," she said. "She called me the other day, in tears, begging me to come to see her. She's been terribly depressed. I didn't know it, but it seems right before the wedding, Cosimo came to tell her that after they were married he and Franca would be moving in with Franca's parents. I don't know how he summoned the courage to tell her. Flora was terribly upset. Dear, dim Cosimo said, 'But, Zia, you can keep our wedding presents here.'

"Imagine, Cosimo was leaving. She, who'd done everything for her mother and for her nephew, was going to end up alone. I think that was what made her decide that in no case, no matter how good my new clothes, was I to be at the wedding. She wanted me out of her life, out of Leo's life. In her frantic state she wanted to strike out at me, blame me. If I had paid for Mamma's coffin, if I had paid for the wedding, as she felt I should, why then Flora would be a signora. She'd have money for a bigger apartment. An apartment where Franca would want to live. Sheer fantasy. Well, she had already shown Leo the sacrificing heart of an Italian woman. Now, she laid down the law. She'd pay for the wedding, but Marcella, that puttana of her brother's, must not stain the occasion by her presence. I guess Leo found a way of arranging that. It was a bit more difficult to eliminate me. But all Flora could do about losing Cosimo was to hate me. She told her brother not one lira if, after all I had made her sacrifice, I was there.

"And Leo being Leo, he had no recourse but to agree. Everything was my fault. Hadn't he said that himself? Hadn't he complained to Flora that I drove him to Marcella, selfish, selfish me. You know, Betsy, I never actually refused to help with the coffin. I simply was not about to discuss lire on the night that Mamma died. But what are facts compared with the heart of an Italian woman who has just given all her money away?

"So naturally, when Flora saw me at the wedding her world crashed in. She was beside herself. Since then, she's had a chance to think. The wedding's over. Mamma's gone. Cosimo's gone. Who does she have to complain to about Leo other than someone who understands him as well as she? Who does she have but me?

"So what could I do, once she called, but visit her? Poor thing. Pale, drawn, disheveled. You would have thought someone had died.

"'Forgive me, Alice. Forgive me.' She threw herself in my arms. 'I should never have trusted that brother of mine. After all these years, how could I still believe what he says? I've spent a lifetime paying for his mistakes. And he still comes to me as big as life with that smile on his face and those lies on his lips, and what do I say but, Yes, Leo. This time it will be different.'"

I watched Alice on the trunk. She was shaking her head. I sat down on a box of books I'd just packed. "So you had to calm her down? That was your job?"

She nodded. "'Flora,' I told her, 'it's not the end of the world, dear.' And she kept holding me, repeating, 'Forgive me, Alice, forgive me.' And I said, 'Calm yourself, listen to me. I forgive you. Think about it, Flora. You've given Cosimo the wedding you wanted to. Can't you accept that?' Then she kept crying, 'How can Mamma ever forgive me? I'll go to hell for what I've done.'

"I told her simply that I didn't think she'd go to hell. I told her I loved Mamma too. I told her I'd speak to Leo and see if it's at all possible to get her a burial space. We'll find a way to cover the costs, Leo and I. I told her that if it came down to it, I'd pay for it myself.

"Imagine, Betsy, all they'd have to do is sell some of those outlandish wedding gifts. But let it be. I refused to upset Flora any more. I sat there in the kitchen with her, afraid for her health."

"So you calmed her down?"

"Nothing so simple, dear. Flora looked at me. 'You and Leo? You'll speak to him? Where is he?'

"'Why, Flora, he's home with me.'

"'You're lying!' she screamed. 'You're lying! He's on location with that tramp Marcella.'"

Alice brought her up short this time. "'That will be quite enough, Flora! Don't you dare talk like that to me.' That's exactly what I told her, Betsy. And she looked at me like a ravaged woman, like a human being who cannot comprehend. 'But, Alice, he promised, he promised. He swore on Mamma. He swore he wouldn't leave me alone. He promised he'd move in with me.'"

"What?"

"Just imagine, Betsy."

Yes, just imagine.

"He told her he was moving in?"

"Oh, he did move in. That's just where he had been the weeks before the wedding, calming her because Cosimo was moving out. Just as he said, he'd been in trouble. He hadn't been with Marcella, just as he said on the day he asked me for the money. On the day he ended up hating me. He took the easy way out. Now, of course, he can't forgive himself."

"But you can forgive him?"

"Sometimes I think Leo's violent needs are like fevers. They take over and he does not know how to control them. He just had too little for too long. So when there is something he must have, he knows no better than to thrash around, and God help you if you get in the way. He sweats it out. This time, when the awful hangover receded, you should have seen him, Betsy, or perhaps you shouldn't have. He was dreadfully sick. But then the fever goes away, he opens his eyes, and he sees. He can't forgive himself for what he's done to Flora. In fact, I'm surprised, with his guilty conscience, that he can afford to forgive me for being me. But he can. And that proves he takes responsibility, finally. He knows how tied Flora is to him. He knows his mother is circling Rome. He knows what he's done to our relationship. He knows he's been just awful. He keeps mumbling, 'I can't do anything right.'"

"Oh, really?" I thought of Leo that day he came to my room at the Center. I saw him once more tearing himself away from me. I saw myself on the cot imploring him, my breasts exposed. "He didn't tell you he's done one thing right in his life?"

Alice looked surprised.

"Come on, Alice, let's go out on the terrace. Go on out, I'll bring some tea."

By the time I joined Alice on the terrace, she was sitting in the shade of my oleanders on one of the two cane chairs I was leaving for her. I was quiet. My packing was done. What was I waiting for? For Leo to come for those chairs? For one last meeting? Suddenly I knew he wouldn't come to see me now. He'd pick up the furniture after I was gone. The day at the Center had been his goodbye. I wondered if I could move up my ticket home. Even a few days. It was time to go.

Strangely enough, for, I'd say, the first time, Alice acknowledged that I was quiet. She looked at me with concern. "Whatever are you thinking?"

"Nothing . . . Everything. Leo. Flora. I guess I was right about her. I had a sixth sense. Her attachment to Leo never did seem too . . . too healthy. I thought you should watch out for her."

"Poor Flora. She's not a modern woman, Betsy. She doesn't know how to be alone. No Mamma, no Cosimo, no Leo — "

"No boyfriend," I cut in rather sharply. "What about a man? She's a handsome woman. Hasn't there ever been a man? Other than poor Leo, that is."

"That's just what I said to her. 'What about Roberto?' She's been seeing him off and on for years. I told her she should be ashamed of herself, not even inviting him to the wedding. Oh, Betsy, it's just priceless. I know I shouldn't joke, but, Betsy, you'll enjoy this. It'll cheer you up."

Alice took a sip of her tea, put it down, and smiled at me. "'Roberto,' she sneered. 'Roberto! Who needs him, Alice? For what?' Then she spread her thumb and forefinger like this, Betsy, as if she were measuring Roberto, and then shaking his family jewels in my face.

"'Why should I see Roberto, Alice? What do I need him for? For the thirty seconds before he snores?'"

Alice stretched her feet out on the cane footstool. "'For the thirty seconds before he snores.' Thirty seconds! Just imagine, Betsy. Poor Flora."

Alice threw her head back. Completely relaxed, she laughed.

PART III

MAYBE
SHE
GO

❧ IO ❧

Y ou'll never recognize Rome," Alice told me. She was sitting
in my living room. "Everything's changed."

"You haven't."

And she hadn't.

This was 1974, and my living room was in Back Bay. I had
moved to Boston with Doug, who had bought into an art auction
house.

The Rome Alice pictured was on the verge of collapse. She
herself had been mugged getting on a bus. "Imagine, Betsy, two
young men came from behind. Ripped my pocketbook from my
arm and threw me down in the street. My arm was twisted, and
I was black and blue all along my left side where I fell. Leo took
his time. One day, two days, and then suddenly there he is at the
apartment, as if he'd just heard. Breathless, as if he'd run all the
way. Well, it wasn't a propitious moment for the only way he
knows of making me feel better. I was sore all over. I could
hardly move. He was terribly offended. He wanted to know what
was wrong with me!"

Leo wasn't living with Alice anymore. He blamed that on the divorce law. The fact that it was voted in appeared to many to be a miracle. I remember Leo joking that by the time he and Alice could marry, he'd have to wheel her down the aisle. But he never thought it would happen. Hundreds of thousands of Italians could now divorce their discarded spouses and marry the people they lived with. The joke was on a lot of them.

When Leo's estranged wife in Genoa immediately divorced him, he told Alice not to breathe a word. But somehow Marcella found out. The way Alice put it, once Marcella got her divorce, she made Leo marry her. Pure party politics. He was still terrified of that cold fish. "Imagine, Betsy, he'd come to me every time he could get away. He'd make love to me like a madman. 'Don't leave me, don't leave me,' he'd say."

"I can just hear him!"

"Anyone else would think it crazy, Leo needing my sympathy because he'd left me! Well, it is crazy, but I knew you'd understand."

"Oh, Rome," I said. "I'm not looking forward to going there, Alice. It's Doug's idea for me to come along with him. It's only for ten days. Things have been strained between the two of us. That's why I think I really should go. I — "

"Just be careful then. It's not safe to walk the street with a purse. Why, I saw a young German tourist who just wouldn't let go. The motorcycle dragged her right through Piazza Campitelli, but she wouldn't let go of her shoulder strap."

"Doug and I . . . It's not the same anymore."

"What is? Why if it weren't for Nano — "

Nano the librarian had become the hero of the American Center.

A well-dressed young Italian couple had come into the vestibule of the library on a day pass. How the armed guard at the front of the Center let them through the gate, Nano did not know. Let them through with their odd-shaped cases uninspected. Nano's assistant asked them to open the cases at the front desk. They rushed past him. From below, Nano heard shouts and scuffling. He came right up the stairs, carrying his gun. He'd heard rumors. He trusted no one. He knew what could happen. He wasn't even surprised. The boy had his rifle unpacked when Nano shot him in the head. The girl picked up the rifle and in stress attempted a wild volley. The readers all ducked into their carrels or under their desks. Not Nano. He kept walking, right through the shots, gun pointed. Closer than he needed to be, he looked into her eyes and shot her dead. He took the other, smaller case they hadn't opened and went with it far out into the back gardens. Put it down carefully. Walked, didn't even run away. Out of harm's range, he heard a section of the city wall blow up at his back.

Nano on the front pages of all the papers. The *Daily American* called him the old partisan who saved the day. The *Paese Sera* called him the dwarf who roared.

Alice had been in the grand salone that day, reading the papers, wondering what to do. Nano walked past her, splattered with blood. "Signora," he said, "even here, even here."

She went out to the back gardens. "Those dead children, the rubble from the wall. I understood. It answered my questions . . . I decided to come home. Now, I even hear rumors that the Center is going to close."

"Really?"

"Americans aren't welcome in Rome anymore. Perhaps it's best we leave. Let the young take aim at all those old leftists who advance their paramours and secure things for their sons. Why, remember the day at Carrara, Betsy? Leo calling me a fascist in front of all our friends? That's what the Red Brigade calls the communists now — fascists. Well, I abhor their methods, but I see them crying out against the corruption of their elders — "

"Alice, don't you think the Red Brigade is excessive punishment for those who have grown too fine for bathless doubles?"

"'No more rooms without baths!' Just imagine, Betsy. Oh, I don't sympathize with the violence. But I've lived in Rome long enough to understand that I'll never understand. Now I've left. I'm not going to contribute one iota to the general rottenness."

"You've left for good?"

She didn't answer. Instead, she took off her hat. Her hair did not look as it used to when she could afford the local Roman beauty parlor once a week. There was an orangey glaze to it, now that she was back to American prices, and beyond the veneer it was thinning. Alice's doing her own hair surprised me more than her strong words. For some reason it upset me that she was stingy enough to face growing old.

"Do you think you might be able to do me a favor while you're in Rome, dear?"

"If I can."

"Leo will be so delighted to see you and Doug — "

"I don't know about Doug. He has so much business, and he hasn't much patience these days."

"But surely you'll see Leo, dear."

"I want to."

"He often asks after you."

"Does he?"

"Why, he asks me to read him your letters. He misses you. He's said goodbye to too much in his life. It's a barren life for Leo in Rome, without me, without his American friends. He knows what he has given up. That's why he refuses to believe I'm gone. He calls my leaving a trip. He insists on keeping up the rent on our apartment. He says he's keeping it for us. Do you know the premium there is on space in Rome? Can you count the thousands of homeless people, while no one in Rome, whether he lives in it or not, gives up his place? Well, I'm not going to plunder poor Italy. It's just not fair. Would you give Leo a letter for the landlord from me? You know how to talk sense to him. You would save me a painful, needless trip."

"Alice — " I was in a quandary because of something that had happened a few months ago. Something I couldn't tell her.

"What's wrong, Betsy?" Doug asked. It was the third evening that I had sat silent through dinner.

"I have a bad period."

I took a glass of wine and went upstairs. The Roman apartment had been my choice. Now we had a house in the city where we had met. We had taken the smallest room for our bedroom so that we could each have a roomy study. To make it look larger, everything but the icy blue rug was chalk white. I propped up some pillows and lay against them on the bed. Sipped my wine. Thought. Stared.

"What's on your mind?" Doug asked when he came up.

"Nothing."

"It's a very heavy nothing."

"I've just been thinking."

"Heavy thoughts?"

"I've been thinking about a lot of the things we don't talk about."

"Patience, Betsy. There's nothing wrong with either of us. We've been to doctors." He sat down on the bed like a doctor.

"It's the moon. Anyway, I wasn't thinking of the baby."

"Oh, no?"

"You sound angry."

"Why would I be angry, Betsy? I'm concerned."

"Concerned about us?"

"Concerned about you."

"Why are you concerned about me?"

"You know how nervous you can get. I don't want you going off the deep end."

"You make me sound as if I'm your patient or your child."

"Do I? I don't mean to."

"Yes, you do. I think we have problems, Doug. Not you. Not me. Us. The two of us, together."

"Name one." He was about to bring his lips to my sweater to wet his way to my nipple. I sat straight up.

"Sex," I said. "We've been married ten years. Ten years is a long time. Have you ever thought we both might need more freedom?"

"I've always thought we have all the freedom in the world. We travel where we want when we want to. You wanted your Ph.D.

You've just gotten it. We've waited to have a child. You've come and gone as you've pleased."

"I said 'sex,' Doug. Not career. Not house beautiful. Not the perfect couple. I mean, we have so much going for us. But maybe we should talk about sex."

"Don't I satisfy you, Betsy?"

It was a plea and it was an accusation. Doug's family had been in America a long time; mine had just come over. But we were raised according to the same ethic. Both Doug and I knew how fragile a man's ego was, how important it was for a woman to support it. His question was as far as we had ever gone in talking about sex.

"I'm thinking of Silas' trust fund," I said. Silas was one of his partners.

"What does money have to do with this?"

"It's not the money; it's Silas' great-grandfather. Remember how we've joked about the way he set the trust up? The money has to go through the male line and only through the children of the first wife."

"He was an archaic bastard."

"But his reason was that the first time a man marries, he marries for the right reasons; the second time, he marries for love. I'm thinking, Doug, maybe we're a bit like that. Wait! Wait! Don't misunderstand. I always thought meeting you was so ideal. It was me you sought, not my body. You were different from other men."

"I *am* different from other men. I've never been one of the boys. You know that. I never boasted I was a Don Juan — "

"I know."

"We have the same interests. Is that what you mean by marrying for the right reasons? If so, you're right. I married you for the right reasons and I'm happy I did."

"Are you happy, Doug?"

"Are you?"

"No."

"Well, what do you want now?"

"I don't know what I want. I want to talk."

"Talk, talk. Talk!"

"Doug, have you ever thought of going to bed with anyone else?"

"Have you?"

"I asked you first."

"What kind of question is that, Betsy? Of course not. I married you and I meant it."

"Okay, never mind. It never, ever entered your mind. Let's forget this. It's off on the wrong foot."

"Not so fast. You want to talk? Have you ever thought of going to bed with anyone else?"

"Yes."

"When?"

"In Rome."

"With whom?"

"Leo."

"Leo?"

"That's right. He was the most beautiful man I ever saw in my life. I thought about it."

"But you didn't do anything about it."

"No. I didn't have a chance."

"You mean, if you had had a chance, you would have done something?"

"Yes."

"Oh, Betsy, Betsy, don't say that."

"Why?"

"You don't mean it."

"What do you mean, I don't mean it? How can we talk together if you keep telling me what I mean? Don't you realize you're patronizing me?"

"I'd rather patronize you than tell you you're talking nonsense. Leo? Are you out of your mind? What does that man have?"

"It's the thirty seconds before he snores."

"What?"

"Never mind. *Never mind.* Don't you ever listen?" I had told him the story of poor Flora. I told him as if we were doing that much better than thirty seconds ourselves.

"What is it now, Betsy? You want more freedom. Do you want one of those open marriages they write about in *Cosmopolitan?* Do you want to be a *Cosmopolitan* girl? Do you want to run off to Italy and make love to a maintenance man?"

"Don't be so damn snide and condescending! Who made you the judge of the world?"

"Leo. Another one of your underdogs. Shades of your old friend Salmanda." Doug sighed and shook his head.

"What do you mean?"

"Salmanda at least had intelligence to recommend her. Or you say she had. Leo doesn't know art from his asshole. Never mind. Suffice it that he's an underdog."

"Art? What the hell does art have to do with it? Maybe you don't need art to make a baby. Maybe it's telling us something. Maybe all the dust on the old masters is bad for sperm!"

Doug blanched. Then clusters of red veins appeared in his cheeks. He began to shake. His fluctuating sperm count was sacrosanct.

"Bad joke, Doug."

Shaking, he looked around the room as if to find something to do. He stood up and slapped the wine glass out of my hand. The wine poured like menstrual blood on the white bedspread. I watched it soak in as he slammed out.

Later, I found him downstairs, sitting in the living room, his overcoat across his lap. I felt a terrible anger.

"You've kept me sane for ten years," he said. He looked at me red-eyed. He didn't say another word.

He didn't have to. A thunderbolt of guilt ripped through my heart and ricocheted through my body right down to the tips of my toes. "Stay here, Doug," I whispered. "Forgive me. Stay here."

And that was that. The name Leo was not mentioned between us again. And now he was insisting that I go to Rome with him.

Why? Was it a punishment? Was I to be in Leo's town and never mention Leo? Wasn't I well trained enough? What was the last trick of a learned mind? To stand at the very edge of the curb and not flinch when experience marches by? I had, then, no idea of my own dependencies, not to mention his. Doug manipulative? Why, no. He just did things right. It was I who screwed things up, who did things wrong.

So that day when Alice asked me to see Leo, I didn't know what to tell her. She was expecting me to say yes. Other people's expectations. The staple of my diet then. I told her I'd do what I could, but not to bring this up in front of Doug. Doug didn't like me to get involved.

I hoped she'd say, "Well, then, don't bother, dear. I don't want to cause you any trouble with Doug." All she said was "Thanks."

"I've been ridiculous," I told Doug in our hotel room in Rome.

"Do you still want him?" Doug asked.

"Oh, Doug. Can't you forgive my stupidity? Can't we forget all this nonsense? Won't you come with me?"

"I have business to do."

"Don't you want to see Leo?" Leo! There, I'd said it. I'd said it beyond the stab of guilt and regret I had felt in Boston every time Alice mentioned his name. Leo. "Don't you want to see Leo?"

"Not particularly."

"Why? Are you going to let some stupid thing I said ruin your friendship?"

"Friendship? What do we have in common? Our sperm count? You go see your friend. I'll go look at art."

"Why don't you rub it in?"

I saw Leo before he saw me. When I got out of the elevator, he was standing in the small lobby of the hotel, talking to the desk clerk.

"Betsy!" He opened his arms. "Let me look at you," he said after we hugged. "You're too thin. Don't they feed you in America?"

I looked at him. To me he was as handsome as ever, though he had broadened in the waist and the chest like a big shot. "You haven't changed."

"Ah, me." He smiled. "I'm dying."

"Still? You see? Some things haven't changed."

He kept one of his arms around me and we left the hotel, walking through the small side streets till we came to Piazza Navona.

"Isn't it wonderful?" I said as the immense oval of the piazza stretched out in front of us. "What a difference it makes, not allowing cars here." I thought, I'm not like Alice. Rome is still Rome to me.

"It's too quiet without the cars. I'm a traditionalist. I prefer the old ways."

"I bet."

We stopped in the middle of the piazza at the caffè opposite the Bernini fountain and the church façade. We sat down, ordered coffee, and began to talk. Immediately we were in sympathy, just as we had been that hot afternoon at the Caffè Greco so long ago. If I thought nothing had happened between us at the American Center a week before Cosimo's wedding, I was wrong. Unstated, it added emphasis to our reunion. It was something we shared.

I told him of my studies, my Ph.D., and of how parts of my Anita Garibaldi manuscript had been published as long articles in scholarly journals. How at last it would be published as a book. He talked about his work, about the union, about Marcella's successes all through the land. I didn't need Alice to tell me things were not going well between him and Marcella; that too was in the air.

He said he had just gotten a letter from Alice. She had written him about my success in finding jobs. I told him it hadn't mattered as much as I thought it would. I had been offered jobs in three universities for the fall: one in North Carolina, one in Lowell, one in New York.

"Which one are you going to take?"

"What do you mean? Lowell's near Boston. Which other one would I take?"

"Which one do you want to take?"

"If I were free, Leo, why if I were free, I'd go to New York." I looked down and saw that my fist was clenched.

"You remind me of someone," he said.

"Do I? Who?"

"Nick Russo."

"Really? Is there a resemblance? Are you joking? Do you know, I always had this feeling right from the first day we met that something about me reminded Alice of Nick Russo."

"Oh, yes. You could be his sister. So alike and yet so different. He took his opportunities. It was because of him that I learned about opportunities. I had no concept of them. Alice had to spell them out for me. Nick Russo, he had opportunities. And he took them. Alice never forgave him for that, any more than she ever forgave me. She won't forgive you either, Betsy. If you take your opportunities, that is."

"What are you talking about? What does this have to do with Alice? Of course I take my opportunities. Of course I take them. Alice knows that."

Leo warded off my words with his opened hand. "One minute," he said. "What job do you want to take?"

"Well, of course, if things were equal, the one in New York, but — "

"But nothing! Why the one in New York?"

"It's by far the best opp—— offer. And New York itself. Doug doesn't like it. But by myself, with my own income . . . I guess it's childish of me. I'd love an apartment there. I'd love to try it."

"Your face lights up. You look like you did the day I first met you, after Signor Sordi shot up your door."

"Do I? I was excited that day."

"As well you should have been, making the front pages of all the papers."

"You excited me."

"I'm an old man, Betsy."

"Leo, come on!"

"Listen to me! Nothing ages a man like a young wife."

"Then why did you marry her?"

"I had to."

"Why, was she pregnant?"

A strange expression came over his face. A confused look that was also amused. It struck me, right out of the clear blue Roman sky, that Carlino, the brat with the orange balloon, might be his.

"I had to," he repeated, the smile coming to the fore. "In life there are things one has to do."

I looked across the little table at Leo, and suddenly I knew something. Leo was a traveler. Without a knapsack, with a few coins in his pocket, and with the luck of his wide smile. I saw him walking through his city, I saw him walking through his life. Call it daring, call it crazy, call it dumb. He took his experience where he found it, carried it along with him. Pigheadedly, myopically, boldly, he refused to learn from it, had it, and went on. There was no plot to Leo's life, whether or not he and Marcella had a son. He lived his life as life conspired. He had to.

"I'm an old man, Betsy," he repeated. "An old man lives on his memories. I watched you work on your manuscript. Alice writes me of your success in America. She writes me you have something to say to me. You bring me her news. Forget her. You worry about you. Take your life. Live it! Things are going well with you. What are you waiting for? For things to go wrong? Do you think when you're older you'll get a second chance? I thought I would. But only Alice, only Alice gets second chances. And she does what she has always done, at fifteen, at twenty-five, at thirty-five, at fifty, now. She starts new lives. You! Don't you worry about delivering messages for her. I don't want to hear them. Do something for yourself. You think Alice cares for you? *I* care for you! Live your life. Opportunities! Do you think I'm blind? You have opportunities. Take them! Move somewhere else. Do what you want to do. Gain some weight! On the day you die no one's going to thank you for not living your life."

I looked out at the Bernini fountain that bordered him. I felt like the figure falling back. I swallowed and burned my throat.

"What about other people?" I murmured.

"They are other people. Come on!" he said, rolling out some of his traveler's coins. "Let's get out of here."

"You see?" Leo said in the apartment he and Alice had shared. "Everything's clean. No signs of Cosimo and Franca and their little son. You can report that!"

"Oh, Cosimo has a son? Good for him!"

"You didn't know? Alice didn't tell you?"

I avoided it. "But why would Alice think they were here?" At the same time I roamed from the small dining room into the small living room. I checked out the kitchen. No anchovies in oil. The place was sad without Alice. I opened the kitchen blinds and light flooded in.

"They're not there either!" Leo called.

"Whatever do you mean?" I asked, back in the living room. He was propped up on a daybed, with a pillow protecting the wall from his head.

"Come here," he said. He stretched his arms out to me without discomforting his sprawling body.

I took a look at him. One word would spoil it. I didn't say a word. I walked over and put my hands in his. He was so easy with his body. He drew me down next to him. I felt my heart tumbling. He kissed me slowly. His lips, his tongue, insinuating the language he knew. It was as if we had all the time in the world. As we kissed I could feel the edges of his irregular teeth. I could taste his smile.

He undressed me. Again, slowly, insinuatingly. He wanted me naked and him dressed. His hands, his mouth, all over my body. I was the sprawling one when he disentangled himself from my legs and stood up. I could see myself imprinted on his raw mouth. I watched him undress. I saw his cock. At attention. When he brought it to me he let me touch it first, then he put it in my mouth. He was incredibly hard. The excitement grew even more fierce. When he entered me I began to have orgasm right away. And no amount of my coming satisfied him. He went on and on and on until we both hit the biggest wave of all and drowned.

We fell asleep together and woke up together too. I said, So it's true. There's a place beyond ourselves where man and woman meet. He said, Is there any way at all we can spend a few days together?

Leo and I went to Florence, because it was a train ride away. I always felt Doug knew I wasn't at Gaeta. We took a room with a bath and didn't give a damn about the view.

And something extraordinary happened to me in those three days. I prayed I'd get pregnant by Leo, and that opened me up physically in an entirely new way. No caution, no diaphragm, no rhyme or reason. Our three days in Florence. We'd walk out at night and cross the Ponte Vecchio, which, with Leo's arm around me, was simply a bridge, a link to an area where we could eat. And when we stopped at the first trattoria that could seat us, we weren't looking for atmosphere and the best deal. We just needed a place to get food, drink wine, and talk. Nothing I ever do again, fully clothed, guidebook in hand, will match those days in Florence with Leo.

Those three days naked with Leo in a hotel room. Sprawled together on a messy bed. Compressing everything we wanted from each other into the only time we had. Naked, wet, hair tangled, I was given an intimation of someone I didn't know very well — me. That's who Leo was looking at and talking about. So close to him, I counted specifically. Leo saw me.

I told him I'd probably go to the Center and say hello to Nano when I got back to Rome.

"Nano! That cretin!" Leo, naked, looked angry.

"You call the hero of the American Center a cretin?" I attempted, stretching.

"Some hero."

"He was brave."

"Brave? It was like war. It doesn't count."

"What do you mean?"

"In war certain people rise to recklessness. They cannot help it. It's in their glands. It's adrenaline!" He brought his hand to his forehead and saluted. "When they come to their senses, they commend themselves. 'I killed a nineteen-year-old boy and a woman!' Me, I'm comfortable with a man who runs."

"Really, Leo."

"Save your own skin. What does the cretin get for his murders? A swelled head he can hardly hold up."

"A sense that he protected the American Center."

"Let him take it home to bed with him."

"What do you have against Nano, anyway?"

"He once got me out of prison."

I did not laugh at this audacity. Leo looked in my eyes. Brushed my hair back. "You knew? Of course you knew. Leave it to the Daughter of the American Revolution. Or did Nano tell you?"

"He just shakes his head and says, 'Leo Conti, he's a phenomenon, that man.'"

Leo brightened. He liked that. "Remember when you were offered that job under him and you worried about the money?"

"I sure do."

"I didn't think you should have taken that job. A girl like you, who makes such good iced tea."

"Oh, great. The Madonna of the Terrace. I should have stayed home to be there in between your adventures with Marcella and Alice. I should have stayed home, your virgin, to comfort you."

He smiled and hugged me. "To comfort yourself," he whispered in my ear. "You didn't need more facts, you didn't need any more old letters. You should have gone to Gaeta and sat on the beach. Or walked around Rome as on the day I met you and we went to the Caffè Greco together. The day half of Rome was following you. Droves of ugly geese gawking after one white swan."

"And you thought I had seen you. You were probably with Marcella, right? You thought I'd tell Alice you weren't at any meeting."

"Yes, that too. But I was also a hero, no? I scattered all the ugly little geese who were after you." He didn't say any more. Brought me to him, instead.

We made love for the last time the day before I left Rome, in Alice's living room. Afterward, I lay down on his naked lap, pushing my hair away so that I could feel his prick against the nape of my neck. I looked up at him, then traced the fine hairs of his chest. "I'm going to miss you. Terribly," I said. He didn't answer.

"Leo, did Alice say anything about Doug and me in her letters? Did she say we weren't getting along?"

"She said you didn't seem happy. But she didn't have to tell me."

"No?"

"No."

"Well, nothing's going right between us. You know, we hardly talk. It's all my fault."

"Is that what he has you believing? Lucky man."

"What do you mean?"

Leo shrugged.

"Don't you like Doug?"

"Do you? That's what's important, Betsy. Do you?"

"He annoys the hell out of me. I know he shouldn't, but he does."

"And why shouldn't he?"

"He's so much better a person than me."

Leo put his head back and laughed. I found myself confronting his Adam's apple. "What's so funny?"

"Next time, Betsy, don't pick so well!"

My head on his lap, I felt him getting hard again. "See what I mean?" he said. And we made love again.

Later we were both sitting on that couch. I kissed him on the cheek, I touched his hair. Now at the edge of the time we had, I wanted much more. After all, perhaps both our lives were changing. "Leo," I said quietly, "you know, don't you, that Alice isn't coming back."

"Betsy, don't tell me you still believe Alice. Don't you realize by now that she lies?"

"She doesn't lie, Leo. In fact, you must know I have a letter she'd like delivered to the landlord. She wants to give up the apartment. She thinks it's foolish for you to keep paying the bills."

"She's afraid I'll let Cosimo move in behind her back."

"I don't know a thing about this. Perhaps for a minute you can be less personal. Cosimo is one of many who can't find a place to live in Rome. That's because people hold on to apartments they no longer use."

"I use it!"

I looked at him and shook my head. "Alice said that for a long time Italy was good for her, and now she wants to leave in accordance with Italian law."

"Italian law? What does she know about Italian law? Where did she find this animal? Has she ever seen it?"

"I guess she'd like to enforce it. She'd like to do the legal thing, which is to give up her apartment, since she is no longer living in it. And the deposit — she wants the deposit given over to you."

He slapped his forehead. "The deposit! A few pieces of caramel! No one has small change to give out anymore. She knows nothing about Italian law. She knows nothing about how much an apartment costs in Rome today. Do you know what a landlord will pay to get back an apartment like ours? Does she know what an apartment like ours is worth today? You give her a message from me. You tell her to come back to Rome and turn over her place personally. If she doesn't want me to have it, I, in my turn, will not stand by and let her lose her money. Let her come back to Rome, go to Zamparelli personally, and collect the two milioni he'll be happy to pay out, if she's so foolish to hand back her keys!"

"Two milioni?"

"Conservative estimate. It's worth at least that for Zamparelli to get rid of her. Do you know what he can rent a place like this for? You go back and tell her that!"

Leo stood up abruptly. He paced, looked around for something to do. Picked up his pants and put them on. Buttoned the fly. "She's a fool!" he bellowed finally. "Why doesn't she take what life has to offer? Her apartment costs nothing. *I'm* in Rome. Why doesn't she live out her life among friends? Why doesn't she live out her life here?"

"I don't think she feels she's wanted here, Leo. As an American . . . even as a friend."

"Absurd! She lies. Didn't I always come to visit her?" For the first time since I knew him, he expected something from walls. Sad walls, drab and streaked without Alice's favorite pictures. He spread his arms. "Aren't I always here?"

I had trouble breathing. "So you still love Alice?" I forced myself to ask compassionately.

"Che miseria," he answered. "Yes."

Two weeks later, in a different world, yet still feeling a stab of fire, I sat with Doug outdoors at a small restaurant in the North End.

"Doug," I said, "I spoke with Martin Gruber in New York."
"Oh?"

"They still haven't filled the nineteenth-century slot."

"It's amazing, what with so many people on the market."

"It's simply good luck."

"Good luck?"

"I have something to tell you. It's not easy. I mean, things have not been going well between us. You see that. You've hardly talked to me since Rome. I think this is what we both need."

"Betsy, what are you trying to say?"

"I'm taking the job in New York."

"What?"

"I'm just going to offer my apologies to Lowell. I'm not going to come out of this looking very good, but I've got to do what I've got to do."

He sighed. "What next? Don't you think you're high-strung enough without commuting to New York every week? And tell me, what about your research? With all that travel, how will you ever get things done? I don't even mention conceiving. The way you're acting, you seem to be relying on an immaculate conception, anyway."

"Not exactly."

He looked confused.

"Forget it," I said. "I can feel my period coming down."

"Well, then, will you bite my head off if I say perhaps, just perhaps, this New York thing is your period talking?"

"No, I won't bite your head off. And I won't be commuting. I'm going to take an apartment in New York for the academic year."

"Never a dull moment. You mean you're going to take a job, you're going to take an apartment, without consulting me?"

"I had to act fast. I did accept a job, and I think I already have an apartment. Martin's getting me a sublet — a fellow going on leave."

"Sight unseen? Did you have a chance to ask about noise?"

"Frankly, my darling, I don't give a damn!"

"Just what does that mean?"

"Forget it!"

"Who's the man?"

"If there were a man, would you find a way to make me go to bed with him?"

"And just what does that mean?"

"It means my nerves are shot. I don't want to say it this way. What I believe is, this is best for both of us; let's give ourselves some time. What do you say?"

"What do I say? This has nothing at all to do with me. It's you who are deciding. Do what you want."

I did what I wanted. The exhilaration of the next months was incredible. My furnished studio apartment in New York, my work at the university, a life of my own. I expected I'd come down with a disease, doing what I wanted. Instead, I found a new source of energy. I thought, or fooled myself into thinking, that all of this change might bring Doug and me back together. Then there was that day when, returning to my sublet, I found a lawyer's letter waiting for me. Doug was suing me for divorce, claiming desertion.

"Why didn't you tell me?" I asked him over the phone.

"I told you I wanted you to come home when we spent Thanksgiving in New York, and I told you by letter as well."

"You know I wouldn't leave in the middle of a school year. I was coming home next weekend. Why didn't you wait?"

"I've been fair with you, Betsy. I could have claimed adultery. I know what happened in Rome."

"Oh, you do, do you? If you think you know so much, why didn't you try to stop it?"

"It was up to you."

"Was it? You had nothing to do with it? You're so pure!"

"Don't make any trouble or you'll see how pure I am!"

"Why would I give you any trouble? We haven't had a relationship for years. What proves it more than your doing this behind my back? If we'd talked about it, we could have avoided lawyers' fees."

"Do you have a lawyer?"

"Doug, I just got the notice. I thought I'd call you first and see what's up. I've never been sued before. I haven't deserted you. I've left for a year. Why did you do this? Why not mutual consent?"

"Have your lawyer contact my lawyer."

I spoke to a new friend of mine at the law school, Caroline. "Well, since he's initiated the action, I'd say he wants the house."

"Oh, no. Not Doug. He'd be fair. The house would be the last thing on his mind."

Caroline has big green eyes. They sparkle when she smiles. "Now you really do sound like a wife!"

He wanted the house, all the contents, everything in our mutual savings account, half of whatever I earned on my Anita Garibaldi book, and a portion of my salary. He contended it was through his support that I had gotten a job and had been able to write.

I made an appointment with the divorce lawyer Caroline recommended. She was in the Lincoln Law Building. I got there early and in the vestibule of the skyscraper I saw the significance of its name. There on a pedestal was a small model of Daniel Chester French's Lincoln, the one in the Lincoln Memorial. I've always loved that statue, the grave look on Lincoln's long, downward-gazing face. If I had been with Doug, this would have been the find that justified the building. It would have been more important than the teeming commerce of the place. Our joint interests began, I often thought, just where other couples' left off. Well, I wasn't with Doug. I sighed, patted Honest Abe as if he were St. Peter's foot, and went over to the directory to check my lawyer's floor.

Something on the directory caught my eye. I went back to it. I was used to this feeling. On handwritten indexes and in card catalogues certain sources often seemed to stand out for me. Blake, I read. Blake, Salmanda. Well, I'll be. No. No, it's impossible.

"Is Salmanda Blake in?" I asked the receptionist. The company name on the door was Fleisher Drugs.

"Do you have an appointment?"

"No. Actually, I was wondering if it's the same Salmanda Blake I went to school with. If you simply tell her Betsy Lewis is here, that will settle that."

The receptionist looked up from the intercom. "Won't you sit down a moment, please? Miss Blake will be right out."

I sat down. My heart was thumping in my chest.

I didn't know from which entrance she'd appear, and I didn't want to. I picked up a pharmaceutical journal.

"Betsy!" I heard her voice first. Not *Behhtsy*, but "Betsy Lewis! Is it really you?"

A very tall, thin black woman in a burgundy suit came over to me. She was wearing a creamy silk blouse. Her hair was in a short clipped natural and she wore golden earrings, complete circles. I stood up. I looked into her almond-shaped eyes. "Salmanda!"

We were in each other's arms. I felt cashmere and wool as I pictured Duke's squalid room. The validity of the past is an emotion.

"Come on in, Betsy. Milly, hold my calls, will you? Unless it's Pierson. Let me know that. Thanks."

Her voice was careful and cool. It was not Bronx gone to Harvard, but it did have that slight nasal audacity of an East Coast intellectual whose parents hadn't been. The modification of voice was as startling as the modification of appearance. I would not have recognized her, this elegant, middle-aged woman. The air about her wasn't the same, the air of efficiency, sophistication. But had I ever pictured her in the Lincoln Law Building, in her own office, behind her bulky desk? Well, she didn't sit behind her desk. We sat at her coffee table. I noticed there that her plain, low-heeled black shoes gaped slightly and could use some polish.

"You haven't changed, Betsy."

By then I wasn't painfully thin, and I certainly had a storehouse of unlived life to keep me looking young. In terms of career, I was going, finally, in the direction I'd set. Where, before I saw the name on the register, had I expected to find Salmanda? Working another night shift? Scrubbing floors? I had left Salmanda the more complete victim of the fifties — I thought. All I had to do was look at my old friend to realize the deepest mystery of history. I don't care whether we call it zeitgeist, fad, fashion, dialectic.

"I think I've changed, Salmanda. I'm living here in New York. I'm divorcing my husband. No. I should be divorcing my husband. But it turns out he's divorcing me."

"That Doug?"

"You remember his name!"

"Betsy and her fellows."

"Yes, it's been one mad romantic whirl."

"Look at that smile. I swear you're still a teen-ager."

"What about you, Salmanda?"

"I guess except for an occasional whirl with the bottle and someone nicknamed Fire, I've put aside my childish ways."

"You sure seem to have. By the way, what the hell do you do here?"

"I know. I should be in the lab."

"I never said that."

"I started there. Now I'm head of technical personnel."

"No kidding!"

"You should see the look on some of the fellows' faces when they walk in here, all buttoned up, and take a look at me. What a place to find affirmative action."

"Does it cost them the job?"

"If it did, I wouldn't be head of technical personnel."

"Fleisher Drugs must be one hell of a shrewd company."

"It's better, you better believe it!" She parodied the Fleisher commercial, including me in on an office joke.

"By the way, Betsy, what the hell are you doing here?"

"You better believe it. I'm here to see my divorce lawyer, one Patricia Cass, and I see your name on the directory as big as life. I think to myself, Could it be? Why, the last time I saw Salmanda . . ."

"I know. The last time you saw me I was going to jail."

"Oh!"

"Don't worry, don't worry. Don't look so concerned, Betsy. I never did go to jail."

"Whew!"

"It was 'whew!' Say, Betsy, you want some coffee? You still have a thing for doughnuts?"

"What a memory! I thought mine was good. No, I gotta go, babe. I have a very expensive meeting. Have you heard of this Patricia Cass?"

"No, but I know it's expensive to keep up this building. When are you free for dinner? I want to take you out."

"Tonight, tomorrow, the day after. As soon as possible, Salmanda. But you don't have to take me."

"Say that after you see Lawyer Cass."

Salmanda went to her desk, looked at her calendar, and we made a date for the following week.

"I never walk through the park at night," Salmanda said, after picking me up at my apartment. She wanted to take me to an Italian place on Thompson Street.

"Hey, come on, Salmanda."

"No, I mean it. Washington Square's changed."

"Then how come every time I go through it, I think of you, I think of me, I think of us?"

"Because your professorial mind's some place else, somewhere on a higher plane. You don't notice those Jamaican boys selling 'ludes and loose joints."

"They don't bother me."

"Well, they bother me. You'd better be careful you don't get hassled."

"I'm no dope, Salmanda. I'm careful. But I don't think Washington Square's changed. I think all the great places stay the same. I think we change."

She sure had. She knew Italian food almost as well as I, though for a moment arugula stumped her. And at a subsequent brunch, my treat, we both knew what we wanted. We were both thirty-five minutes and light years away from Passaic, effortlessly versed in Black Forest ham omelettes with Brie, spinach salads, quiches of the day, French toast made with challah. Though the night at the Italian restaurant, it was more noticeable that she could order fried calamari, which was not on the menu, and that she insisted on the Barolo red. She liked red even with fish, she said. And now, years away from the Albani hills and the Roman white, so did I.

She was wearing jeans and boots and a light blue turtleneck sweater. A heavy gold chain hung around her neck. This time, she wore gold earrings shaped like pearls. They added a certain grandeur to her tight-skinned, high-cheekboned face. Slim as she was, she was no longer the boyish athlete. She was too sophisticated for basketball.

"I'm sorry," I said when she confirmed that Auntie was gone.

"She wasn't herself the last years of her life. I don't think I helped her any, though goodness knows I was there at the end."

"I'm sure you helped. She was so proud of you."

"My being arrested didn't help her." She paused. "Of course, she knew it was whitey's fault. If she guessed any more about me, she didn't admit it. But I always had a feeling at the end that she knew. I mean, she knew her people went to jail. That was part of what she wanted to save me from. It's me. I never got over the arrest."

I looked at my old friend. I said, "I know."

"You always knew. Betsy, I didn't believe they could do what they did to me. Arrest me. Treat me the way they did. Get me kicked out of school. You know, I think a lot about my little town in Georgia lately. My mother raised six of us, and she raised us to know we were as good as anyone. Segregation? Well, I'll tell you, it was a funny town. One day, right before I came north, I was in town. It was very hot, and I decided I wanted an ice cream soda. So I go into the pharmacy and sit right down at the fountain. And don't forget this is before civil rights had a name. I don't care if it's white only. I'm Salmanda Blake. Mr. Higgins knows me since I'm born. I ask for a strawberry ice cream soda, please."

"No black and white? Sorry."

"Very funny. I didn't want to be that obvious. Mr. Higgins doesn't blink an eye; he fixes me one. Then, you know what he does? Lord, Behhtsy, I think about this a lot now. I must be getting old, even though you're not. While I'm eating my ice cream and drinking my soda, he's unscrewing all the other seats at the counter. The whole place closes down so I can be served. Discrimination? What a joke. I had to come north to understand it. You were right about the North. You always used to warn me. How ever did you know so much?"

"I don't think I knew much. That's what I've been thinking about lately. How much I didn't know, growing up, getting married. You know, I tried to call you when I was getting married. Up to now I'd forgotten that you even knew I was going with Doug. I thought I reached Auntie. But she hung up. She hung up; I gave up."

"She wasn't all there the last years. It wasn't pretty. You want some more wine?"

"Sure. I'm sorry. She was such a good woman. She knew a lot. You could see it in her face."

"What she knew was taken away from her at the end. Anyway,

I figured you'd be getting married to that straight type, Doug. It wouldn't have been news to me."

"It seemed the right choice, up here."

"You always did have a good head."

"Don't rub it in."

"Don't look so sad. We went our ways. My lawyer found out good old Vinny didn't even have a liquor license. The powers that be were so busy hushing that up that I never did go to jail. Maybe she don' go. Remember the record shop on Eighth Street where we used to listen to Odetta?" Salmanda laughed her old deep-throated laugh.

"They don't have sound booths anymore."

"Sound booths? Of course not. Where have you been, girl?"

"Away."

"You've become quite a traveler."

"No more than you."

She had been like Leo in the beginning. She had picked up and gone down along her road. But experience had taught her something, made her wary, and kept her thin.

She missed my meaning. "Oh," she said, "I don't have time to travel anymore."

"When did you?"

"Right after I was acquitted. Before I went back to school. I was so bitter, Betsy. Just plain old bitter and drinking too hard. That reminds me, let's order that wine. I don't drink hard liquor anymore. Well, there was this Constance and her friend Joyce. Two middle-aged ladies from Holland. You remember Holland, don't you, Betsy, the home of the dykes? They just fell all over me. Couldn't do enough for me. Anyway, I was in the middle of a disastrous affair. That Gail, the same one I got in trouble with, was down on her luck and came back. Constance and Joyce, they just begged to take me to Europe. They'd pay and all. After Gail did me dirt, I went."

"When was that?"

"Right after President Kennedy was assassinated. That's all anyone asked about."

"Before me. I was there for the next round of assassinations. Where'd you go?"

"Name it."

"Italy? Rome?"

"I spent a month in Rome. You should have seen where we stayed. We had this old queen's penthouse right near the Spanish Steps all to ourselves."

"You want to hear something? I have this very good friend in Rome. Leo. I used to talk a lot about you, you know. Out of sight, but definitely not out of mind. Well, one day he tells me he's seen you. I'd say this was nineteen seventy. He said he saw you with two white women, right at the Spanish Steps. He tried to get your attention, but you didn't understand him."

"I didn't understand any of them. The men there do not quit. I swear I couldn't walk down a street without everyone eyeing me, curious as can be. And they didn't care if you caught them at it. I was even an extra in a movie while I was there. They had a call out for blacks. I liked it there. I felt I could stay."

"I felt that way too."

"But I came back. Did what I could for Auntie."

"Funny, I wonder if Leo really did see you. I bet years ago he really did."

"All I can tell you, Betsy, is if I passed by his eyes, he'd remember."

"I'll bet."

"Did you like him?"

"Did I? I do. Very much. Without him, I doubt I'd be here now. He gave me something, call it advice. He changed my life."

"You stuck on him?"

I shrugged. "It wouldn't matter. He was, is, I don't know which, the lover of my friend Alice. She's over there now with him. Straightening out her affairs. I wonder what he'll tell her. Whatever. I have no regrets . . . I guess."

"Same old Betsy."

"How?"

"Wrapping yourself round some guy."

"Salmanda," I said, deciding to joke it away, "believe me, he was worth the wrapping."

"I can see that."

"Enough of me. After you came back, you went back to school?"

"That's right. Things were different then. I had a choice, three schools, three scholarships. I chose Rutgers Newark."

"What did you do about Englehurst?"

"Forgot it. Transferred some credits over later on."

"Clever."

"Oh, they would have shut their eyes to my troubles there, anyway. They really wanted me."

"Things have changed in this country."

"Yes," Salmanda said. Her eyes glinted. "In this year of our Lord, it's easier for a black man to be a brain surgeon than a construction worker. It doesn't do much for the unemployment rate."

❦ II ❦

When Alice and I were in Rome together, we used to joke about how "busy" Americans became once they went home. With so much to do, there was hardly time to write letters. But I did find time to write to Alice when she went back to Rome. I wrote to her of meeting Salmanda, of my courses at school, of my new research on nineteenth-century revolutionary lovers, of the progress of my divorce. I wrote to her about my divorce lawyer, Patricia Cass, and of how she had connected me to a literary agent. It was to Alice I wrote when I signed a book contract. On the basis of what I had already completed of *Revolutionary Lovers*, I got a cash advance!

Alice answered, full of her own adventures, and acknowledged, with relish, my description of meeting Salmanda again. She didn't say a word about my book contract. About opportunities, had Leo been right? I wondered if she always associated success with the deviousness of her mother. I felt very uneasy. For there in Rome, Alice had good enough reason for suspecting me. Still, I was relieved by the easy flow of her letters. Leo hadn't said anything. Leo.

There'd be evenings I'd sit in my sublet, looking at the off-white walls that needed to be painted, drinking Russian vodka straight up and cold. After I stared long enough, the wall in front of me loomed like an overcast sky or a dingy ghost. The wall included the past, the present, and all that would be. I wondered if this was what Alice was looking at the day I met her, the day she was staring at Garibaldi's wall. It was on nights like this that I brought my drink over to my desk and wrote her letters. There must have been a strange intensity to them. "Send my best to Leo, this letter is for him too."

When Alice returned from Rome, she was off to Saratoga Springs to visit friends. I wasn't able to see her during the few days she'd been in New York. I was in the process of moving into my own new illegal sublet, marking exams, seeing my lawyer. I had turned busy. Over the phone I asked about her trip, and found myself annoyed when she told me that sooner or later she'd have to go back again. "You *have* to, Alice?" I asked pointedly. This was a few months after I had begun analysis with Dr. Gianetti. Caroline had recommended her. "Why, yes, dear. Things are still not settled. By the way, Leo sends his love."

How did she mean that?

In early September Alice came to New York. By then, Salmanda knew the whole story. I told her how uneasy I felt about seeing Alice. I didn't know what Leo had told her. "Bring Alice here for dinner," Salmanda said, though I hadn't been to her place before. "Neutral ground. Don't worry about a thing. Fire loves to cook."

Alice rang my bell promptly. I paused, breathed deep before I answered the door. When I look back at it now, I wonder whether Alice was uneasy too, for we seemed to meet on a level of confusion. She was in the hall, encumbered by two plastic bags labeled STANDA and a wide-brimmed hat. We couldn't embrace. "Let me take these for you," I said. "No, no," she said as she walked in.

She put the two bags down on my table. She extracted her

pocketbook from one. This concealment was an antimugging device. She fished in the other until she found what she was looking for. She unrolled a slightly damaged poster. "I found it in this condition, can you imagine, Betsy? Do you think Salmanda would like it? I didn't know what to bring. Or do you think you'd like to hang it here?" She stood in my apartment in her antique hat and her three-season coat. Her bright museum poster unfurled, she smiled at her luck. "Once it's framed," she said, "these few creases will relax."

Salmanda owned a brownstone in Brooklyn. There was a steep stairway to the front door. She met us at the top. She was in a khaki jumpsuit that added bulk to her body and made her belted waist appear even more slender. You had to remark the startling blackness of her long neck and her fine-boned face. She reached to shake Alice's extended hand. "I've heard so much about you," she said. "And I've heard so much about you," Alice answered.

Salmanda led us into the house and then down the stairs to the dining room and kitchen. Past the kitchen, there were sliding glass doors that opened on a garden.

Fire was by the stove. She didn't look more than twenty-two or -three. Extremely pretty. She was big-breasted and at the same time tomboyish in her jeans and T-shirt. She had extraordinary large fiery blue eyes — lit up by her bushy black eyebrows and curly mop of purple-highlighted black hair. I had had no idea before meeting her that Fire was white. How could I? I hadn't seen Salmanda that much, but one night she came over when she was really down in the dumps. It was during one of her many breaks with Fire, and she was regretting the past. "You know, Salmanda, you're very hard on yourself. That's the way I've always been. But Dr. Gianetti, she's really helping me. Have you ever thought of analysis?"

"Well, if I ever did, you'd better believe it wouldn't be with anyone white."

"No? You think it would matter?"

"Would it matter? Do you think a white woman could understand me? There are some things — some hurts — you can know only if you're black."

As Salmanda brought me over to introduce me, I wondered whether Fire was a nickname because of her eyes, or whether it was because Salmanda was playing with Fire.

"And this is my friend Alice Blanders Russo," I said after I was introduced. Fire had been almost mockingly shy, saying hello to me. Now, an uncomprehending look came into Fire's eyes.

I avoided it.

"What a beautiful space, Salmanda," I said.

"It's been a lot of work, but the minute I saw this house, I had to have it."

"Do you know what this downstairs kitchen reminds me of?"

"Sure. Auntie's place. Here, come, look at this." We followed her to the refrigerator. She opened its freezer door. There was an ice machine spitting out cubes. "Big or small? What's your pleasure? I don't know what it is about these gizmos that makes me buy them."

"So you can show them off!" Fire said.

Alice stood by the open refrigerator door, feeling the cold come out and watching the electricity consumed. I felt guilty about Salmanda's refrigerator, as if it somehow implicated me. At the same time I was glad I told Alice I'd keep the poster and we'd bring my bottle of Spumanti from the both of us. "Put this in," I said, handing Salmanda the bottle. "It's for later."

"What do you want to drink, Alice?"

"What are you offering?"

"Everything."

"Some white wine would be nice, if you don't have to open a bottle."

I wonder if Alice had a sixth sense with that request. She had to settle for vermouth.

She took her glass over to the sliding door. "My goodness," she said, "what a nice garden." I joined her. In Italy, we would have sat out and chatted. We both looked at the garden with nostalgia. Salmanda called out, "Here's your drink,

Betsy. Come on, I'll show you two around."

"What do you think of the rat trap?" Fire asked, when we had settled in the living room. She'd come up with a tray of cheeses and put it on the coffee table around which we sat.

"Fire likes the country," Salmanda said apologetically.

"Where are you from, Fire?" I asked.

"Everywhere and nowhere. Not here, that's for sure." She walked over to the front windows.

"Well," I said, "these cheeses look delicious."

Salmanda brightened. "There's no place like Dean and De-Luca."

"Nor are there such prices. Though I must say, in Rome, now, Betsy, everything is going up. You should see what cheese costs. It's outrageous. I don't know how people live."

"Oh, well, it's for friends," Salmanda said modestly.

Alice looked at Salmanda knowingly. I remembered her saying of Bev in Rome, Of course it's easy to cook if you can throw in a pound of butter.

"I didn't ask about the cheese," Fire said. "I asked about the trap." She gave up the windows, came over and sat down.

"You mean the house," I answered. "It's a beauty. The woodwork, the staircase — "

"It reminds me of my old brownstone — " Alice started.

"It wouldn't be a bad idea for you to look for something to buy in the city, Betsy," Salmanda said. "Right now, while the market's still a little off."

"Not real estate, Salmanda!" I turned to Alice. I wished we were talking of something else. Say Martin Luther King. Then I joked with the truth. "Real estate, Alice, is *the* conversation in New York."

"I'm serious," Salmanda continued. "There are ways of doing it without having to put that much down."

"Real estate." Alice sighed. "You know, Salmanda, it's difficult for me to realize now that I once owned a brownstone in New York."

"Can you imagine what it would be worth today?" Salmanda said. "Alice, you should have held on."

Alice smiled. "Now, I couldn't even rent here. Why, I thought the apartment situation was complicated, not to say corrupt, in Rome. You know, I have such a nice apartment there, Salmanda . . ."

And Alice was off. I watched her, sitting on the couch, her skirt spread around her, her long thin hands on her lap. I saw the compassionate look in Alice's eyes as her face reflected the tragedy of her story. Alice sailed away from sound systems and fuzz busters, perpetual ice cube makers and a full bar except for white wine. She spoke of Italy, of postwar poverty, and of the scandals of the construction industry there. She knew what she was talking about. I wondered how many articles she had clipped from magazines and papers and added to her mind and to her files. As she spoke of the mysterious fires that burned the way for the Cavaliere Hilton, as she spoke of all the walls of the modern Roman apartments that amplified your neighbors' sounds, she interwove the story of Leo.

That was her magic, I thought, though I had heard these stories before. They had befriended me. She was a born historian, tracking her own seemingly modest path of passion and intrigue through the wars, poverty, and desolation of her times. The magic of Alice was that when you first met her, you slowly became engulfed by the vastness of her experience and her knowledge. As she talked, I kept hoping she'd somehow tell us all. Here was the Alice I had met in the American Center's back gardens. Show Salmanda, show Fire, what I've always seen in you.

I looked at Salmanda. She seemed entranced. I saw her become intense, almost anxious in her absorbed concentration. But she was looking at Fire. And Fire suddenly stood up.

"Where you going, babe?"

"You listen. I gotta cook."

Salmanda said into the dead silence left in Fire's wake, "Fire's nervous about her meal. Excuse me, Alice. What was that you were saying?"

Dinner was a disaster. First of all, Fire couldn't cook. She knew she couldn't cook, which was why, during this particular reconciliation with Salmanda, she had to do it. I got the feeling that the taste of the scorched rice, the occasional bite of the raw garlic in the paella, were saying, "See! It's not enough that I try." Salmanda made it worse by saying, "Boy, baby, this is good."

"No, it's not. Yours is better."

"This is really good. Ask Betsy."

Thanks, Salmanda. I looked at Fire. "It's good, fresh food. And food's food. My almost ex-husband was such a gourmet that he used to drive me crazy with perfection. Tell me, how are things coming with your work? Salmanda tells me you're going into modeling?"

"Lousy," she said. "Things are lousy. I'm no brown nose, and in this town you've gotta suck — brown-nose if you want to get ahead. Anyway, I'm no model, really."

"I know just what you mean, Fire," Alice said. "I had my opportunities for a life like that."

"You?" Fire asked in total disbelief.

"Yes, as ludicrous as it apparently sounds." And Alice shut down. The only Alice Fire saw was the one in front of her eyes. She did not come to her with a full mind. Alice was my friend. And I was the middle-aged friend of Fire's middle-aged lover, someone who had introduced her to an old lady in a hat.

I looked at Alice, past the silverware, the tablecloth, the good wine, the botched meal on expensive plates. Was she thinking, Who is this Salmanda? Who is this Betsy? I saw recrimination in her eyes. Was it for tonight? Was it for Leo? The candlelight flickered over her face and her neck. She wet her full lips, smiled slightly at me, and lowered her eyes to her plate.

Back in the living room, Alice excused herself to go upstairs to the bathroom. "I think we should be going soon," I said. Salmanda said, "Come on, let's have some cognac first."

Fire rolled her eyes. "Can we smoke in front of your friend?" she asked.

"Of course," I said. "Does she look like a narc?"

Alice took her time, as I knew she would. When I heard her on the stairs, we had finished the joint. I was more mellow, and the cognac was tasting exceptionally good.

I watched Alice descend the stairs. She was slow and she had her bearings. Was she following after the image of a former life or the stiff body of her father? She came back to us, sat down, watched Salmanda pour her drink. When it was handed to her, she didn't say thank you; she said, "Nothing but the best."

Fire stood up.

Salmanda yelled, "Relax, will you? I'll put the dishes in later."

"I need some cigarettes. I'm going out."

"Nothing's open."

"I'll take a walk."

"Wait for me. We'll take one later."

"Alice and I should be going."

"Drink your drink!"

"You guys stay," Fire said. "You've got stuff to talk about."

There was some relief in her wake. Salmanda poured herself another cognac. "You have to excuse Fire. She gets very nervous. I told you, she's been shy about meeting you, Betsy, you being a professor and all."

"Oh, damn! Did I talk too much about the Risorgimento again?"

Salmanda threw back her head and laughed. "Betsy and I go back a long way," she said to Alice. "You want to hear something?" She got up and went over to her elaborate sound system. "Remember this?" she asked, pulling out the old Odetta album.

"Remember it? I still have the one you gave me. That is, if Doug doesn't repossess it. Put it on." I turned to Alice. "That's the record I told you about. The story of my youth. Salmanda, can you find 'Maybe She Go'? I want Alice to hear it."

> There's somethin' that say she stay where she be
> Somethin' say go
> But nothin' that say what somethin' will be best
> Nothin' she know of.

I asked Alice, "What do you think of it?"

"Why, it's very nice, dear."

Salmanda was back on the couch and we were both listening to the song as if we needed something from it. I needed something I could cup in my hands and show Alice. What was I trying to find? What was I trying to show?

"I want to hear that again." I got up, went over to the turntable, and carefully returned to the song.

> Maybe she go
> Maybe she don' go
> Many a time she afraid to go
> Many she do go.

Salmanda laughed. She poured more drinks. "Remember, girl? Remember the first day I saw you, Behhtsy? Alice, she walked into the cafeteria of Horace High with Paul D'Amato. You keep up with him, Behhtsy?"

"God, no. I'm amazed you remember his name."

"I remember everyone from Horace High." And Salmanda showed us, recalling names, incidents. She had a kind, happy look on her face. Once more she was the basketball player, the class joker, the matchmaker, the class wit, the scientist, the example of her race, the lithe boy.

"You walked in with Paul and I thought . . . you know what I thought, Alice? I thought, That girl's so pretty. And then she turned out so nice and so smart. I sure remember those days. They were the best. Do you remember, Behhtsy?"

"I remember a lot," I said. "How young I was. How naïve."

"We were going to save the world," Salmanda told Alice. "Behhtsy here's still trying. But I, I've done nothing."

"How can you say that, Salmanda? How can you sit there after all you've done and say that?"

She shrugged. "Remember how I was in the old days, Betsy? I wanted to do things, help people. I've ended up helping myself."

"Maybe you should help yourself some more."

"Oh, sure," she said, pouring again. "Maybe I never wanted to help anyone, do anything. Maybe I just wanted to impress you. I really didn't know the way I was in those days. The friendship

I felt for you, I confused it with other things. Now I can look back on it. But then, then it was heavy."

"It wasn't just you. The thing was, back in Passaic, back then, Salmanda, I was half in love with you. I wouldn't let myself know it then; I couldn't admit it. I say it now."

Salmanda shrugged. "You never gave me a turn. You were half in love with all the things you thought I'd do."

"That's true too."

"And I never did them."

I looked at Alice. She nodded involuntarily. But she didn't have a word to say.

"If she's not back in fifteen minutes, I'm going to have to go after her. There's so much that kid doesn't know about herself. She's always getting in her own way. Pazienza, right? I remember that from Italy. You need lots of patience there. Betsy and I go back to the days when we thought we were going to have this old world or save it," she said bitterly. She got up unsteadily.

"No, don't rush," she said, illogically, when we got up too. "We haven't had the Spumanti. Where the hell are my shoes? This place is too much, isn't it? Too many floors. Fire's right. This place sucks."

Alice was staying in her friend Ben Clancy's rent-controlled apartment in the Village; he was out of town.

"Your friend was certainly upset," she said, pouring us some of the good decaffeinated espresso he'd left for her.

"I've been thinking of her all the way here. I hate to see her in such pain. I don't know, it's as if she has a talent for finding the kind of young white girl who'll get her in trouble."

"Perhaps that's what happens to many of us when we have more than enough."

"Do you really think it's that simple, Alice? Do you think she's being punished for her ice cube machine?"

"Well, dear, maybe she is. Why, it's similar to Leo and our apartment in Rome."

Leo. I wanted to be on that subject and at the same time I

wanted to avoid it. "Did you get the two milioni?" I asked sharply.

Alice looked surprised. Around her I was usually careful not to blurt out money.

She began to talk about what two milioni could do. How it could buy textbooks, ensure the education of the children of an Italian friend. She spoke of Bev, who offered to put things in a lawyer's hand. As she talked of the lire she could get for her apartment, I realized she'd turn collars, choose rooms without baths, and back in America give up the beauty parlor, cut and bleach her thinning hair. But she would never take charge of the two milioni. It was the wrong kind of money. Alice lived her life on the threadbare edge of an overabundant system, be it Italy or America. She was not about to allow conspicuous consumption to pay off in her hands. Not the way Salmanda had? Did she mean that too? Not the way I had?

I thought of her mother and all I had heard of her mother's greed. Alice lived her life to be different. I wondered, Toward the end, did Maple Blanders salvage slightly damaged posters? I could see Alice, an eternal house guest, rummaging toward salvation.

And at that moment she started to talk of Leo, to picture for me the two of them in the apartment together. "Can you imagine Leo saying, 'How can you think of giving up the only place in the world where I have ever been happy?' As absurd as his words were, we were more absurd. Imagine the two of us, standing there in the buff, crying."

"I doubt his words were absurd."

"Do you?"

"You know and I know he means them."

She looked at me carefully. "Yes, he means what he says while he says it. It's that he's indiscriminate with his honesty. I thought that was something you might already have found out."

I shrugged. "Leo's Leo."

"Why, my goodness, Betsy, you're still his champion. You have to admit that he did leave the only place where he'd ever been happy."

"Are you sure you didn't force him out?"

She looked up from stirring her demitasse. She hadn't even begun to drink it. "Whatever are you saying?"

"Would you have married Leo?"

"He didn't ask me."

"Did he ask Marcella?"

"Don't you think I've been married enough? Leo and I were happy once. That's what was important."

"Yes, you were happy. Then things went wrong. Then perhaps you thought, The happy days in Rome are over, it's time to come home. You'll forgive me for speaking my mind? You're here the way I'm here, because you want to be. And you're doing well."

"Why, you sound like Leo. Whatever did he do to you?"

"He didn't do a thing to me. We — "

She cut me off. "Then what did he say against me? It's apparent he said something to turn your head when you went to Rome."

"He never talked against you," I said quickly. "The worst he ever said . . . was nothing. God, I'm tired. Salmanda and Fire, they got me upset."

"What was the worst he ever said?"

"Nothing, I told you; I don't want to get into this. Isn't the evening botched up enough? I keep thinking of Salmanda. I'm sorry she's with that girl."

"So am I, dear. But what did Leo say?"

"Alice, the worst Leo ever said about you is that you do what you want to do. Like now. Is there anything wrong with that? And he said on a waiter's tip you would split a lira. Is that any different from 'no more rooms without baths'? You tell that yourself. You know your being so thrifty got on his nerves. I mean, look at you. You won't even spend on your hair!"

"How dare you!"

"Alice, I'm tired. We had a lousy night. We ate shit. We drank too much. I apologize for having taken you there. You can't see the girl I used to know. I can't either. But I care for the woman

I see. I'm glad she knows about real estate. I saw the look on your face. I'm glad she learned how to do business. Believe me, she was inspired by a good woman. She's changed, I've changed. I thought she was a genius, that she'd save the world. Now I hope she'll save herself. I'm glad she's making money. I'm glad I have a job and a book advance. We're educated women. We can't help fitting into our times. When I look at you, I see some sort of disapproval. The way you phrase your life, it's as if you're always doing something for other people. But don't you think, all along, you've been doing a lot for yourself? Leo's not far wrong. But there's nothing wrong with that. Isn't that what we're supposed to do? Find our own lives? Live them. Would you believe I needed Leo to tell me that? That's what he did for me. That's what Dr. Gianetti is doing for me."

"Did Leo say I'd split a lira? Were those his words?"

"Damn, Alice. Haven't you heard a thing I've said? Yes, he said that. Is that such a big deal? Is it so awful? Is it so untrue? What do you want to hear? That you're an angel? That there's nothing of your mother in you? It seems to me that you're going to make sure you're out two milioni. Maple Blanders' daughter is a good girl. She has to be poor."

"And to think I worried."

"Worried?"

"Yes, watched it and worried and begged Leo to be careful with you."

"Careful?"

"Careful as he charmed you the way he has to charm all women. You were so impressionable. I was afraid of what would happen once he turned your head. Apparently, I needn't have worried."

I stood up. "Who do you think you're condescending to? Flora? Do you think there was nothing real between Leo and me? Do you think I settled for thirty seconds?"

"And I begged Leo to be careful with you."

A few months later I received the most remarkable letter from Alice. She was staying with her son, Brad, in Florida. The letter was very long. She talked of her life with Maple Blanders, she talked of her first husband and how she had to be responsible for them both in the end. She talked of the birth of her son and the years of hard work supporting him. Of Nick and of how she had always had to earn her own money. Of Leo's family, "her" Italian family, and of all she had given to help them after the Second World War. "Whatever little I've had," she said, "I've always shared with those who have been more needy."

She went on: "To me this has always been the meaning of money and the meaning of life. So you can imagine, Betsy, how affected I was to hear you say such things. If Leo in actuality said I would split a lira, why then I really must say he has lost himself, he has forgotten. And I must say your words were cruel. There's nothing in my life that's like my mother's. She had a natural ruthlessness that sprang full blown from the power she was able to exert over others. She fed on the weak. She pampered me as long as I remained what she intended: a pretty, very little, girl. It was not in her plan to lie down beside a dead husband. I doubt she ever forgave him his escape. (I did, except when I had to yank him out of the elm tree!) But I can imagine her, inspiring pathos, while planning a very big service and a very small coffin for me. Yet I escaped from her lavish life. Perhaps there really is no strength like that of the weak when the weak rise up strong."

Alice went on, many pages, single-spaced. Afterward, I scanned the letter. Not one mention, one allusion, to what she had said about Leo charming me, or my retort that hinted an affair.

"Why don't you ask her for clarification? Get it out in the open if it bothers you." That's what Dr. Gianetti said.

"She's away," I told her.

"You could call her up."

I did.

"Hello, Alice?"

"Why, Betsy."

"I got your letter."

"Did you, dear?"

"Yes . . . Uh, I hope we're still friends."

"Why, of course. What would I do without you, Betsy? There's so much I wish I could tell you. Letters don't do."

"No, they don't. There are things I want to tell you too. But . . . but phones don't seem to do."

"Well, why don't you come down over your Thanksgiving vacation? We can have a nice visit. There's always room for you!"

"Well . . . why not? Okay."

"Good for you! Why, I was saying to Brad, just the other day, How I miss Betsy Lewis. With Betsy, I can always laugh."

"She can laugh?" asked Dr. Gianetti.

"I told you I was funny."

Alice was sitting behind Brad's condo, facing the developer's lagoon. She was wearing a wide skirt and scoop-necked top and a wide-brimmed straw hat that protected her from the sun. As I approached, I saw that she was staring past the slow stream of water, beyond the condos that stood like Quonset huts on the opposite shore.

"Hi," I said. "Remember me? I'm Betsy Lewis."

She turned her head. There was a pause. "Why, Betsy, dear Betsy."

"Don't get up."

But she did, spryly, and we were in each other's arms.

She held me. I remembered a day when we had toured Paestum. I had tripped on the temple's step. She was in front of me, grabbed me, and saved me from a fall.

"You look very good, Alice." Around her, especially when I was first seeing her again, nothing seemed changed. The straw hat shadowed her face, emphasizing the soft, lean contours of her jowls and shading, deepening her large blue eyes, obscuring the light hairs she hadn't seen under her chin. Freed from the incomprehension of Fire's stare, there was something — I was going to say timeless — about Alice. But it's not really timeless or ageless. There's something about Alice that fits into time.

"Do I look good, dear? I feel good. And I'm very glad to see you."

Brad came down from the back porch. Alice introduced us, and he said hello, shyly; he seemed a diffident man. I told him how nice it was to meet him finally and he said just about the same. He looked a little lost, like the widower he was, and excused himself. He was going off to play golf. I watched his sloped shoulders, his careful step as he walked. Alice had a son old enough for early retirement.

It was a very sunny, very mild day, and you could smell Florida coming to you around the new complex, springing over the dull lagoon. We sat outside. After a while we ate sandwiches Alice had prepared and drank gin and tonic. "Wonderful weather," I said. "Are you planning to stay the winter?"

"I don't know, dear. Is your gin strong enough?"

"Sure is."

"Goodness knows, we've got plenty of gin."

"Brad likes it here, huh?"

"He'd like to buy the apartment he's subletting. He'd like me to invest in it too. I'd have my own room and a place to keep my things. Then I'd be free to come and go. Of course, I'd never spend all my time here."

"Are you going to do it?"

"Why, I'll invest in it, if that's what Brad wants."

"What do you want?"

She didn't answer. "I'm thinking of Leo," I told her. "He used to say he never did what he wanted to do."

"While always doing it, of course."

"Yes."

"I've heard from Flora recently. Do you know that Marcella is divorcing him?"

"I'm not surprised," I said. "I wonder if he'll be the first man in Italy to be divorced twice!"

Alice laughed.

"And the union? Is he still the head?"

"Yes, dear. Through all the intrigues and scandals, he seems not to let go. Well, if Brad buys the condo, I imagine I'll go to Rome next summer and finally sort out my things."

"Sort out your things?"

"Well, there are still things at the apartment I plan to ship over."

"Alice, is it worth shipping anything here?" I felt like saying, Buy something new. I could just hear Flora.

"Well, there are a lot of my books and my files, and there are still some pictures. And then there are a few good pieces."

"I don't know. Is it worth the trouble? For example, Doug, thanks to Patricia Cass, is being reasonable. He's no longer asking for any of my salary or my nonexistent royalties. And I'm relinquishing my claim to half the house. Let him have it all! I never wanted it anyway. And the books? Except for the absolute essentials for my work, he can have them all. I've made a vow that I'll never again be followed around in this lifetime by thirty cartons of books. I'll travel light."

"That's nice, dear. But you see, the things I left are part of my life."

I was quiet.

"You know," she continued, "I read the most extraordinary account of Picasso. He meets an old friend he hasn't seen in years. And do you know what he asks her? Just imagine, he's ancient, absolutely ancient by then, and so's she. He asks her, 'Do you still love life. Do you still love love?' Isn't that wonderful, Betsy? Can't you just see the two of them on a Paris street? 'Do you still love love?'" Alice asked the weather.

"Alice, would you think of moving back to Rome?"

She turned and looked at me. There was a gleam in her eye. "Would you, dear?"

"Would I what?"

"Move back to Rome again."

"Me? Why would you ask me that? Don't you think my life is here?"

"It's for you to decide where your life is."

"I know that. At least I'm paying to get to know that."

"It's when we lose the simple things that we find ourselves paying the most."

"So you think I've lost my grip on the important things?"

"I didn't say that. But I do think it can be easy to lose one's perspective. To forget about the feelings of others. Why, I remember when Nick got the offer from Keeger's firm . . ."

Alice's generation, my mother's generation, generations of women who did not do things for themselves. Circumstances shifted them; their lives were created out of what they did for others. And for each of these generations there had to be a Maple Blanders. Perhaps, to my mother, I with my ideas was one myself. I heard Leo's voice through Alice's. "Alice does only what Alice wants to do." Why was it an accusation? Because it was anathema to Alice and therefore sacrilege to the people she loved.

I found myself nodding as Alice talked about her life, and I realized it would be easy for me to go along, listening, letting our relationship settle into the accustomed grooves.

"Alice! Listen to me!" I said suddenly. She stopped talking. "Alice. Your letter. You didn't mention something that happened in our fight."

"What fight?"

"The night we saw Salmanda. Afterward, at Ben Clancy's apartment. Surely you remember?"

"You were tired, dear. So was I."

"You were tired enough to say Leo charmed me and you knew he was doing it."

"Why, that's like saying Leo's Leo and you're an intelligent, good-looking woman."

"Then why did you send me to him with your letter to the landlord? Sometimes I think you sent me there as a gift."

"Whatever are you talking about?"

"I'm talking about all the things you gave him in your life together. Your view of things, your friends. Maybe I was sent there to bring back the old days, to rub it in."

"My goodness. Do you think I had a plan?"

"I don't know. I don't know why Doug insisted I go with him when I didn't want to. I don't know why you sent me straight to Leo."

"Why shouldn't Doug want you along? Why shouldn't I send a letter through you? All you had to say was no, if you didn't want to. To be honest, Betsy, I think you have a guilty conscience."

"Do you know about what?"

"No. No, I do not." Her eyes fluttered for a moment. I saw red rise to her face. Her lips closed tight.

My hand was shaking. I put down my glass. "But you do know I was crazy about Leo."

"Yes."

"How did you feel about that?"

"Why," she said slowly, "you saw what I saw. It made me love you more."

She looked away from me. I had seen her suffused with pink the night in Pietrasanta when I found her naked in the hall. But I had never seen her cheeks grow red. It wasn't girlish, and it wasn't pretty.

At that moment, in the Florida sun, I realized I wouldn't scream my truth in Alice's ear. I wouldn't say what was on my mind. I wouldn't confess I had slept with Leo. Our friendship was formed in Rome and our discretion often said a lot of things. I felt my body relax. It was as if I had just had orgasm with a phantom.

"There's something I didn't tell you about my last visit with Leo, Alice. Something you should know. I almost said it that night after we saw Salmanda. But it got stuck somewhere, it came out wrong. It's about your apartment. I know Leo has a lot of reasons for wanting it. It's a hideaway, it's cheap, and maybe, if you never do go back, someday he could give it to his son. I don't know. List the disagreeable reasons. They are all there. But the real reason he doesn't want you to give up the apartment is that without him paying the rent, without Flora dusting it, without him going there . . . without that, he loses you.

"We were there, in your apartment. The day before I left Rome. I'll never forget it. He had avoided the issue every time I'd brought it up since I'd been in Rome. And that day — we knew we wouldn't be seeing each other again for a long time, maybe forever — we talked and talked. You know, it was Leo who gave me the advice to take the New York job. It's as if he sensed how unhappy I was. He wanted me to do something for myself. He gave me real advice, Alice. Advice I could use. Take your life, he told me. Live it. Seize — seize your opportunities. Meanwhile, he was looking around the living room as if somewhere there he'd find you. I mean, he exploded when I talked about your letter to the landlord. I told you that. He felt you should at least get the lire. But I realized of course it wasn't the money. After all, couldn't he take the letter to the landlord and somehow get the money for himself? All he wanted was for you to come back to Rome. He didn't want to admit it, but I couldn't help seeing through him. 'Leo,' I said. 'You still love Alice, don't you?' 'Che miseria,' he answered. 'Yes.'"

Alice turned from me and looked past the lagoon. Her concentration reminded me of that day in the back gardens of the American Center, when I first saw her and she was staring past Garibaldi's wall. On that day in the Center's gardens I had so much to tell her. How she listened to my story of Salmanda. How she followed my thoughts about nineteenth-century Italy and my ruminations about prejudice in the States. What was I like then? I was young and enthusiastic and searching. My roots were not far different from those of Nick Russo. Neither, according to Leo, were my coloring, my features, and the cleft in my chin. And like the articles Alice saved, I had a concise, passionate, yet abstract point of view. I was so untried, so magically young.

We would not start again, Alice and I. I could feel myself separate from her that day in Florida. Alice has Alice. Betsy has me. Tears came to Alice's eyes. She was looking at her own life through her own tears.

"You know," I said to her finally, my voice wavering, "I've always wanted to ask you, Alice — you've had so many lives. You've had such strength. What kept you going through the bad times? What makes you so wise?"

"Me, dear? Oh, Betsy, I never thought about it that way. I doubt I think. So many things happen. I remember Sidney Sladiz once saying when we were in Egypt together. He was a young architect then. Before he made his name. He said, 'Alice, I wonder how smart you'd be if only you had learned to read and write. You'd have us all beat.' I had no formal education at all, dear. You see, I got married at fourteen just to get out of that dreadful house. Then imagine Nick saying, when he was so confused and decided he had to have a divorce, that I looked down on him intellectually. I? What did I know? I never tried to figure things out in an all-encompassing way, the way he did, the way you do."

"Me, Alice? I've changed a lot from the days in Rome."

"Why, have you, dear?"

Only Alice could say it that way. It wasn't argumentative. She simply handed the statement back to me. I could see what Nick had meant.

For a moment, I was disappointed. Then I remembered her telling me how she brought two of everything to Rome. So much love to share. And I wanted to tell her how much I had loved her during those days in Rome. I wanted to tell her I still loved her. But it didn't come out that way.

"I've always admired you," I said.

"I don't know why. Look at my life. One marriage after another. Poor Leo too. He loves me so much that he makes it impossible for me to stay in Rome. At least he *did*. Imagine. He and Marcella being divorced. What next? I remember Ed Mills saying to me — have I mentioned him to you, Betsy? He was at the Center in the early fifties, and I kept up with him. It was in New York, we were having dinner at a little Ukrainian place. 'Three husbands?' he said. He leaned over toward me. 'Three husbands. Whatever do you do, Alice, eat crackers in bed?'"

I smiled. I let Alice go on without me. My thoughts went to

Leo, wading for me at Pietrasanta when I swam out too far. I felt him rubbing my back with lotion. I felt his sex in the Florentine hotel. I looked up at the sky. I watched a cloud till I made out Leo. I saw his face. Like a child, I watched him ride past me in a cloud formation. I said goodbye.

"I really must leave crumbs in bed," Alice continued.

"I'd admire you if you left a whole pie!"

"Oh, Betsy!" She smiled. Her smile said she knew I should admire her. She was her own story.

It's midsummer as I finish this account. Putting it all down has made me feel very good. I'm staying at my friend Owen's farm in Connecticut until the fall. I've been seeing him for four months. He's a nice-looking guy, muscular, sympathetic and independent, and some years younger than I. He buys old barns and sets them up for rich people. We met by the sheerest chance, because of a rather complicated real estate deal of Salmanda's that fell through. "Behhtsy's got a new boyfriend," she teases me in the old Horace High lingo. Occasionally we meet at moments like that, then months go by.

I like Connecticut a lot. I can feel the spirit of the Indians who used to inhabit the hills. Seriously. Route 7 and the diners and the shopping centers and the El Cutesy Shoppes haven't blotted them out. Every once in a while, especially on a hot summer day, I think of a trip to Rome. Then I think, Europe's a vacation. Betsy, your travels are here.

ABOUT THE AUTHOR

Julia Markus's novel *Uncle* won the Houghton Mifflin Literary Fellowship Award in 1978 and it was followed by *American Rose* in 1981. The author teaches fiction workshops at Hofstra University and divides her time between New York and Connecticut. At present she is at work on a new novel.